WICKED SOUTH: SECRETS AND LIES

Stories for Young Adults

Edited by
EMILY COLIN

Edited by
KATIE ROSE GUEST PRYAL

Goldenjay Books

Publisher's Cataloging-in-Publication Data
Colin, Emily A. 1975-.
Pryal, Katie Rose Guest. 1976-.
Wicked South : Secrets and Lies, Stories for Young Adults / Emily Colin and Katie
Rose Guest Pryal
p.____ cm.____
ISBN 978-1-947834-28-6 (Pbk.), ISBN 978-1-947834-29-3 (Ebook)
1. Anthology, Fiction. 2. Young Adult Fiction. I. Title.
808.83 | LOC PCN 2018907466

Goldenjay Books

Published by Goldenjay Books
an imprint of Blue Crow Publishing, LLC
Chapel Hill, NC
www.bluecrowpublishing.com
Cover Design by Lauren Faulkenberry

WICKED SOUTH

SECRETS AND LIES

For Mrs. S

~ Elizabeth Tellido

Praise for WICKED SOUTH: SECRETS AND LIES

Menacing fairy folk and locker room monsters. Forbidden love and time-traveling adventures. The nine twisty tales in WICKED SOUTH: SECRETS AND LIES take readers to atmospheric corners of the American South (and beyond) filled with heartfelt characters and alluring mysteries. You won't be able to pass a lonely roadside produce stand or dig into our native red clay soil without wondering what magic and secrets are hidden in plain sight.

-John Claude Bemis, author of THE WOODEN PRINCE and
The Clockwork Dark Trilogy

A collection blazing with seduction, trickery, conflict, and grief, WICKED SOUTH: SECRETS AND LIES is a saga of bitter deceits and breathtaking victories.

-Heather Ezell, author of NOTHING LEFT TO BURN

WICKED SOUTH swept me in from the first page. I devoured the heartwarming stories of romance, kindness, and grief—then discovered (to my delighted surprise) that I also enjoyed tales with magic, mystery, or horror. WICKED SOUTH will enthrall you and linger in your thoughts long after you finish. A gripping, glorious anthology.

-Julia Day, award-winning author of THE POSSIBILITY OF
SOMEWHERE and FADE TO US

A captivating collection of unique and eclectic stories—poignant, twisted, adventurous, and everything in between. Tales of love, obsession, magic, and more, all with a secret simmering beneath.

-Mary Fan, award-winning author of STARSWEPT and editor of the BRAVE NEW GIRLS anthology series

The stories in WICKED SOUTH: SECRETS AND LIES delve into dark hidden corners of a landscape you only thought you knew. These nine tales flirt with magic, love, death, and identity, all with a delicious Southern flavor.

-Megan Shepherd, NEW YORK TIMES bestsellling author of THE MADMAN'S DAUGHTER

Clear your schedule, pour a glass of sweet tea, and curl up under the nearest magnolia tree to read this delicious and delightful collection of short stories. You won't want to close WICKED SOUTH until the last lie's been told and the last secret revealed.

-Nina de Gramont, award-winning author of EVERY LITTLE THING IN THE WORLD

WICKED SOUTH: SECRETS AND LIES is a juicy, engrossing, and always surprising read for anyone who loves that deliciously wicked feeling of being in on a secret no one else knows. Story after story, this anthology sucks you in and keeps you reading!

-Kelly Harms, author of THE GOOD LUCK GIRLS OF SHIPWRECK LANE

Contents

From Emily:

Previously I have dedicated books to my boyfriend. My parents. My son.
This one is different.

This one's for the thoughts
Dimly remembered
That drift, half-formed
Between sleep and waking
The lies we tell without meaning to
The secrets we keep even from ourselves
The wounds, half-cleansed
That we seek, desperate
To transform brokenness
into art.

From Katie:

For my boys, for whom I wanted to write stories
For my sister, who always made the team

WICKED SOUTH: Introduction

The *Wicked South: Secrets and Lies* anthology came to be because Emily and Katie once took a fateful university fiction-writing course together many years ago. In this course, the professor teased us both terribly because we enjoyed—and wrote—stories that weren't (in his dubious opinion) literary enough. He gave us both nicknames: Emily's was "Anne Rice." Katie's was "Soap Opera."

We were both horrified.

In retrospect, had we landed jobs writing like Anne Rice or for soap operas, today we'd be happy as clams. But when you're nineteen or twenty and you want to be a writer, and being a good writer has a very narrow definition set by a stodgy teacher whose good opinion you are desperately seeking, an experience like ours can turn you from your path.

Indeed, we both stopped writing fiction after that course—for years and years.

And then, separately, we drifted back to fiction. Before embracing fiction again, we'd both become writers—just not *fiction* writers. But fiction was easy to find again once we grew up a little bit and realized what a small man our professor had been.

We realized we were good at writing stories. We also realized that there is room in the world for many kinds of stories.

Best of all, we reconnected with each other, and we became friends.

Oh right—we're supposed to be talking about this anthology! Here's what happened. On the phone, Emily said to Katie, "Young adult anthology!" And Katie said to Emily, "Great idea!" And we said to each other lots of words that brought this seed of an idea into a full-grown azalea of stories.

And here we are.

Why "Wicked South"?

While the word "wicked" can have negative connotations, if you look in the dictionary (such as the OED), there are also less negative ones. Wicked can mean "playfully mischievous," or even, in more recent slang, it can mean "excellent," or "wonderful." While this anthology features young adult stories of any genre, all of the stories are playful, or tricky, or mischievous. And all of them are wonderful.

And the "South" part? All of the contributors are from the southern United States, in particular the states of North Carolina, South Carolina, and Georgia. Emily and Katie live in North Carolina.

Who Is Here—and Why It Matters

This anthology is not perfect. We tried, and failed, to include authors from diverse racial and ethnic backgrounds. Representation matters in fiction, and we recognize the importance of racial and ethnic diversity in a short story collection such as this one. We are pleased to have included short stories by disabled authors and LGBTQI authors, as well as emerging authors who have never before been published. We are deeply committed to including diverse racial and ethnic voices in the second volume of our *Wicked South* series.

A portion of the proceeds from *Wicked South: Secrets and Lies* will be donated to benefit literacy programs at El Centro Hispano in Durham, North Carolina. We selected this organization because of its commitment to literacy, including its Motheread program, which works with Spanish speaking mothers and their children to cultivate a shared love of reading, as well as the adult literacy classes the organization offers as a vital component of its mission. We hope that this anthology will be the first of many in the *Wicked South* series to benefit this worthy cause.

Why "Secrets and Lies"?

The theme of this *Wicked South* anthology is "Secrets and Lies." Each story has, at its heart, a secret kept or a lie told. For example, in Katie Pryal's "Alex and Lora," a neighbor isn't at all who she seems, and in John Klekamp's "The List," the narrator keeps a secret list that carries a delightful surprise.

For good or ill—on the page or in life—few things are more alluring than the siren song of a secret. Conflict and possibility are embedded in a secret's very nature; betrayal and conspiracy are encoded in its DNA. Secrets can transform; they can alienate, anger, or inspire. One thing is for sure: They make a great story.

And so—let us begin.

E.A.C. and K.R.G.P.
October 2018

An Unkindness of Ravens

EMILY COLIN

Emily Colin is the *New York Times*-bestselling author of *The Memory Thief* and *The Dream Keeper's Daughter*. Her diverse life experience includes organizing a Coney Island tattoo and piercing show, hauling fish at the Florida Keys' Dolphin Research Center, roaming New York City as an itinerant teenage violinist, helping launch two small publishing companies, and serving as the associate director of DREAMS of Wilmington, a nonprofit dedicated to immersing youth in need in the arts.

A 2017 Pitch Wars mentor, she is the 2017 recipient of the North Carolina Sorosis Award for Excellence in Creative Writing and the 2018 recipient of the North Carolina Greater Foundation of Women's Clubs Lucy Bramlett Patterson Award for Excellence in Creative Writing. Originally from Brooklyn, she lives in Wilmington, NC, with her family. You can find her on Twitter at @emilyacolin or on her blog at www.emilycolin.com.

He first came to me in the woods, in the cruelest days of summer, when the heat lay close along my skin. It was a day for reading in the air conditioning, curled up on the couch in cut-offs and a tank top, with a sweating glass of lemonade and a plate of Thin Mints straight from the freezer. But Mom had been at the whisky again, and so we were having a picnic outside, Cora and I. Outside was safer. Vodka made her mean, but whisky made her cry. She'd been sobbing over her wedding album when I shepherded Cora past her, a packed-full picnic basket in my free hand. "My two little girls," she'd said when she'd noticed us, tears rolling down her cheeks. "My babies."

I tried never to show scorn for Mom in front of Cora, but when she'd said that, I couldn't help but snort. I was two weeks short of eighteen and pretty sure she'd stopped seeing me ten years ago, right after the accident that took Daddy's life and brought Cora early. Don't get me wrong, she knew I existed—but in the absent-minded way you'd pay attention to a piece of furniture that had been in your living room forever, oblivious to whether it was covered in scratches or polished to a sheen.

Mom was a bit more solicitous of Cora, but in a maudlin, devoid-of-practicality way that made me grit my teeth. (Or would have, if I didn't know I'd have to earn the money to pay for my dental bills.) I'd raised my sister on my own, with only the most perfunctory help from her. Had worked at the veterinary clinic every day after school to make sure we had money for groceries, after I was old enough and the settlement money ran out. I hadn't been her little girl for a long time.

Cora's lower lip trembled, and I hustled her past our mother, out the door. "Come on, Care Bear," I said when she hesitated. "Mom's just sad right now. She'll feel better later." It was a lie, and both of us knew it. Still, it was enough to get Cora moving.

We went to our favorite spot in the woods. Years before we'd moved here, this grove had been an apple orchard, and many of the trees still stood. I unpacked the picnic basket—ham sandwiches, a thermos of lemonade, and the Thin Mints, in a regrettable state of meltdown—while Cora spread out the blanket. Afterward, I wove a crown for her out of daisy stems and lay back, head pillowed on my arms, as she set up a tea party for imaginary friends on the stump of an oak. The cups were acorns; the plates were broad, glossy leaves.

"Cassie?" she asked, without turning to look at me.

"Yeah, Cor?" It was my secret nickname for her, so much more than a simple abbreviation. In Latin, it meant heart; she was mine.

"Do you think the apples are any good to eat yet?"

Drowsy and sated, I was on the verge of telling her no, that it was way too soon for them to ripen—but her voice was so hopeful. "I'll check," I said, taking a gulp of lemonade and getting to my feet. Standing up was an effort; even up here in the mountains, the humid air was so thick, it was hard to breathe. I'd worn the cut-offs and tank top after all, and braided my long red hair to keep it off my neck. Still, the heat lay on me like a weight.

I strode out of our small clearing toward the nearest apple tree. And then I saw him standing there, a man-shaped shadow among the streaks of dappled light. He was staring past me, toward my sister, a strange avidity emanating from him. His eyes gleamed as they fixed on Cora, his lips parted. It occurred to me that he looked almost . . . hungry.

Our woods were secluded, deep in a North Carolina mountain valley—what the old folks around here called a holler—accessible only by the trail that led from our house. I'd never seen a stranger here. And the way he stood—so still, as if he'd been spying on us, devising a plan of attack . . . if he were simply lost, why wouldn't he have said something, let us know he were there? No, he meant Cora harm, I was sure of it. Why else would he be looking at her that way?

Rage trembled in me at the thought, making me bold. I didn't care what happened to me. He would never touch her. Furious, I strode forward to tell him so.

On second glance, the man didn't look like a vagrant or a serial killer. Up close, he seemed no older than nineteen or twenty, more of a boy than a man, with a fall of black hair that brushed his collar. His clothes were unremarkable—dark blue jeans and a red T-shirt. Still, something about him struck me as unmistakably *other*.

Cora didn't look up. Didn't notice him. I wanted to keep it that way.

"No," I told him, stepping between them. His moss-green eyes widened.

"You see me," he said, and his voice sent shivers rippling through me. It was a voice like wind rushing through grass, like water over rocks. It was not human. But it was beautiful. When he stopped speaking, I wanted more than anything for him to do it again.

I didn't know what unnerved me more—the boy's presence in our neglected apple grove, or the fact that his voice moved me so deeply. After a brief flirtation with Tommy D'Angelo at the end of junior year, I'd sworn off dating until after I graduated . . . and maybe not even then. I had to study, to work and watch out for Cora. I didn't have time for distractions—particularly not dramatic ones, like romance and heartbreak. Distractions were for girls who had energy to spare.

But here in the woods, with this boy who seemed carved from the wilderness, I felt my heartbeat quicken, and hated myself for it. He was a stranger, and a peculiar one at that. I had no business being drawn to him this way, not when he was staring at my sister like she was a tasty afternoon snack.

"Of course I see you. There you are." Fear made my voice tight.

"Most cannot, unless I will it." He tilted his head, bright-eyed, a bird regarding its prey. "What are you?"

I opened my mouth to scream, to tell Cora to run. But curiosity got the best of me—as usual—and what came out instead was, "I don't know what you mean."

He took a deep breath, letting the air out bit by bit. With horror, I realized he was sampling my scent. "Ah," he said, voice thick with satisfaction. "That young one—she is yours?"

"Cora? Yes. My sister. You can't have her. Leave us alone."

"Such bravado," he mused. "But she brought the offerings, did she not? Gifts to the forest. Gifts to my kind."

"Your kind? What kind are you?"

His lips curved upward in a shark's grin, hungry and predatory. His teeth were bone-white and sharp. "The Fair Folk, they once called us—for our beauty, if not our sense of justice. Though your people have a saying, do they not—all is fair in love and war? So it is with us."

"And you think you can have Cora? You think that's fair? Well, it isn't, and you can't." My voice shook with fury.

"She made the offerings," he pointed out, gesturing at Cora and her stump. "A gift, once given, cannot be undone."

There was weight to his words, a ritualistic formality that sent an icy chill down my spine. "The acorns? The leaves? She's a little girl, playing. They mean nothing."

"Not so. But perhaps I would be willing to bargain." His gaze swept over me, considering. When it came back to rest on my face, I felt the blood rush outward, heating my skin. "The Folk will risk much for bravery and beauty. You possess both. Care you so for your sister? Then offer me a trade."

"What do you want?"

He stepped closer, his eyes fixed on mine. In their depths I could swear I saw another world: cities overrun by rampaging armies and storm-churned oceans crashing into distant shores, the debris of broken ships littering the sand. I saw blood and pain and loss, the shadows of outspread wings soaring past the impassive face of the moon, and a man falling to earth, shackled to the ground against his will.

The boy shifted his weight, small branches crunching beneath his feet. The vision shifted with him and I saw myself, gray eyes fierce and hair flaming bright in the gloom of the forest. I breathed in, tasting the tartness of apples on the wind and the richness of leaf-turned earth, the top note of my fear and a baser, thrumming note that I could only identify as desire.

Horrified, I stepped back, breaking the connection between us. I was myself again, inviolate. But in the back of my head a voice echoed, as resigned as it was satisfied: *What is done can't be undone.* For one absurd moment, I wondered if it was his.

A smile curved the boy's lips. "I ask only the pleasure of your company, on the longest night of the year. The Winter Solstice. A small gift, is it not, for your sister's freedom? For otherwise I would surely take her as my pet, my prized companion. In the land under the hill, time slips and spills. And one day indeed she might return to this place, only to find all she loved had passed to dust."

"She's an eight-year-old child," I hissed, hands clenching into fists. "She's not your pet."

It was his turn to regard me with curiosity, as if my indignation puzzled him. "I meant no offense. What say you? Do we have a bargain?"

"One night," I said, turning to glance at Cora, with her bird's-wing shoulders and her crown of daisies. "That's all you want?"

The boy reached out, bridging the space between us, and ran the tip of his finger down my cheekbone. His touch was ice and fire. I could feel its trace long after his hand had fallen away. "I spoke nothing of what I wanted. But as for what I ask—yes. Will you grant it, or no?"

"One night," I said again, dubious. "To do what?"

He coughed a laugh. It bore more resemblance to the bark of a dog than a sound that might emerge from a human throat. "At the core of every bargain there is risk," he said at last, the smile gone. "Will you take it, for your sister's sake? I won't ask again."

"Tell me your name," I countered. "I won't go to meet a boy who's a pure stranger."

"Ah," he said, eyeing me. "But I am not a boy."

I'd known he was more than he seemed. Still, hearing him admit it sent a rush of terror through my veins, pooling low in my stomach. "Tell me, or no deal."

He bowed low, a mocking gesture. "Even so. You may call me Reuben. And you? Will you return the favor?"

I paused, unsure whether I should answer him. But then Cora called to me, concern clear in her lilting voice. "Who are you talking to, Cassie? Is someone there?"

"Just myself," I called back, forcing levity into my voice.

She giggled. "You're so silly, Cassie. Are the apples ripe, or not?"

My eyes flicked above his head to the tree. The fruit was green and small, still weeks away from eating. I opened my mouth to tell her so. But then Reuben gave a low, musical laugh, and around him the tree rustled. The apples swelled, their color deepening to a blushing red. He plucked one, and held it out to me. "For your sister, Cassie," he said.

"You—how did you do that?"

He smiled, flashing those predator's teeth again, and dropped the apple into my palm. It lay there, sun-warm and heavy— ordinary, not like a miracle at all. "Is it short for Cassiopeia, your name? Or Cassandra?"

"Cassiopeia," I said, before it occurred to me that telling this bizarre not-a-boy my name might be a mistake. "My father was an astronomer. He named me."

"The study of the stars is an admirable pursuit." He plucked another apple, this one for himself. His teeth sank deep into its flesh. I watched him swallow, wondering what else such teeth were capable of. "What say you, then? Do you agree to our bargain, or no?"

Behind me I could hear the trample of leaves as Cora got to her feet. It occurred to me that he'd never answered my question; I still didn't know what he wanted from me. But if the price was my sister's life, there was only one thing to say. "All right," I said hurriedly. "I'll do it. Now you have to go. If I can see you, then she probably can too. You'll frighten her. Go away."

"As you wish," he said, and the air around him began to shimmer. The leaves of the tree shook, the branches bent. The apple fell from his hand. And then Reuben was gone. In his place stood a huge black dog, its green eyes fixed on me. It scooped up the fallen apple in its mouth, nodded its head once to me in acknowledgement, and then faded into the forest.

I was still staring at the place where Reuben and the dog had been when Cora came up beside me. "What are you doing?" she scolded. "Oh look, the apples are ripe after all. Can I have one?" She closed her small hand around the fruit I held, trying to pry it loose.

"No!" I said, startled back to myself. "Something's wrong with these, Cora. They never should have ripened this early. I don't want you eating them. The tree could be sick, or—I don't know. Let's just go home."

I hurled the apple as far as I could into the woods, ignoring her shrieks of outrage. As it landed in the brush, I could have sworn I heard Reuben laugh—but maybe it was just the wind that had suddenly risen to stir the trees.

I did my share of research on the Fair Folk after that—learned that they were famous for their beauty and their charm, that they never lied but twisted the truth to suit their will. I thought of how Reuben hadn't answered my question when I'd asked what he wanted, and my blood ran cold . . . for surely he'd avoided it deliberately, knowing I wouldn't care for his reply.

The rest of what I learned about the Folk didn't make me feel any better. They were known for spiriting human women away, luring them into a circle of frenzied dancers, where the women would gyrate until the flesh fell from their bones and their hearts gave out. They stole children and gave back changelings. *Never enter into a bargain with the Folk,* website after website cautioned. Yet I had, and if the price were Cora's life, I couldn't regret it.

Reuben brought me gifts all that fall and into the winter, small tokens left behind where only I would find them: a wreath of holly berries on my bedroom windowsill, a single fragrant pansy crushed between the pages of a book, a ring woven from the stems of lavender-blue daisies, slipped onto the passenger seat of my Honda. Next to the ring, he'd arranged more petals so that they spelled out a single word: SOON.

A thrill ran through me, chased by a rush of terror. I stared at the petals, heart pounding, then gathered them up, intending to dump them on the ground. But instead I crushed them in my palm, then stood and tossed them to the wind. "Soon," I said aloud, willing my voice not to shake. "But not now. Why can't you leave me alone? This isn't romantic. It's creepy. Why can't you see that?"

There was no reply, but that night I got home from work to find a large black dog lying on the worn rug in front of the fireplace, an abashed expression on its furry face. "I found him," Cora said, head pillowed on the dog's side. "He was just waiting on the doorstep when the bus let me off from school. Isn't he sweet, Cassie? Look at his eyes, they're the most amazing color. Can we keep him? Please, can we?"

The dog placed his great head between his paws and gave an imploring whine, looking as innocent as could be, but I knew better. While Cora stroked his fur and chattered about how they'd given him the leftover chicken—chicken I'd worked hard to buy instead of studying for my chem midterm—I fumed. "Get away from him, Cora," I said when she finally wound down. "He probably has fleas. Mom, tell her."

But my mother was no help. She was sitting at the kitchen table, staring beatifically into her glass of red wine as if it contained a tiny, explicable version of the universe. "I think he's sweet," she said, sounding a thousand miles away. "Every child should have a dog."

"See?" Cora sat up, her face lit with one of those smiles I hardly saw her give anymore—the kind that wasn't just for my benefit, to reassure me that she was Okay. As if on cue, the wind gusted around the house, and she wrapped her arms around the dog's neck to protect him—the irony of the century. "We can't just put him out in the cold, Cassie. At least let him stay with us tonight. Just one night, okay? Please?"

I flinched, nearly dropping the mug of coffee I'd just poured in an effort to stay awake long enough to finish my calculus homework. The dog flinched too, and his moss-green gaze dropped to the floor. "He's sad," Cora crooned, hugging him tight, her copper curls bright against his dark fur. But I knew better.

I didn't have the heart to put him out, even knowing what I did—not with Cora looking happier than I'd seen her in months. She cleared a special spot for the dog on the floor when I refused to allow him on the bed and insisted that I read her bedtime story out loud to both of them. I obliged, glaring daggers at the dog whenever Cora glanced in the other direction. After an eternity, I tucked her in, switched on her nightlight, and told her I loved her to the moon and back. And then I turned to go. The dog padded after me, as I had known he would.

"He likes you," Cora said sleepily. "Please can we keep him?"

"Let me think about it, Care-Bear," I told her, shutting her bedroom door behind me. Down the hallway I went. The dog, of course, followed.

I walked into my room and closed the door. The dog sat on the throw rug, his eyes on my face, the picture of obedience. "Drop the act," I said to him.

For a moment nothing happened. Then the air wavered, flickering as if shot through with an electrical charge. One moment there was a black dog sitting on my floor. The next, Reuben was standing in front of me, buck naked.

"What the hell." My heart was pounding, and not just from the shock of having a dog transform into a man right into the middle of my bedroom. Well, a male, anyway.

He glanced down at himself. "Oh," he said, as if it had just occurred to him that I might find this state of affairs offensive. "My apologies. May I?" He gestured at the quilt on my bed, which I could only just see out of the corner of my eye because I'd looked away from him and was staring studiously at the floor.

"Please." Possibly, my voice could have contained more sarcasm. Like, if I were telling my mom how thrilled I was that she'd managed to miss Cora's fourth cello recital this year.

Reuben grabbed the quilt off the bed and wrapped it around himself. "I don't suppose you have anything I could wear," he said.

Disgusted, I stomped past him. "Wait here."

My dad's old clothes were boxed up in the garage. I found a pair of jeans he hadn't cared about and a Georgetown Hoyas sweatshirt he'd hardly ever worn, stuck them in a paper bag so my mom wouldn't ask any questions, and hauled them back upstairs.

He was sitting on my bed. I locked the door behind me, handed the clothes to him without a word, and turned my back. The paper bag rustled, and I heard Reuben give an amused chuckle. Then he said, "You can look now."

I turned, blushing despite myself. Reuben was occupying himself with folding the quilt. "I apologize again, Cassiopeia," he said in that unsettling voice of his. I told myself I hadn't been waiting for months to hear it again.

"What the hell do you think you're doing, pretending to be a dog and worming your way into Cora's heart like that? What am I supposed to tell her when you're gone in the morning? I thought I told you to leave me alone. What happened?"

He abandoned the quilt and came to stand in front of me. The sweatshirt and jeans looked ridiculous on him, a costume. I focused on that, so I wouldn't get sucked in by the vivid green of his eyes and the tempting curve of his mouth. This close, he smelled like the forest after a heavy rain. "First," he said, holding up a single finger, "I'm not pretending to be a dog. That is my other form. Secondly"—he extended another finger—"I do not have to be gone in the morning. I can stay here tonight, with you."

"As a dog?" I snapped, unnerved. "Or as yourself?"

His voice dropped lower, into a decadent purr. "Whichever you prefer."

"Knock it off. You can't stay here. We had a bargain, Reuben. One night—the longest, coldest night of the year, right? As nasty as it might be outside, this isn't it. I've got homework to do. I don't have time for this."

His eyes flashed wide in bewilderment and he stepped back, giving me space. When he spoke, his voice was careful. "It has been a long time since I had much to do with humans, Cassiopeia. I can hear that you are angry with me—I can smell it, radiating from your skin—but the reason escapes me. What have I done? Tell me, so I can make amends."

If he'd been a human guy, I would have accused him of manipulating me—but Reuben could only speak the truth. It occurred to me that maybe he was doing his best to apologize, within the only framework he understood. "How long," I said, and had to stop to clear my throat. I wasn't sure I wanted to hear the answer. "How long has it been?"

"Since I consorted with humans in a meaningful way? Hundreds of years." His voice roughened and his eyes slid from mine, focusing on the bone-white wedge of winter moon visible through my window. For a moment his expression was as bleak as the faded night sky, promising snow. Then he smiled, and it was wicked, a slice of sin. "You might say that I am out of practice. But I learn quickly, Cassiopeia."

"I just bet you do," I muttered, trying for nonchalance despite the shiver that eddied down my spine. He was hundreds of years old? I was so out of my depth here. For all I knew, he'd been around at the signing of the freaking Magna Carta. I stifled a hysterical laugh. "The hell with your damn daisies. I could've used your help on my AP history test last week. Now *that* would've actually been useful."

His brows drew down in puzzlement. "I do not understand."

"Of course you don't." I rolled my eyes. "What does that mean, exactly, 'consorted in a meaningful way'?"

The smile broadened. "It means what it means."

"Oh, come on, Reuben—"

He stepped closer, lacing my fingers with his. "It has been a long time, Cassiopeia. I beg you, have patience with me."

He made no effort to pull me toward him. Still, I could swear I felt his heartbeat, pounding wild and frantic against my skin. An electrical shock prickled everywhere we touched, and I felt the fine hairs on my arm rise, heard myself gasp. I pulled away, shaking, but the damage had been done.

Reuben inhaled, scenting me as he had that day in the woods. His eyelids sank to half-mast as if he'd been drugged, dark lashes casting shadows on his cheeks. "You told me to leave you alone. But you are alone so much already, beautiful one. I want only to please you. If my gifts do not, then show me the way."

Beautiful one. The endearment should have offended me, but instead I felt that traitorous spark again, kindling in my belly, racing through my blood like fire. When I spoke, my voice was harsh. "You don't need to please me. You don't need to do anything. I'll keep my promise. What else do you want from me?"

"This," he said, and before I could reply, his hands were cradling my face and his mouth came down on mine. He tasted like berries and sunlight. I meant to step away, but his body was warm against mine, and his hands roved in my hair, and I forgot about all the reasons why this was a terrible idea. Instead I kissed him back, letting the taste of him flood through me. His hair was silk beneath my fingers, and I tugged at it, urging him closer.

A low growl rumbled in his throat, and he murmured my name, ducking his head so that the sharp edge of his teeth skated along my throat. He untangled one of his hands from my hair and traced a path downward, from my face to my neck to my shoulder, so that I trembled in his arms. "Let me stay," he whispered.

It took everything I had, but somehow I pushed him away. "No," I said, my breath coming short. "This—it can't happen. We had a deal."

For a moment hurt showed clear on his face. Then it was gone, hidden behind the impassive mask he'd been wearing the first time we met. "As you wish," he said, and, pushing my window open, slipped through it without another word. It was a two-story drop, and I half-feared, half-hoped I'd find him shattered on the ground. But he landed easily, gave me a mocking wave, and disappeared into the dark.

I dreamed that night of a narrow, twisted path, suspended in midair. Beneath it raged the ocean I'd seen the first time I gazed into Reuben's eyes, the water surging upward to lap, freezing, at my feet. Above, the sky was on fire, as if the sun had unfurled into flaming ribbons that spiraled into the depths of the white-capped sea. But the path itself was impossibly dark, as if it had been cut from nothingness.

I'm not fond of heights, to put it mildly. When I was in sixth grade, my class took a trip to Grandfather Mountain, complete with a trek across the Mile High Swinging Bridge. It was windy that day, and every time the bridge swayed, I was convinced I was going to topple over the edge, leaving Cora sister-less and alone. Only the thought of her crumpled, tear-stained face gave me the strength to unlock my death grip on the railing and shuffle the rest of the way to safety. Every inch of the bridge's 228 feet felt like a marathon, and the next year, when my class went back again, I made Mom let me stay home.

But Grandfather Mountain's suspension bridge paled in comparison to this path over the abyss. Between the height, the ocean, and the flaming sky, it was sort of a choose-your-own-adventure near-death experience. For a moment I simply stood there, frozen with fear. And then—as if things weren't bad enough —I saw a shadowy, hunched figure dart from the blackness. It extended a hand to me, mouth open in a plea, just as the road behind us dissolved in fire.

I fled, the flames licking at my heels, sweeping over the path so that there could be no retreat. My breath sobbed in my lungs, tasting of ash and salt. I tried to remind myself that I was safe in my bed, that none of this was actually happening—but the dream felt so lifelike, the bite of the fire and the briny scent of the sea impossible to dismiss as fantasy. I ran faster, ignoring the shadows that had slipped from the night to keep pace with me, wailing in an awful, desperate way that reminded me of the stories the priests had told us about Purgatory, back when my father was still alive and we'd gone to church every Sunday.

The shadow-creatures reached out to touch me, wrapping my wrists in their icy grip, the flames a wall of heat at my back. Panicked, I tried to wrench free, but they held me fast. I was going to die here, I realized. I'd made a bargain with one of the Fair Folk for nothing, and after I was gone, Reuben would make a meal of Cora anyhow.

"Let her go." The voice rang with conviction, deep and hauntingly familiar.

Speak of the Devil. I jerked my head up, panting. Reuben was standing on the path, silhouetted against the flaming sky, so bright it hurt my eyes to look at him. A sword dangled from one of his long-fingered hands. "Step away from her," he said, and his voice was iron. "Let her go, or I will drive all of you back into the shadows you came from."

Slowly, the shadow-creatures' implacable grip on me loosened. They retreated, obsequious in the face of his fury, and it was just the two of us, the fire blazing up behind him, my heart stuttering in my chest like a starved thing. "What the hell are those—" The words died in my mouth, choked with smoke and terror.

Consternation marked his face, and his dark brows drew down. The hand that held the sword was gloved with blood. "Lost souls. It isn't safe for you here. I thought—" He shook his head, his lips a tight line. "I was wrong."

I forced the words through the pinhole of my throat. "But where—"

His head tilted upward, as if scenting the air. "Run!" he said, and now I heard them, coming fast: the pounding of hoofbeats, the howl of dogs, the mournful cry of a horn.

I turned to do as he said. But there was nowhere to go: The path behind me had been eaten up by fire, and beyond where Reuben stood, it fell away into the dark. As I watched, thornbushes rose from the earth, growing across the path from either side to block my passage. The air filled with the thick, cloying scent of roses.

The hoofbeats grew nearer, and Reuben's hands gripped my shoulders, the fingers biting deep. He shook me, hard enough to hurt. "Wake up, Cassiopeia. Wake up!"

And then I was falling—off the path and toward the ocean, plunging deep into the waves, Reuben's arms wrapped around me. We hit the surface of the sea and sank into its depths, past pale faces and reaching hands. Air was a lost commodity, and through the haze that filled my mind, I spared a thought to wonder how a sea that was on fire could be so terribly cold.

As if from a great distance, I heard Reuben calling me, telling me again to wake up, begging me to stay with him. But his voice was a curl of ash, a ripple amongst the waves. It dissolved beneath the pounding of the surf, and took me down with it into the dark.

I woke at last in my bedroom, the sheets pulled up to my chin. For a moment I just lay still, breathing. The dream had felt so real. When I swallowed, I could still taste soot and salt.

Reuben had rescued me, like a prince in an old-fashioned storybook—which irked me, even though it had only been a dream. I'd never liked those stories, where the prince woke Sleeping Beauty with a kiss or delivered Cinderella from a lifetime of servitude. I'd always saved myself. But there on the path, I'd been beyond grateful to see him. And when we'd fallen—in an awful reenactment of my worst fear, other than something happening to Cora—he'd kept me safe.

It had been so long since I'd felt that way—protected—I hardly remembered the sensation. What did it mean that my subconscious had hand-delivered a dream about my second-deepest anxiety, and then conveniently inserted Reuben as my savior? I didn't need a savior. In fact, if I were to star in one of those stupid fairytales, I'd rather be the prince—making something happen, instead of waiting around for something to happen to me.

Of course, in those fairytales, the prince hadn't shown up to resuscitate Sleeping Beauty covered in someone else's blood.

Frustrated, I sat up, the sheets pooling at my waist. And then I froze . . . again.

In the dim light that filtered through my blinds, I could see the pale skin of my wrists easily enough. They'd been unmarked when I went to sleep, after Reuben's unexpected visit. But now, across the inside of both wrists, just where the shadow-creatures had grabbed me, were five angry red marks. I turned my wrists left and right, examining them carefully, hoping the marks had been a trick of the light. But no matter how many times I looked, they were still there.

Holy crap. Did Reuben have the ability to invade my dreams, like some kind of freaking incubus? Or had the mere fact that I'd met him—that I'd struck a bargain with him—opened me up to a Faerie mind invasion?

I leapt out of bed and ran to the mirror. My face was streaked with ash, my hair tangled. On my cheeks, there was an unmistakable scrim of salt. And when I looked down at the hardwood floor, I saw that I'd scattered a trail of sandy, man-sized footprints, leading from the window to my bed and back again.

Incubus or not, he'd brought me home.

I followed the footsteps to the window, then glanced beneath it, at my desk. On it lay a single folded piece of paper, my name written on it in rounded, distinctive print.

Teeth gritted, I snatched it up and opened it. Inside, using one of my blue Bic pens, Reuben had written: *I am sorry. It was never my intention to endanger you. Wear this charm with my blessing, and dream no more. R.*

My eyes fell to the desk. Between my stapler and my hole-punch lay a round metal locket inscribed with three interlocking circles, attached to a chain. I picked it up and almost dropped it again—it was unexpectedly heavy, and cold, as if I held a piece of winter itself in my hand.

With shaking fingers, I undid the latch. Inside was a drawstring silk bag—moss-green, the color of Reuben's eyes. I tugged it open, peered inside . . . and then coughed, my own eyes streaming. The bag was filled with crumbled, strong-smelling herbs, a pinch of dirt, and—upon further examination—what looked like bits of bone.

Eeugh. I debated tossing the damn thing out the window—but what was I supposed to do? Never sleep again? Resigned, I dropped the locket over my head. It settled next to my heart like it was meant to be there, icy against my skin.

I wanted to scream—and I would've, if it hadn't frightened Cora. I grabbed some clean clothes and headed to the bathroom instead, the locket swinging back and forth beneath my pajama top like a tiny clock's pendulum. It was early enough that no one else was awake; I wouldn't have to explain myself. Thank goodness it was winter—I'd be able to hide the marks on my wrists with sweaters and long-sleeved shirts. But as for the rest of it—how had he gotten inside my head? And what if it *did* happen again, charm or no charm?

For a moment I wanted nothing more than to tell my mother about the promise I'd made. But then I came down to earth with a crash. My mother would think I was losing my mind, and it would break her. And if she broke, then Cora—

It was my secret. I had to keep it. And so I would.

I kept my secret, and Reuben kept his promise. If he appeared in my dreams, it was only because my subconscious had conjured him to be there. I told myself such dreams didn't matter. Who wouldn't dream about a gorgeous boy who kissed you like his life depended on it and called you 'beautiful one'? I was only human, after all . . . unlike the boy in question.

The winter grew colder. The nights grew longer. I kept expecting to find Reuben waiting for me, kept thinking I caught glimpses of him—in the study carrels at the library, standing outside Blue's Diner the one time I allowed Tommy D'Angelo to talk me into going on a date. It wasn't fair to Tommy, not really. If I was honest with myself, I'd only done it to chase Reuben out of my mind. But it didn't work, and after we'd made awkward conversation and eaten fries and shared a chocolate-mint milkshake—my favorite—I'd excused myself, feigning homework as an excuse. Hurrying through the chilly air to my car, hands deep inside my pockets for warmth, I'd seen a tall, lithe figure leaning against the hood, gotten a glimpse of dark hair and a sardonic smile. But by the time I'd reached the car, the figure was gone, as if I'd imagined him. Maybe he'd never been there at all.

I was relieved—but disappointed, too. It scared me, the way Reuben had burrowed his way into my heart. I found myself thinking of him at odd moments, wondering what it would be like to come home and find him waiting for me, with his wicked grin and his grandiose pronouncements. I *missed* him, which appalled me. I'd never even had a boyfriend, and here I was, lusting after a guy that wasn't even really a guy at all, to whom I'd promised God knew what in order to keep my sister safe. Clearly I needed to have my head examined.

But when I thought about seeing him again, my pulse beat too fast and hard for comfort, and it wasn't entirely from fear.

The clock ticked down. I took my last final and came outside to find a note pinned under my windshield wiper. *Tomorrow night,* it read in Reuben's graceful handwriting. *Midnight. The playground on South. Yours, R.*

I looked around, but he was nowhere to be seen, in either form. Amidst the cheerleaders and jocks, the tech-heads and drama geeks, all celebrating the start of winter break—whooping, revving their car engines, making plans for the weekend—I felt more alone than ever. *So,* I imagined saying to Tommy D'Angelo, *what're you doing tomorrow night? I'd hang out, but I'm off to fulfill a bargain with a tricky and potentially murderous—but hot!—faerie who can transform into a dog when he feels like it. Catch you later.* A hysterical laugh escaped me, but no one was listening. I slid behind the wheel and drove to work.

Sleep was elusive that night. I tossed and turned, waking convinced that I saw him standing beside my bed. But when I blinked my eyes clear, no one stood there at all. A rich scent filled the air, and I turned my head to find sprigs of rosemary tied into a bouquet on my pillow, their stems bound by a deep blue ribbon: the first of Reuben's gifts since the ring of daisies, unless you counted the cords of firewood I'd found neatly stacked by the toolshed the day after the first snow. Rosemary, for remembrance. As if I could forget.

Cora and I spent the day together. I made her chocolate-chip-and-banana pancakes and didn't even fuss when she ran her finger through the puddle of syrup on her plate and licked it clean. We went to the mall and got pedicures—wine-red for me, pale pink for her. I took her to Aranti's, our town's best coffee shop, and splurged on mochas for both of us. We spent hours that rainy afternoon sunk into the cushions of the old couch at the back of the bookstore on State Street, me pretending to read but really sneaking glances at my sister over the top of my book: her wide gray eyes, so like my own, her copper curls in need of cutting, her fingernails, gnawed to the quick with worry, the way she pulled her sleeves over her hands, as if trying to hide them. My heart swelled with love for her, love and loss and fear. *Please,* I thought desperately, *please let me have done my best for her.*

It was a miracle of a day: We got home and Mom was halfway sober, pot roast simmering in the oven and apple cider bubbling on the stovetop. Cora peeled off her wool socks and boots to show off her nail polish, and made me show Mom mine, too. I did, even though I felt silly, and Mom made a big fuss over both of us. When I went into the living room to feed Reuben's wood to the fire—the house was old and drafty, and keeping up with the heating bills was more than I could manage—she followed and wrapped her arms around me, holding me tight. She smelled of cider and cinnamon and roasted meat, with just the faintest undercurrent of whisky. "I love you, Cassie," she said fiercely. "Even when it seems like I don't. I see everything you do for us— for Cora. Your father would be so proud of you."

I couldn't think of a single thing to say, and after a moment she let me go. When she was halfway to the door, though, my throat unstuck, and I managed, "Mom?"

"Yes?" She turned. On her face there was such hope. It slayed me.

"Just—take good care of her, okay? If anything were to ever happen to me, like it did to Daddy—promise you wouldn't let anyone take her away."

My mother's brows knitted. "Why are you saying this, Cassie? Are you—is everything okay?"

This was a laughable question. Everything had been about a thousand degrees south of okay since I was Cora's age. Of course, now it had taken a new and disturbing swerve off the beaten path. But I hadn't confided in my mother for the past decade, and I wasn't about to start now. "Everything is fine," I lied. In the fireplace, Reuben's logs crackled and spit. I watched them burn and imagined I could see his face in the flames. "Never mind. Forget about it."

I heard my mother take a tentative step away. Then she stopped. "I promise," she said, her eyes clearer than I'd seen them in a long time. "I wouldn't let anything happen to her."

I nodded, not trusting myself to look at her. "Thank you."

"Don't thank me, Cassie. Don't you dare. You're my babies. I just wish—"

But I never found out what she was going to say, because Cora came bouncing into the room, asking was the cider ready and could she have some and did we think it was going to snow, and the moment fractured into pieces.

We ate the pot roast and drank the cider, sitting around the old wooden table that had belonged to my Grandma Celie. *Not bad for a last meal,* I told myself, in a last-ditch attempt at humor. It didn't work.

Cora read her bedtime stories to both of us that night. Afterward, I took a bath, a long one. I shaved my legs and conditioned my hair. If I was going to my death, I reasoned, I might as well look good. I put on my favorite jeans and my softest sweater.

Time crawled. I tried to read. Tried not to think of what Reuben might demand in exchange for our bargain, about the curiosity that consumed me and the traitorous excitement I felt about seeing him again. Waited some more.

At 11:45 I pushed the door of my room open and looked up and down the hallway. The house was dark. I tiptoed down the stairs. The TV blared from the living room—Mom had fallen asleep watching, as usual. I put on my coat and my boots and eased the front door open. Locked it behind me. Started to walk.

The playground on South was five blocks away, set in the midst of a grassy field, bordered by a creek. No one was outside but me. No one drove by. The streets were silent. Even the trees were still. I walked on.

I came to the basketball court first, forlorn with its cracked asphalt and torn nets. Reuben was not shooting hoops. I looked across the field and waited.

The playground was pitch-dark, deserted. One of the swings swayed back and forth as if under the influence of the wind or a child, even though there was no child and no wind. Shivering, I scanned the park for any sign of him. It was eerie, what with the unnatural silence and the self-propelled swing. I might as well have been anticipating the advent of the apocalypse, or a man with an axe, or the appearance of a tiny, oblivious ghost.

One moment, I was alone. The next, Reuben separated himself

seamlessly from the dark. He stood with one hand wrapped around the chain of the swing, urging it to stillness, a reverse etching against the ink of the night.

"I don't suppose," I said into the empty air between us, "that you'll ever tell me how you do that."

His lips lifted in a smile. He shook his head.

"You know it's not natural, right? Real people make noise. Or announce their presence. Or meet somewhere else other than a playground in the middle of the night. Like a coffee shop. Or a diner." I heard the petulance in my voice, but it was better than the bone-deep fear that warred with want inside me. Show him either, and I was doomed.

"Do they?" He sounded amused. "I assure you, Cassie, I'm real enough. And I'd meet you at a diner, if I could. I quite like diners, actually."

I laughed at this, trying to imagine him sitting across from me at Blue's, dipping salted fries into a puddle of ketchup. His smile widened.

"What, you don't think I eat?"

"I can't imagine it."

"I eat all sorts of things." His voice was mild enough, but still I shivered. I told myself it was from the cold.

He saw it, and shook himself all over, in the manner of a horse shedding flies. Then he held out his free hand. "We've talked enough. Come."

But still I balked. "Are you going to kill me?"

His mouth fell open in surprise, the most human gesture I'd ever seen him make. He threw back his head and laughed, the sound ringing like the bells of the old Catholic cathedral downtown, the one we'd gone to when Dad was still alive. "Why would I want to kill you, Cassiopeia? I have done much to keep you safe." He raised an eyebrow, and I thought of the path and the shadow-creatures, his arms around me as we plummeted through the dark. The charm was a sudden weight, its metal icy against my skin.

I thought of retorting that I wouldn't have been in danger to begin with if it weren't for him—but I was far too cold to debate semantics. "That's not an answer, Reuben."

"Yes," he said, "it is. Now. Come."

I stepped off the basketball court and into the grass. The blades were thick with ice, *shushing* a warning against my boots: *Go back. Go back. Go back.* But I thought of Cora, and kept walking.

I don't know what I was expecting—for him to whisk me away to some kind of faerie dun, for him to draw a knife and chop off my head as a sacrifice? Neither one would have surprised me. But instead he led me to the old carousel that sat at the edge of the playground, left behind by some long-ago fair that had called the park home. In the summer, the town hired bored teenagers to run it and charged a dollar for a ride.

Now, in the dead of winter, the carousel was still. But Reuben helped me up onto the platform anyway. Together we lay down on the metal floor. "What—" I began, but he only shook his head. A strange electricity emanated from him, a cold and stinging wind.

"Don't be afraid," he whispered as the carousel began to move, spinning slowly beneath the star-pricked sky. "I will be with you."

"That's what I'm afraid of," I whispered back. By my side, I felt him laugh, but he made no sound.

The carousel spun faster, the brightly-colored horses a blur. Reuben lay next to me on the icy metal floor, his hand gripping mine. "Watch." His voice was a breath of air.

At first I saw nothing, save the familiar constellations. I lay there and played connect-the-dots the way my father had taught me when I was a little girl, trying to slow the beat of my heart. The wind rose, baying, and suddenly the night seemed desolate, the park a wasteland. Clouds scudded across the sky, whipped one after the other as if in frenzy, exposing a baleful scrim of moon in their wake.

"What are we waiting for?" I asked Reuben, but he hushed me with the press of his fingers.

And then I saw them, bursting through Cassiopeia's constellation, rending her body asunder: A pack of men, their hair streaming, mounted on black horses whose bodies seemed carved from the fabric of the night, hounds keeping pace at their sides. The one in the lead let out a cry, full and mournful as a horn's wail, and a shudder ripped through me, despite my best efforts to lie still.

"The Wild Hunt," Reuben whispered, his lips cold against my ear. "To see them is a gift few mortals survive. For they take what they will, do the Hunters, and bring it not home again. Come to their attention at your peril, Cassiopeia Jorgensen. Forever afterward, you ride with them. All save one, and he is doomed."

"But who are they?"

"They have many names. The Furious Host. *Asgårdsreia. Odens jakt. Cŵn Annwn.* They are dreadful to behold, are they not? And yet, a wondrous sight."

He stared up at them as if mesmerized. I stared too, wondering if I was still asleep in my bed, if all of this was no more than another dream. "You said they had many names. What do you call them, Reuben?"

A tremor coursed through his body, and for a moment I could have sworn the metal horses that surrounded us transformed into living creatures, their painted bodies shading to the color of night, breaking free of the stakes that anchored them to rear back with a full-throated, stallion's cry. The skin of Reuben's hand prickled against mine, but when I tried to pull away, he only tightened his grip. When he spoke, his voice was the wind through the trees, the crystalline shattering of ice. He whispered, "Home."

Fear took me then. I closed my eyes and when I opened them, the horses were only horses and Reuben was himself again. "When the night is darkest, they ride," he said, eyes fixed on the Hunters. "When the world is cold and the storms rage. Many are the mortals who fall under the cold eye of the Hunt, only to find themselves wandering a foreign land, devoid of all they knew. Many are the mortals who never return."

He rolled on top of me, shielding me from view, and his mouth came down on mine. Over his shoulder I could see the Hunters, shrieking through the sky. "I would keep you safe, Cassie. Open to me. Let me mark you. Let me in."

His tongue traced along my lips. I felt that dangerous tug of desire again, the same way I had the first time I saw him, and again, that night in my room. What was to stop us now? It was too late for regrets, and so I returned the favor, nipping at his lower lip in a moment of daring. Dimly it came to me that I should ask him what he meant. But instead I whispered, "Yes."

He made a noise low in his throat and knotted his fingers in my hair. They tangled with the chain of the locket, and he drew back, inhaling sharply. "If you would have me, Cassiopeia, then take it off."

"The locket? Why?"

His voice was tight. "It is forged from cold iron. Poison to the Folk."

"But you made it for me," I protested. "Or you gave it to me, anyhow."

"I did. At a cost." He held up the hand that had touched the chain; the fingertips were an angry red, as if he had held them over an open flame. "I told you I would keep you safe. If such is at a peril to myself, then let it be."

His words seared through me, branding me as surely as the iron had scorched his skin. I thought of how I'd felt when we'd fallen from the path in the dream-that-was-not-a-dream: protected, watched over for the first time in years. There was no reason for me to trust him. Yet, somehow, I did.

Holding Reuben's gaze with my own, I pulled the locket over my head and tossed it aside. With an inarticulate sound, he came into my arms.

Time slipped and rolled and turned. The world came to me in glimpses: His lips on my neck, sharp teeth grazing my skin before they closed on my shoulder. My hands fisted in the silken material of his shirt. The cold air whistling in the space between us before he dropped his weight against me, murmuring in a language I didn't understand. My own voice, urging him onward, until he stopped my words with his mouth. The two of us moving together as the carousel revolved beneath us and the Hunt cleaved the starry vault above us and feeling rushed through me like the tide.

"Always sought," he whispered into my mouth. "Never found."

The Hunters crossed the moon, outlined one after the other, wild hair and dark horses and hellhounds and horns. On their faces there was a terrifying sort of ecstasy, teeth bared with the thrill of pursuit. As if he could see them, Reuben made a small, desperate sound. "*Huesta de Guerra.* They ride to war," he said, and in his voice I heard the basest sort of longing. "They go to reclaim what was lost."

Clouds swirled around the Hunters, hiding them from view. The wind roared and snow began to drift down, dusting the horses and the trees and ourselves, and suddenly I understood. I knotted my fingers in his dark hair and pulled his head back, so I could see his face. He ducked down again, hiding, but it was too late.

"Always sought," I repeated to him. "Never found. Do you keep me safe, Reuben of the Fair Folk? Or is it the other way around?"

Above me he trembled. "If you ask the question, Cassiopeia, the answer is already yours."

I dug my fingernails into his scalp, drawing blood, but he didn't wince. "Who are you, really?"

His lips drew back in a snarl, showing me his gleaming teeth, filed to points. Teeth meant for tearing, for the kill. Yet he had marked me carefully, leaving only the barest impression behind. "For centuries, I rode with the Hunt, a warrior at Gwynn Ap Nudd's side. Lord of the Otherworld, King of *Tylwyth Teg.* White

Son of Nudd. I did his bidding, I was a vessel for his will. I stole wine and women, ripped spirits from their bodies, tore the world asunder and laughed in the ashes."

I tried to turn my head away, but he cupped my face in his hands and held me still. "Aye, there is a freedom in it, Cassiopeia. Riders of the Hunt are bound to none but the Son of Nudd. They roar and ravage as they will. But love they do not. There is naught but the Hunt, Ride of Asgard, *Hueste de Animas,* Troop of Ghosts." His green eyes grew hard, distant. Snow silvered his dark hair. "One night I came upon a woman standing by a moonlit window, hand pressed against the glass. I should have taken her, tossed her upon my horse as I had so many others. But I could not. Instead I went to her. Instead she took me in."

"You left them," I said, my voice a rasp. "You left the Hunt behind—for love."

He nodded. "You are the very image of her. Your eyes like a gathering storm. Your hair like flames. You have her scent, like violets."

I swallowed hard. "So then Cora—"

"I was not there in the woods for Cora. I was there for you. May the gods forgive me." He moved against me, restless, and I felt that peculiar electricity course through his body again, transmitting itself through his flesh to mine, so that we became a single, burning thing. For an impossible moment I saw the bones shift beneath his pale skin, morphing into something both more and less than human. "I have watched you grow up, Cassiopeia. Far-flung descendant of the woman at the window. In you I see her bravery, her curiosity. In you I see her beauty."

Anger flooded me then. "You tricked me. If you've been watching me, you knew I would protect Cora. That her life means more to me than my own. You knew that I would come here, tonight. To you."

He lowered his head, brushing my lips with his. Beneath them I felt the threat of his razor-sharp teeth. "I have waited long for this night. Every Solstice since I abandoned the Hunt, I have taken solace with a mortal woman, letting her scent mask mine. But it is as Gwyn foretold long ago, when he cursed me for leaving my brethren behind. Always I left the woman's bed less satisfied than when I'd come to it. Always she pursued me, haunted by my touch, desperate for what I did not have to give. Until tonight."

The Hunt surged through the clouds above us, circling overhead. Some wore gleaming silver armor; some rode bare-chested, heedless of the frigid night. The head of their leader bristled with antlers, and over his saddle there lay the limp body of a white deer. Behind him rode a man whose skin was as green as the leaves of the apple tree in springtime. A crown of brambles graced his head. An owl soared beside him, wings outstretched, riding the currents of the wind. The sight was magnificent and terrible at once. And yet I was no longer afraid.

"Look," I said to Reuben, my voice filled with wonder, but he shook his head.

"I dare not. They cast me out, when I sought to rejoin them after I lost her. Offered me shelter only as the meanest of curs, trapped forever in my other form. And if not—then barred evermore I would be from *Tylwyth Teg*. Exiled to the mortal world, lost to all my kin. It was my punishment to walk the earth, searching evermore for something I could not reclaim. When the Host rode once more, I would be naught but their quarry. And so I have been. So I am."

I stared up at him, his inky lashes dusted with snow. "You want—to go home?"

"More than anything." The yearning in his voice was terrible to hear. I felt it thrum through me, as if it were my own. "I have not seen my homeland in centuries, since Gwyn banished me. He cursed me, as I said. Only when I fell in love with one who was worthy of the love I'd felt before—the love for which I'd given up everything—and was loved the same way in return . . . only then could I go home. And until such a time, he and his warriors would hunt me, forcing me to seek a pale simulacrum of what I had lost in the arms of another."

"But then—you lied to me. When you said you'd take Cora with you—that I might be dead by the time you brought her back again—"

Reuben gazed down at me, his expression grave. "I cannot lie."

"But you did! You said—" I could feel my eyebrows knit as I tried to remember what his exact words had been, that day in the woods. He'd threatened to take Cora as his pet, yes—but he hadn't said where he'd take her, exactly. All he'd said was that creepy thing about time slipping and spilling in the land under the hill. And I, in my foolish, reductive humanity, had connected the dots, just as he'd intended.

I pushed at him, my hands against his chest, and he retreated, obedient. Snow sifted through the space between us, coating the boards where we lay; with his index finger, he traced the shape of a star. "I would not have hurt your sister, Cassie. For in so doing, I would have damaged your heart beyond repair."

"Then—" My voice caught in my throat. "I never had to come here at all?"

"You made a bargain." His face was grave. "Once it is met, you may have naught to do with me, if that is your wish."

"I still don't understand. Why me?"

He slid closer to me once again, one eyebrow raised in question. I didn't shy away, and when he touched me, his hands were gentle, cradling my head, his fingers woven in my hair. "Like me, you know what it means to sacrifice for those you love, Cassiopeia. Like me, your heart is marked with loneliness. You look up at the stars each night, just as I do, and wonder what could be. There is a strength in you, a resilience. You have lost, and yet you endure."

I slid my hand down the pale line of his neck and felt his pulse pounding, an insistent beat against my fingertips. Slid my fingers further, and traced the line of his collarbone, marked with the black ink of a tattoo I'd never noticed before: a necklace of brambles, crossed with a sword. He gasped, a tiny noise devoured by the snow and the wind.

"Do you love me, then, Reuben?" The voice was mine, but the words seemed to come from somewhere far away—as if the night itself was speaking through me.

One of his hands tightened in my hair. The other slipped lower, leaving a tingling sensation everywhere he touched. "Cassiopeia—"

I drew my nails across his tattoo, beneath the silk of his shirt, and felt him shake against me. Somehow the power between us had shifted; it didn't matter what magic he possessed, or how sharp his teeth might be. I held his heart in my hand, and knew it. "I know you can't lie, Reuben. So tell me the truth. Is this a trick, a curse? Or do you love me?"

The snow drifted down, a blanket covering both of us. Above me he trembled, and I knew it was not from the cold. "No trick," he said against the hollow of my throat, his breath gusting warm on my skin. "And the curse is mine, Cassiopeia. For I am a damned soul."

"Answer me." My voice was fierce. "Do you love me?"

He raised his head and looked me in the eyes then. His own were wild, and in their depths I saw something unfamiliar—fear. "My heart is yours, should you want to claim such a shattered token as your own." The words came hoarse, barely audible over the roar of the storm and the howls of the hounds. "For yes, I do."

Surely I was dreaming. And in my dream I allowed myself to feel triumph for his admission and an echoing call within myself —after all the years of sacrifice, the grief and the weight of responsibility holding me down, finally there was this: A beautiful, broken boy who was not a boy at all, a boy who said he loved me and could not lie, a world of magic, where faeries led a hunt across the winter sky. I looked up into Reuben's haunted eyes and saw the thing I had never dared to admit I wanted most. I saw freedom—my own, and his.

"With you at my side," he whispered against my lips, "the

doors to *Tylwyth Teg* will open for me once more—that is, if you feel the same."

It was a dream. It had to be. And in my dream I felt pity for his loneliness, for the woman he had lost and the world he had left behind. In my dream I opened my mouth and drank down the night, in my dream I clutched Reuben to me and kissed him, the snowflakes melting to nothing on our tongues. Our mouths tasted of sorrow.

The Hunters dove, and an unkindness of ravens rose from the treetops to meet them. The birds' raucous cries resounded through the night, and the dogs echoed them, heads thrown back, jaws stretched wide to reveal an eternity within. The clamor was deafening, but it was lost in the fury of the storm. No lights came on in the houses that edged the park; no curious neighbors came to investigate. But between the ice-laden blades of grass I could have sworn I saw a dozen pairs of glowing eyes, as if tiny creatures crouched there, heads tilted upward in curiosity or veneration.

Reuben shuddered against me, and when he spoke again, his voice was a growl. "For centuries I have waited. For generations I have wandered. And I will not go back to them. I will be his hound no more." His body arched over mine, sheltering me from the worst of the storm, but I understood now, as I had not before, that I was the one who sheltered him. "In my dreams, I ride with them still. The Hunt calls to me. I feel it in my blood. But here, with you, under the open skies—I can bear its call. Always sought. Never found. Unless you cast me out."

I thought, later, that I should have done just that. But instead I pulled him closer. He came to me willingly as the Hunt passed us by. The night and the drifting snow and the ice and the wind, the revolutions of the carousel and the flight of the Hunters across the sky—all of it fused into one, so that I understood how Reuben had disappeared into the darkness, how it had claimed him and relinquished him again. The world was geometry: the hexagons of snowflakes, the perfect orb of the moon, the parabolas of his eyebrows, the angles and planes of his face, lost in shadow. "What warmth I have is yours," he breathed against my skin, and I felt the snow around us melt, the metal beneath me heat. "Our bargain is fulfilled."

I woke alone and half-frozen on the floor of the carousel hours later, when dawn had already creased the sky. The wind had ceased to howl, and the snow came down in silent drifts. It lay thick on the backs of the horses, weighing the branches of the trees, bending them low.

There were no Hunters. Reuben was gone, as if he had never been. And maybe he had not. Where, after all, was the proof? Who would believe me?

I struggled to my feet, bracing myself on a palomino's icy neck, and surveyed the park. It was empty. The swings hung motionless from their metal bar. But on the banks of the creek, I saw him: a massive black dog silhouetted against the snow, his eyes fixed on my face. He growled once, in warning or recognition, and paced backward toward the bridge, looking over his shoulder in a clear indication to follow. Again, he stopped. And then again.

I knew what he was offering me—and what he would give up, if I refused. For love, for the sake of one of my ancestors, he had wandered alone for more years than I could imagine. If he'd been telling me the truth—and as far as I knew, he had no choice but to do just that—he felt for me as he had for her, that woman he'd known so long ago.

He loved me.

But what did I feel for him? Fascination, yes. Attraction, definitely. Blood heated my cheeks when I thought of what we'd done the night before, the feel of his hands on my body. But love?

The black dog regarded me, as somber as it was possible for a dog to look. Its body flickered, shifting—and then Reuben stood there, pale against the snow. His clothes lay at his feet; he pulled them on, and stepped toward me. "Cassiopeia—"

I put up a hand, stopping him where he stood. In my heart, a strange and dangerous seed took root. I'd never imagined leaving Cora. She was my responsibility. But now—with Reuben—I'd be doing him a great service, and in return he would open the doors to a world full of possibilities. A world where I would be responsible for no one but myself.

I would be free.

I'd never dared to admit how much I wanted such a thing. For what was the point of admitting your desire for a thing you could never have?

But I'd come to meet Reuben tonight thinking I might never go home again, never see my sister grow up. If I chose to go with him —if the quicksilver obsession I felt for him was really love—I'd just be embracing the future I'd imagined all along.

Reuben stood motionless, a still life against the snowy bank of the creek, his face impassive. He was a statue of a boy—but I remembered the heat of his lips on mine, the tremor in his voice when he'd said he loved me, the way he'd held me tight when we'd tumbled from the path into the sea. *Like me, you know what it means to sacrifice for those you love, Cassiopeia,* he'd said. *You have lost, and yet you endure.*

For the first time in as long as I could remember, I wanted to make a selfish choice—a choice purely for myself. What did I want . . . just for me?

I'd never had the luxury of asking myself that question before. Never imagined I could.

Reuben didn't speak, didn't say another word. He didn't have to; my choice was stark enough. All I had to do was cross the park to him. Or crook my finger, and he'd come running, eager. He could go home. I could be free. And we could be together, in this strange and brutal world that existed alongside the one I'd always taken for granted.

I felt the call of him in my blood, as he had no doubt felt the lure of the Hunt. Torn, I swayed. But then I remembered what he had said, that first day in the woods: *In the land under the hill, time slips and spills. And one day indeed she might return to this place, only to find all she loved had passed to dust.*

By the feet of one of the horses, the charm glinted in the morning light. I bent and slipped the chain over my neck, feeling the weight of the iron locket settle once more over my heart. Rubbing my hands together for warmth, I set off across the field toward home.

Finders Keepers

ELIZABETH DEVIDO

Elizabeth DeVido has a taste for dark stories, strong heroines, and bad people as protagonists. She is a two-year selected playwright for Big Dawg Productions's Youth Play Festival. She is currently attending UNC Asheville to pursue a degree in English. When not writing, she is drinking sweet iced tea, doing theatre, and excessively daydreaming.

I know exactly where Dylan Carver is.

He lives on 433 Appleton Lane. He has a signed poster of LeBron James above his bed, and it's torn at the corner. He's wearing his basketball jersey (number 13) in his driver's license photo.

I also know who took him.

I was there when it happened, standing outside his window, peeking from behind the tree near his room. The guy came in through a different window in the house. He looked about forty. White. Dirty scruff on his face. About six-foot-three. He wore a gray hoodie and faded black jeans and white Nike sneakers.

Dylan is six-feet, three-and-three-quarter inches tall. He is young and muscular, and when I saw the intruder, I thought Dylan would easily defend himself. But the guy knocked Dylan out and threw him over his shoulder with hardly any scuffle. I hid around the corner of the house as the guy climbed out the window and carried Dylan to a black van parked at the very end of the street, out of sight of any of the Carver house windows.

The next morning, I ride my bike through the Carvers' neighborhood. A squad car is parked in front of their house. An officer stands in the driveway with Dylan's parents, notepad in her hand, asking them questions. Mr. and Mrs. Carver stand in perfect parents-of-the-victim position. Mr. Carver has a comforting arm around his wife, who weeps quietly. They look like models posed for a reenactment of a crime. Even when grieving, the Carvers always have to appear picture-perfect.

I never liked Dylan's family. They aren't good enough for him.

As I approach the house, I hear the officer ask if there are any possible witnesses.

"No," Mr. Carver says. "Everyone in the house was asleep. No one saw what happened."

I can't help but chuckle as I bike past. Pastor Carver is lying to a cop and doesn't even know it. The truth is that there is one witness. There's me. His classmate who has a drawer full of his chewing gum wrappers, his outgrown shirts that still smell like

him, and his hairs plucked from the comb he keeps in the left
drawer of his bathroom.

But I don't tell them any of this.

As I pass them by on my bike, I try not to look like I'm paying
much attention to them. I saw the captor's face. I have a
description of him and a good idea who he was and why he
was there.

I can't tell the police what I saw. What I know. If I do, they'll
ask why I was standing outside his window the night before. Why
his parents don't know who I am. How I know about Dylan's
gambling debts. How I knew what he was doing before any of his
friends and family did.

This is what I hate about the police. This is what I hate about
people. They ask too many questions.

Other people are nothing but nuisances that get in the way.

They get between me and Dylan.

I went home from school with Dylan every day since I first
saw him my sophomore year, and he never knew. I followed
him while he left home, letting his parents know he was
going to "work." What he told his parents was the movie theater
was actually a local pub, whose owner was too dumb to tell that
Dylan's ID was fake. (I knew it was fake because he wasn't
wearing his number 13 jersey in it.)

I stared through the front windows of the pub and watched
him return over and over to the poker table in the corner. The men
he played with were older, a lot older. Either old men with silver
hair tucked under hunting caps and puffy camouflage jackets, or
middle-aged men with five o'clock shadows. The first day they
offered him a cigarette, he said no. Just a week ago, I saw him
smoke six in the boys' locker room when all the other players
had left.

I also heard the conversations Dylan had with these men. And

I know that for every game he won, there are at least two or three guys he owes money to. One of them is a middle-aged guy named Silas who wore the same grey hoodie and faded black jeans as Dylan's kidnapper.

The Carvers don't know any of this stuff about Dylan. Funny how parents can know less about their kid than a classmate who never talked to him. They always thought they raised him right. They thought he was the perfect, golden boy. The athletic, cherry-pie, all-American boy-next-door who got perfect grades, played sports, went to church on Sundays, read his Bible, and would one day have a white picket fence with a beautiful wife and two cherub-like kiddos running around.

They couldn't see the boy who was crying himself to sleep every night worried about his mom's breast cancer treatment they couldn't afford. The boy who knew prayers at his family's church weren't going to cure his mom. The boy whose job wasn't paying enough, who turned to gambling to try to fix everything. The boy who won one poker game and thought he could win them all and save his mom. The thrill that filled his eyes with each thump of a card on the table.

Only I know these things. Only I have walked the lengths of the labyrinth in his head, all the dark crevices he never dared to show his parents. I stood outside his bedroom window watching him cry. Watched him angrily rip pages from the Bible his dad gave him and throw it across the room. I followed him to the pub at night. I saw him sneak a flask of cheap whisky into the bathroom after giving a sermon to children at his father's church. I saw the gambling his family didn't see, and I saw the nights crying the men at the pub didn't see. I was the only one who saw all of him.

I watched over him like a guardian angel would.

Dylan is admired by everyone.

But no one admires him as much as I do.

In our math class, I chose a seat in the back so I'd be able to look at him undetected. Traced my eyes down the golden-tan curves of his shoulders, his shoulder blades, his collarbones, his Adam's apple. I walked through the gym after school one day during a boys' basketball practice, saw him lift his shirt to wipe his face, and nearly threw my arms around him.

That's when I decided that he would be mine one day. I would not allow any twist of fate to decide otherwise. If I were Pygmalion, he was my perfect Galatea.

I make a plan to get Dylan back from Silas, his kidnapper.

I fix myself some coffee and wait until my parents are asleep. Around one a.m., I peek into their room to check. Both dead silent asleep. I slip over to the drawer next to their bed. I've sat through plenty of my dad's rants about the government's heavy-handed regulations threatening to take away his right to own a gun. I think of his misguided words as I pull his pistol out of his drawer, drop it into my backpack, and sneak out of the house.

I know from trips following Dylan to the pub that Silas has a hunting cabin out in the woods. I know this because Silas never drives to the pub to play cards. One day, I followed him, too. The cabin was walking distance. I filed that information away, like all information I kept about Dylan.

Silas's cabin is made of wood siding painted white. It gleams in the early morning sun. The black van is parked out front, so I know this is the right place. As I suspect, the door is locked, but when you're in love and there's a house between you and your beloved, you'll research the hell out of lock-picking.

Once I'm in, I hear the scuffling. The creaking of the floorboards above me, and a muffled voice. Dylan.

I quickly make my way up the staircase, clenching my teeth against every groan of the boards. My eyes dart across the place checking for signs of anyone around.

I make it up to the second floor, an attic. On a bed by the

window is Dylan, hands bound by a pair of handcuffs and his feet bound by rope. Duct tape covers his mouth.

I stare at him. The sunlight from the window illuminates his bronze curls. I've never been this close to him while he's awake. Once he sees me, his beautiful blue eyes widen, and he begins to struggle harder, his voice muffled under the tape.

Does he recognize me from school? I'm not sure. He must have, or else he is just relieved to find help. I don't care. I've been craving for him to look at me like that like a carnivore craves meat.

I approach him, watching his body bucking on the bed. I pull my dad's Swiss Army knife from my pocket and cut the ropes at his ankles. Then I wrap an arm across his shoulders, my nerves burning at finally touching his skin. I help him out of bed and to the stairs.

As we descend, my blood goes hot. He will love me after this. This event will be instilled in his brain for the rest of his life, and I will be forever linked to it. Maybe he doesn't love me now, but this event will forever intertwine us. And with time, I will make him love me.

I will.

He will.

I know all of his secrets. I know more about him than everyone else. And rescuing him is the only way to assure things end up the right way.

The police would have only kept us apart.

As I open the front door of the cabin, I see headlights through the trees. My heart lurches, and I hurry Dylan towards the van. My free hand reaches for my dad's pistol, and I aim it in the direction of the truck approaching the hill. I open the back of the van, and I don't need to give him any instruction as he flops himself down. I shut the van doors just as a rusty red pickup truck pulls up a few feet from us.

"You!" a voice calls.

Silas slams the truck door shut and starts toward us. I bolt around to the driver's seat and shut the door, my hands fumbling for the keys in the cupholder. I hear his fist grip the rear door handle. Adrenaline fills my chest.

No. I grit my teeth. No one is taking him away from me.

Not Silas.

Not the police.

Not his parents.

Not his friends.

I've watched Dylan Carver from afar long enough. I've been patient. Now I'm taking what's been denied to me for so long.

I shove the key in the ignition just as Silas begins to open the back door. I put the thing in reverse, slamming my foot on the gas. The rear of the car hits his body, slamming the back door shut. I hear his skull slam against the windows, and the tires rumble over his bones.

I don't look back to check for blood. But Dylan's muffled screams from under the duct tape tell me I've left a mess. I put the van into drive and rumble away from the cabin toward the highway.

I've been driving for about an hour now. The sunlight through the window is making the vinyl seat hot, and I'm twisting and untwisting my fingers on the steering wheel. My heart has stopped beating in my ears, and the events of the past forty-eight hours are on perpetual repeat in my head. I check over my shoulder, and I see Dylan seated quietly in the corner, before turning my face back to the road.

Dylan built up so many secrets. And so did I.

But now I have a new secret.

The last sign we passed said we were approaching the state border. Dylan's probably starting to wonder why the drive is taking so long.

Dylan Carver is exactly where he should be.

Girl in Pieces

LAUREN FAULKENBERRY

Lauren Faulkenberry is author of the Bayou Sabine series, which includes *Bayou My Love* (2016), *Back to Bayou Sabine* (2016), *Bayou Whispers* (2017), and *Just the Trouble I Needed* (2017), all from Blue Crow Books. She is also the author and illustrator of the children's book *What Do Animals Do On the Weekend?* (Novello Festival Press 2002, reprint edition forthcoming 2018).

Lauren divides her time between writing, teaching, and printmaking. Originally from South Carolina, she has worked as an archaeologist, an English teacher, and a ranger for the National Park Service. She earned her MFA in creative writing from Georgia College & State University, and her MFA in Book Arts from The University of Alabama. She was a finalist for the Novello Festival Press First Novel Award, won the Family Circle short fiction contest for her story "Beneath Our Skin," and was nominated for an AWP Intro Award. She's a sucker for a good love story and is happiest when she writes comedy and romance.

The water around us is black and cold. It stings my skin and fills my nostrils, making my head buzz as I struggle to hold in the last bit of air. My arms flail, my feet kick, and my sister Kylie is motionless in the car next to me. Her dark hair billows around her, like a cloud. We are stuck in the darkness, pulled down by something I can't see. Above us, the moon pierces the river, but to me, so far below the surface, it's no brighter than a dimming bulb. My chest stings, but I can't steal another breath. The car has filled with water. This time the glass is not broken.

I awake on the floor by my bed, my heart pounding and my shoulder throbbing from my impact on the hardwood floor. My feet are still tangled in the sheets.

Across the room, my older sister Kylie snores in the other single bed.

I have this dream all the time. Some nights I make it out. Some nights I don't.

Some nights I don't save either of us.

Some nights I can't remember who saved whom.

Then I look down at my thighs, trace my finger over the scars that curl around my knees and down my calves to my feet, and I remember.

My sister breezes into the studio an hour late, peeling her rain jacket from her shoulders as if it's a skin that no longer fits. She sighs as though this day is the pinnacle of her discontent, and I look away, knowing that if she catches me scowling she'll start telling me all about whatever disaster made her late for the fifth day in a row. I sit up straighter at my work table and focus instead on the blank fiberglass face in front of me. Off-white and smooth as an egg, it will later be attached to our most popular body, Number 7 in the series.

If someone had asked me last year what I'd be doing during my last high school summer, I'd have told them I'd be working in the library, maybe a bookstore—but I never would have pictured myself working as a face painter in a mannequin factory.

And I never, ever, would have guessed that Kylie would be here with me.

Kylie sighs again, draping her jacket over a Number 9 next to her desk. Number 9 was modeled after a ballerina, with shoulders slightly rotated, one foot forward, as if dipping her toe into a stream. She has a serene grace that is obliterated by Kylie's plastic pink leopard-print jacket.

Kylie plops down in the chair across from me and says, "I need to use the car tonight. I have somewhere I have to be." She swivels from side to side in the chair, her knee-high boots squeaking as they rub together. Her skirt rides high up on her thighs, showing off legs toned from years of running track back in high school. It's only June, but she's already had a spray tan.

"What if I have somewhere I have to be?" I say.

"Oh, Maggie. Like you have anywhere to be." Laughing, she grabs a head and spins it on the table like a top. "This dummy sees more action than you do."

She's been saying things like this ever since she came home. One year at college only widened the gulf between us. She's always telling me about the parties she went to, the clubs she snuck into, the reckless risks she took.

"We're supposed to take Mom out for her birthday," I tell her. "Or did you forget already?"

She rolls her eyes, putting enough torque on the head to send it wobbling towards the edge of the table. "Dammit," she says. "I have a dinner date at seven-thirty. He's a total fox."

"Guess you'll have to cancel."

"Mom won't care if I leave early. It's not like she never sees me."

"But it might be her last birthday," I say.

Kylie leans on the table, resting her chin on her arm so that her face is squeezed in among the row of heads I've been tasked with painting. They're fresh from the production room downstairs, where they were airbrushed with a base coat of pale gray paint. Next to their faces, Kylie's looks like a brown egg that got shoved into the wrong carton.

"Way to be positive," she says.

"I'm being realistic."

She's been here for only a month, but already I want her to quit, be fired, be yelled at in front of everyone for being late and screwing up orders. This factory was my sanctuary, the one part of my life that was supposed to be devoid of her. For a while, it had been—but then she dropped out of college in Columbia and moved back in with Mom and me. Then our mother insisted that I get her a job here. *She can't just loaf around the house doing nothing,* Mom told me.

There weren't many jobs for teenagers in our tiny corner of South Carolina, but Mom seemed to think if Kylie hung around with me long enough, she could get scared back on track. *She needs you,* Mom kept saying, as if that absolved Kylie of every careless and hurtful thing she'd ever done to me—those things that made us stop speaking to each other after the night that ripped us apart.

Kylie complained about the job for the first three weeks she worked here. She whined about our supervisor, Luke, because he actually expected her to work—and he'd put her in the packaging department because that was the only open position. She bemoaned having a shift that started at eight in the morning and a tiny workroom with gray walls. Then she met Fischer, the sculptor, and quipped in the darkness of our childhood bedroom that sleeping with him was the only thing she could see that would make the rest of the job worthwhile.

"Leave him alone," I told her. "Don't make him one of your casualties."

"You like him," she said.

"Of course I do. He's a good guy."

"No," she said, her voice deepening. "You *like* him."

I frowned, hating that she could always see right through me. I didn't care who she slept with, as long as it wasn't Fischer.

Fischer, the college student with the brooding stare and the big square hands, who hardly spoke to those of us not made of fiberglass. Fischer, who had the most adorable crooked grin and blushed when someone told a dirty joke. He was in an art program at the community college across town, sculpting mannequins to pay his tuition. He was apparently some kind of prodigy, at least in South Carolina. Luke was thrilled to have him, because he worked fast and made beautiful figures that had increased the factory's sales by sixty-eight percent.

Englehart's was a family-owned business that had been making mannequins since the 1960s. Now they specialized in high-end mannequins that cost over four times what most mass-produced mannequins did. It was mostly because of Fischer that the company was able to charge what they did—a big-time New York designer had found Englehart's by accident last year, and commissioned a group of specially-made figures sculpted by Fischer.

"That man has an eye like no one else," the designer had said. "If I could take him back to the city in my suitcase, I'd do it."

Fischer had no intention of moving to New York, but he happily sculpted a dozen models for the designer's new fall launch, and Englehart's had retained the rights to use those models—in a slightly different form—for their future sales.

After that launch, Englehart's sales had increased ten-fold.

Fischer was unfazed by all the attention. He just seemed happy to not have to worry about tuition ever again.

I keep hoping Fischer will suggest that he and I go out somewhere, talk outside of these gray square rooms, but he never does. A bunch of us go out as a group sometimes, all of us from the factory—usually to a dive bar that won't card me—and Fischer and I circle each other in that strange way that's just past the orbit of friendship, but not close enough to be more. Now that Kylie's fixated on him, I hardly ever have time alone with him.

She's an expert at squeezing into spaces where she doesn't belong.

Before Kylie, I'd wander down to Fischer's side of the building a couple of times a week just to see what he was making. Sometimes he'd come by my office and bring me a coffee, or offer me a doughnut before he took the box to the break room where they'd be devoured in seconds. Now, whenever he came to my corner of the factory, Kylie was there, wedging herself between us like a third person squeezing onto a love seat.

She wanted him to chase her, mostly because she was bored, but also to prove she could still take anything from me that she wanted. She got more reckless with each passing day, and she didn't seem to care who she took down with her. For her, Fischer was just something she could use to make her crappy job a little more bearable, and mine a little worse.

This is the pattern with Kylie and me: she shoves herself into my space and I disappear next to her, like a faint star next to a full moon.

"You can't skip Mom's dinner," I tell her, mixing a pale blue paint for eye shadow.

She rolls her eyes and spins the mannequin's head with enough torque to send it skidding off the table and into the doorway, where it collides with a sneakered foot. She grins when Fischer steps over the threshold and bends to pick it up.

She shamelessly stares at his ass and I bite my lip.

"Morning, ladies," he says. "Maggie, I need a favor." He swipes a bit of dust from the head with his sleeve and places it back on the table. Kylie's eyes track his every move.

My heart thumps against my ribs when he says my name. He leans against the doorframe in his usual faded jeans and pearl-snap shirt, looking like he just rolled out of bed. His muscular frame fills most of the doorway. His dark hair stands out in tufts, and for the hundredth time, I wonder how soft it would feel between my fingers. As he slides his hand over his stubbled cheek, I think of how those hands mold lumps of clay into lithe bodies with tiny waists. I imagine how those fingers press into the surface of the clay, and how they would feel pressing into my skin. I am not lithe, nor particularly lean like the models. I have broad shoulders, full breasts, and thighs that rub together when I walk. Unlike Kylie, I do not turn heads.

That designer had been right: Fischer was the reason that our mannequins weren't soulless and vacant, like all the others out there. It was like magic, the way he captured something from each model—but it wasn't in her face: rather it was in the curve of the shoulders, the arch of the back. Any good sculptor could replicate the human form, but what sold our mannequins was the current of something we couldn't quite explain that coursed through their bodies, warm and electric. Our best seller—Lucy, we called her— had a melancholy line in her shoulders that made your heart sting around the edges. She looked tough, but fragile. Everybody wanted to take her home.

"What is it?" I ask him.

"My model didn't show up," he says. "Could I borrow you for a couple of hours? Would you stand for me?"

His eyes are a glacial blue. When they're fixed on me, I can barely breathe.

It's his job to study a body's curves and angles, and he could no doubt distinguish all of mine, despite the layers of flannel and denim I try to hide under. I want to say yes, but then I freeze, thinking of the scars that crisscross my legs like the seams in a patchwork quilt. He'd want to know what happened, and I'd have to tell him about the accident, and then he would look at me the same way everybody else does.

Like I'm broken.

I don't actually mind the scars myself. Not anymore. I just hate the way people look at them, and then look at me, full of pity. I fantasize about making up stories: *It was a tiger shark*, I'd say. *A motorcycle dragged me for a mile. I was trampled by circus ponies when my act went awry.*

But usually, I just say nothing at all. I can't talk about the accident without talking about Kylie, and I'm tired of being connected to her.

I swallow hard, trying to come up with an excuse to satisfy Fischer. Before I can, Kylie slides next to him and says, "I'll do it, Fischer. I always wanted to be a model." She actually bats her eyelashes.

I want to throw that head at her and knock her off the stool.

He looks at me for a moment, as if waiting for me to come through. When I say nothing, he glances back at Kylie and shrugs. "Okay," he says. "Why not?"

He leads her out of the studio, and she walks with an exaggerated sway in her hips. She's lean, like the models he's accustomed to. When their voices disappear down the hallway, I throw the head against the wall. There's a loud *thunk* as it bounces off the sheetrock and rolls across the floor. Of course it's indestructible, just like her.

Kylie could become the center of anyone's world simply by walking into it. It's been like that all of our lives, and I figure it'll be that way until both of us are buried. I'm the smart one. She's the good-looking one. Everyone always said so, until both of us believed it was true—like we could only be one or the other. I thought she was selling herself short when she spent more time worrying about being Miss Richland County than raising her GPA enough to get a scholarship. She always accused me of being jealous because I scared boys away with my brains. "You think you're so much smarter than everyone else," she'd say. "You keep pushing people away, and one day there won't be anybody left."

She said that on the night she drove our mother's car into the Catawba River—she, tipsy and stubborn, and me with too little spine to stand up to her. We were driving home from her friend's party, and she was furious because I'd embarrassed her. She told me I'd said something to make her look stupid in front of her friends, and I'd told her she could look plenty stupid without anyone else's help.

She'd had too much to drink, and I should have taken the

keys, but I didn't argue hard enough when she climbed into the car—I just wanted to get myself inside before she drove away, and I wanted out of that house, away from those people who were nothing like friends. She hollered at me, choking back tears as we sped around the curve toward the bridge, and I realized in an instant that I had been the stupid one. Metal clanged against concrete and the earth tilted. My head banged against the window and Kylie screamed as the car crashed through the guard rail and plunged off the bridge and into the black water below.

The old Ford was built like a tank. It only took a few seconds for the headlights to disappear beneath the waves, for water to start gushing in. I pulled the door handle, but it wouldn't budge.

"Kylie!" I yelled, "Hurry!"

She didn't reply. Her head lolled to the side.

I clawed at my seat belt, jamming the button until it finally released. The water was up to my waist, my skirt billowing around me. The car's nose pointed straight down.

I shook Kylie's shoulder and she mumbled something I couldn't make out.

The water was freezing, up to my chest. The car had tilted so the seats were pinning us, pushing us under. I gasped, kicking at the windshield as hard as I could.

"Kylie!" I yelled again, but she didn't wake.

When I looked at her face, I saw it. A crack in the driver's side window, running almost the full width of the glass. I grappled with the steering wheel, fighting to keep my head above water, and kicked with everything I had.

At last the glass collapsed under my feet. I kicked at the corners, trying to knock out as much of the window as I could. Water poured in through the opening, forcing the car downward. I took a breath and tore at Kylie's seat belt as we plunged below the surface.

When the belt snapped open, I pushed past her and scrambled out the window, felt the sting of the jagged glass against my leg. My lungs burned, and I wanted so badly to swim to the surface, take a breath, and swim back down. But she didn't have that much time.

I fought the urge to breathe. My hands gripped the frame of the car, my legs splayed against it to hold myself in place while I grabbed fistfuls of her leather jacket, then forced my hands under her arms. I pulled as hard as I could, my knees splaying, my feet scrabbling as I dragged her through the window. The car shifted again and I felt the frame scrape one leg as I used my feet to push us away from the car and towards the surface.

My chest felt like it was collapsing in on itself. When my head burst from the water, I gasped, coughing and choking.

I dragged Kylie through the water. It was like trying to uproot an oak. When I finally pulled her onto the bank, I turned her on her back and slapped her.

"Wake up!" I yelled.

I knelt next to her and put both hands on her chest, heaving my weight into them, pushing in sharp thrusts like I'd seen people do on TV. Tears streamed down my cheeks, but still I pushed, calling her name.

At last she coughed and spat out what looked like a gallon of water. She sputtered and coughed, rolling onto her side. I smacked her on the back and at last she took a few ragged breaths.

"Stay here," I said, and scrambled up the bank to the highway. My body swayed as I stumbled along the shoulder. I just wanted to lie down and rest. My knees buckled and I tumbled to the ground. My head throbbed and my vision blurred. I wanted so badly to lie in the grass and just go to sleep.

Then there were headlights, two tiny golden orbs, and I forced myself to stand again, to get onto the pavement, to wave my arms as hard as I could. The car pulled off onto the shoulder, the headlights blinding me. I collapsed, landing hard on my tailbone, my legs splayed out in front of me.

In the pool of white light, I saw the gashes that covered my legs, the streaks of dark blood.

I was in pieces.

It took over four hundred stitches to patch my legs back together, but my sister emerged from that river with tiny scratches that only she could see.

I n her underwear, Kylie stands in what I recognize from my junior year art class as a *controposto* stance, her body in a gentle S-shaped curve. In her satin bra and panties, her long dark hair falling over one shoulder, she looks more like a pin-up girl than a master painter's muse. She's in the center of the room, standing on a wooden platform. It's chilly, but Fischer has placed a small space heater next to her.

The back of the room is filled with dozens of mannequins, all facing straight ahead, waiting to be sanded in the room down the hall. The seams are still visible down their sides, across their waists. Their faces hold clear expressions and blank eyes. I used to avoid looking at their eyes, but now it doesn't bother me so much. A metal bin in the opposite corner holds separated torsos, arms, and legs. It reminds me of those wire cages in the dime store that hold beach balls. These are the imperfect pieces that Luke will try to salvage later.

Fischer stands a few feet from Kylie, a rack of willowy arms dangling behind him. He's working on a skeletal armature made of wire and wood. It's already covered in a base layer of clay, so he's just using Kylie to finish the details. To his right sits an enormous block of tan clay, flecked with tiny bits of mica. He shears a piece off with a strand of wire, then uses his hands to wedge it against the table as if he's kneading dough. All the while he stares at my sister, his head cocked to the side as if he doesn't quite understand what he's looking at.

I watch from the doorway as he shoves a handful of clay onto the frame, pinching and pulling with his fingers. He adds lumps to the midsection, shoving them into place until he has enough flesh built up, then sliding his thumbs along the surface to mimic the contours of her belly, her hips. The armature trembles as he holds it steady with his left hand, grasping the neck or the shoulder as he shoves the handfuls of clay onto the frame with his right. Then his touch softens, smoothing out the curves of muscle. This is my favorite time to watch—when he takes the lumpy, vague shape and coaxes it into lifelike contours.

Kylie complains about a stitch in her side, grabbing her ankle behind her to stretch. The motion thrusts her chest forward and my jaw tightens.

Fischer frowns and drops his hands to his hips, leaving beige handprints on his jeans.

"Sorry," she says, blinking slowly, as if trying to hypnotize him.

"Just ten more minutes," he says. "You're doing fine."

She sighs, stepping back into a pose that doesn't quite match that of the sculpture.

Fischer shakes his head, motioning with his fingers. "Turn your right hip out a little more."

She moves slightly, staring at him through her lashes, and he says, "Your other right."

She frowns, over-exaggerating the pose. Fischer arches a brow and walks over to her, placing his hand on her hip to move her into place. Staring straight at me, she purses her lips as he moves her shoulder, her knee, leaving smudges of clay on her skin.

When at last he walks back toward the sculpture, he says, "Hey, Maggie. Your big sis might have found her calling."

Kylie smirks, and I feel like my chest is caving in. I hope that he said that because he thinks complimenting her is being considerate to me, and not because he's hoping to take her home on the back of his bike so he can see the rest of her. Not that she's left much mystery.

"It's coming along well," I say.

Fischer smiles, brushing his hands off on his jeans. "Saved my skin today. How will I ever return the favor?"

"I'm sure I could think of something," my sister purrs.

He pretends not to hear her, but blushes from his cheeks to his collar as he steps behind the clay Kylie.

"Being immortalized is probably enough," I say.

"You going to name this one after me?" Kylie says.

Fischer turns back to his sculpture and digs his thumbs into the clay, carving out the collarbones. "This might have to be our little secret," he says. "Don't want to get the boss angry." Smoothing out the shoulders, he says, "He might get upset, thinking he has to pay you more." He winks at me, his back to my sister. For a moment, she is forgotten.

Kylie squirms, scratching her shoulder blade, and Fischer says, "I can manage the rest by myself. You can take off."

"I don't mind," she says. "I'm getting the hang of it."

He taps a finger against his temple. "I've got the rest committed to memory. But if you wanted to come back tomorrow, I could finish up the face."

Kylie grins, and steps off the platform to admire her likeness. She stands so close to Fischer that her bare skin brushes him with each tiny movement she makes. He pretends not to notice, but steps away from her when his eyes rest on mine.

"What happens to it when you're done?" Kylie says.

"This is the master. They make a plaster cast of it to use for the mould," Fischer says, wiping his hands on a rag. He glances at me as Kylie twirls a lock of hair around her knuckles.

I trace my fingers down the bicep, the clay cool and pliable. My fingernail leaves a mark.

"Then they smash it," I say.

From my bedroom, I hear Kylie and my mother maneuvering around each other, trying to get dressed. There's the clack of a toothbrush against the sink, the rattle of perfume bottles, the smell of singed hair—no doubt from my mother holding hers in the curling iron for too long. The chemo made it so thin, she always burns it trying to make it curl. I stand in front of my closet, tugging on a pair of pants. My mother sticks her head in the door and says, "Why don't you wear a skirt tonight, darling? Those pants make you look like you work for the government."

"They're comfortable, Mom."

"It's a shame to have youth on your side and not take advantage of it once in a while. You get to be my age, and you'll regret not showing more skin when it still looked good."

"Kylie shows enough for both of us."

My mom frowns at my words. "You look so nice in skirts," she says.

"Mom."

She sighs. "It's my birthday," she says. "It's the one day I'm supposed to get whatever I want."

Without waiting for an answer, she leaves me to rummage through the closet to search for a skirt. Her walk sounds angry, even when she is not. Her steps fall like stones, echoing in the hollow between my ribs.

The longest skirt I own falls just above my knees, but it's a little too tight now. I zip it over my hip and tug at the hem, trying to cover as much skin as I can. Even with a pair of boots, my scars are still visible, winding around my knees and disappearing into the folds of the fabric. They're darker than the rest of my skin, and when I look closely I can see the tiny dots where the needle pierced me over and over.

I've often wondered how long it took the doctor to sew all of these bits of me back together. Was it just one doctor? Was it a whole team? They must have thought they'd never finish, moving all the way from my ankles to my thighs.

I dig through my dresser looking for black tights, but all I can find is one of Kylie's pairs of fishnets. I pull off a boot and am struggling to get one foot in the hose when my mom comes back around the corner.

"Oh, honey," she says, frowning at the boots. "No."

I yank the hose up over my thigh and she says, "You can't wear those in the summer. Do you need to borrow a pair of heels?"

"No."

She sighs, walking into the den. I battle with the fishnets until it becomes evident they aren't going all the way up to my waist. I huff, stripping them off, then dig through the drawer to look one more time.

"Okay," my mother calls, a cloud of Estée Lauder trailing behind her. "Let's get a move on."

Kylie prances down the hallway and stops dead in front of me. She's poured herself into a short wrap dress that make her legs look like they go to her chin. "You're not wearing those Franken-boots are you?"

"What do you care?"

"What's the problem?" my mother says, digging in her purse. "We're going to be late."

"I guess you won't be able to see them under the table," Kylie says, putting on her lipstick. "Since this is a nice place, with tablecloths and all."

"Forget it. I'm going to change."

"We don't have time," my mother says, herding us into the living room. "We'll lose the reservation."

"If we don't leave now, I might as well not even go at all," Kylie says. "Max is picking me up in an hour."

My mother's eyebrow arches at that, but she says nothing.

"Fine," I say, offering Mom my arm.

"I'm okay," she says, shrugging it off. She leads us out the front door and hands me the car keys.

"You look nice," my mother tells me. "You should wear dresses more often."

Kylie scoffs, her heels clacking on the concrete. "Did Maggie tell you they're making mannequins of me at the factory? I'm going to be famous."

Halfway through dinner, Kylie is still talking about her burgeoning career as a model. When I can't stand it anymore, I go to the bar to see if I can sneak a drink. Sometimes I can get by without being carded, but this place is upscale enough to worry about their liquor license. The bartender is a stout older guy, his face all angles and hard edges. I might have to settle for a soda, if I can ever get his attention.

After a few moments I feel a hand on my arm. When I turn, I'm surprised to see Fischer standing next to me, leaning against the bar. He's wearing dark jeans with a blazer over a tee shirt, the clothes more tailored to his shape than what he usually wears in the studio space. He smiles his adorable crooked smile and says, "Hi, Maggie. I almost didn't recognize you. You look nice."

"Um, thanks."

"Wait," he says, "that didn't come out right." His cheeks turn pink and he runs a hand through his hair. "What I meant was, I never see you all dressed up. Those boots are killer."

I ease onto a bar stool. Waving to the bartender, he says, "What are you having?"

"How about whatever you're having?" I say. I smile, but feel completely awkward.

His lip turns up, and I can tell he's giving the idea serious thought.

"I think they call that contributing to the delinquency of a minor," he says.

"People always think I look older than I am. I might as well benefit from their misconceptions."

"You're very unusual," he says.

"So I'm told."

He climbs onto the stool next to me. "What are you doing here?"

"Family outing. Mom's birthday."

"So why are you hiding over here?"

"I'm just giving them a few minutes alone before Kylie has to leave on her date."

When the bartender comes our way, Fischer says, "Two whiskey and Cokes, please." The bartender barely glances at me, nodding as he hurries to get two glasses. He has a bar full of patrons and is in a rush to get back to a blonde woman in a slinky silk dress at the other end of the bar.

"What are you doing here?" I ask Fischer.

He shrugs. "I like their buffalo wings. They're half price until seven." He smiles again, and I feel something in my chest loosen. His knee brushes against mine and I want to move closer, to feel more of him against me.

The bartender sets our drinks down and scurries back to the blonde, who is motioning him toward her with one finger. Fischer clinks his glass against mine and says, "To your mom. Cheers."

I down half of my drink and his eyebrow arches. "Thank you, Fischer. I've been thinking too much lately. I find whiskey helps with that. Quiets the voices."

"About earlier today," he says. "Are we okay?"

"Fine," I say with a shrug.

"You seemed a little—"

"Really," I say. "It was nothing. And now Kylie thinks she's found her purpose in life. It might actually keep her out of trouble for a while."

"We should all be so lucky, I guess," he says, sipping his drink.

"Seriously? You're like a prodigy."

He snorts, shaking his head.

"You're amazing," I say. "How can you not know that?"

"My parents think I'm throwing my life away. Maybe they're right."

There's a sad arch in his brows. He isn't just being humble.

"Then they're a couple of loons," I tell him.

He smiles.

I glance at our reflection in the mirror behind the bar, and see Kylie getting up from the table. Her date must be outside.

"I should probably get back over there," I say. When I stand, my skirt clings to the chair and rides halfway up my thigh. Fischer's eyes dart downward as I yank the fabric back into place.

He stares at me for a long moment. His eyes look more green than blue in this light, and I'd keep staring at them if they weren't filled with something that looks way too much like pity.

I knock back the rest of the drink, wincing as it burns a path all the way down my chest. "I don't want to leave Mom over there alone. Thanks for the drink."

"Sure," he says. "See you tomorrow then."

I slink past him, my cheeks burning. As I near the table, Kylie trots back over to get her purse from the back of her chair. She looks toward the bar and waves. I turn back, but Fischer sits motionless.

He isn't looking at her.

In a few weeks there are models of my sister everywhere: an army of pale, svelte Kylies with their forty-inch legs and twenty-inch waists. They have no steely eyes to fix on me, no lips to twist into a smirk. But they don't need them—the curves in their hips and the set to their shoulders say everything.

Kylie, of course, loves the idea of hundreds of her being shipped to department stores all over the country. Her hair's been pulled up like Audrey Hepburn's ever since she declared herself a model.

"You think they ship international?" she says, perched on the far corner of my work table. "I could be all over Europe."

I ignore her, painting the hazel eyes of a face that I hope will not be stuck on one of her bodies. It's sickening to think that somewhere in twenty different states, these mutant creatures, partly me and partly her, might lurk in business casual and formal wear. My heads attached to her bodies, like some horrible genetic mutation that was never meant to be.

Today, Kylie has been tasked with counting our inventory. Having counted all the heads in my room, she tosses her clipboard onto my work table and tells me again about how she ran into Fischer when she was on her date with some guy she'd met in the grocery store. The guy turned out to be married and smarmy, both of which I could have predicted; after Kylie sent him storming out of the bar in a huff, she'd sat down next to Fischer and let him buy her several martinis. How many, she couldn't remember. Or at least that's what she wanted me to think.

"He's playing hard to get," she says. "But I like a good challenge."

"I know this may be difficult for you to believe," I say, "but maybe he's just not interested."

"Oh, please. Why wouldn't he be?"

"He's a nice guy, Kylie. Not exactly your type."

"Oh, Maggie," she says, laughing. "Sometimes I wonder what it's like to live in your world. That magical land where everybody makes love and nobody just screws."

When we were teenagers, we shared everything— clothes, friends, and cigarettes behind the garage. Kylie was two years older, but sometimes it only felt like two days, two heartbeats. We used to play this game we called Speedbumps—we'd lie in the road at the end of our lane, out by the cow pasture, staring up at the stars. There was only one rule: you could ask anything you wanted, and you had to tell the truth, but there was no judgment or anger allowed. We'd confess all of our secrets there at the end of the lane, but no cars ever came by, as late as it was when we were out there. We could tell each other anything, and we couldn't get angry over any of it. That was the rule.

Now, I hate the idea of sharing anything with her—the car, the house, the air between us. Two years has become as vast as two oceans. After that night in the Catawba, I did whatever I could to make myself look less like her. I chopped my hair, dyed it bright red. Gained twenty pounds, then thirty. People don't mistake us for twins anymore.

After lunch, I push a cart full of heads down to the assembly room, where Fischer and Gordon are busy finishing the last shipment of the day. This room is the largest, by far, with a half dozen aisles of ten-foot shelves and a loading dock in the back. Hands and feet are wrapped in plastic, stored in bins labeled with model numbers. Dozens of arms and legs hang from hooks on clothing racks. Torsos take up four aisles themselves, and the heads take up the rest. The back third of the room is where assembly happens, where limbs are attached and the finished mannequins are stored in neat rows, like soldiers. They're arranged by model type, so it's easy to see how many different variations we have. Some have a hand planted on one hip, some turn slightly to the side. Some are specially made to sit, to semi-recline in aloof repose—like women in Renaissance paintings.

Fischer finishes taping up a box and Gordon slaps a "Fragile" sticker on the side. Gordon is one of those guys that would be broke if all the women who should have sued him for harassment had realized they could have. Wiry and boyish, he looks younger than his years, which makes his jokes seem more innocent than he intends—sometimes.

"Oooh," Gordon says, eyeing the cart I'm pushing. "My favorite time of the day. If only good head always came this easy." He grabs a body from behind, his hands gripping the breasts, and walks it over to my cart. "You got something for me, Maggie?"

"Take your pick, Gordon."

"I need two blondes," he says, reading a purchase order he pulls from his pocket. "And a few for this store in Dallas, too."

Fischer brings another body over, his arm looped around the waist.

"Hey," Gordon says. "I think this is your best one yet." He

eyes Fischer's model, then drapes his arm over the shoulders. "We look pretty good together, don't you think?"

"She is the perfect girl for you," Fischer says, attaching a head he's selected. "The only one in the world that won't shoot you in your sleep."

"Fish, you and me need to work out a business of our own." He wiggles his eyebrows at me while he slides his hand onto the mannequin's backside. "I still say that with a couple of anatomical adjustments, you and me could corner the market on girlfriend facsimiles. We'd put blow-up dolls out of business and make enough millions to buy ourselves neighboring islands."

My eyes roll so hard they actually ache.

Fischer shakes his head. "One of these days, Gordon, someone's going to smack you for saying stuff like that. I gotta get back upstairs." He looks at me sadly, as if this entire scenario is just too difficult to endure.

"I've already come up with a name and everything," Gordon says. "Applied for a patent, too. I'm telling you, Fish, we gotta move on this before somebody else does."

When Fischer waves him off, Gordon turns back to me. While he leans on the mannequin, his eyes follow its legs to the floor. "So Maggie," he says, "is that sister of yours seeing anybody?"

I glance at Fischer, but he's already turned and started for the door.

"Yes," I say to Gordon. "I'm afraid she is." I despise my sister, but not that much.

At home that night, I find my mother sitting in a lawn chair in the back yard. She coughs, holding a fragment of a joint in a pair of tweezers. She looks like a ghost, sitting there pale and blue in the moonlight.

"Bad day?" I ask her.

"Today hurts."

I sit in the chair next to her and say, "Share?"

She hands me the tweezers and says, "Just promise you won't make this a habit after I'm gone. Don't blow your inheritance on weed."

"Deal."

"I'd expect that from your sister, but you know better."

"Right. Always the smart one."

She smiles, running her fingers through my hair. "Thank heaven for that."

"I'm always going to be stuck taking care of her, aren't I?"

"Oh, Maggie." Her words come out in smoke. "Bless her heart, Kylie thinks that all she has is on the outside. She'll need someone to look out for her until she figures out how wrong she is."

"I can't do it. I'm not strong like you."

"Yes, you are."

"Half the time I want to kill her. The other half, I want someone else to."

She laughs. "Better than not caring at all."

"There you are." Kylie comes around the corner of the house. "I'm going out. I'll be back later."

"What are you doing wearing that?" I say.

She looks down at herself and says, "What?"

"Take that off this second," I say. "That's the one Mom made."

She glares at me, her hands on her hips. Of course the dress fits her perfectly. It's the one Mom made for me to wear to the prom back when I was a sophomore. But I didn't go because of the accident. I never wore the dress—it's a cute polka-dot fit-and-flare, off the shoulder and above the knee, something she patterned after one I saw in a magazine. It didn't look like a prom dress at all, which is why I loved it. I felt like a movie star when I put it on, but I'd only worn it around the living room when she fit it to me, and then later, out in the moonlit backyard while everybody else was dancing in the school gym.

"Give me a break," Kylie says. "You'll never wear this again. It won't even fit you now."

"Take it off!" I yell, striding towards her. I grab her arm and she yanks it away.

"What's your problem?" she says. "It's a great dress. Somebody ought to be wearing it."

"Not you," I say, grabbing her again.

"What? You can't be happy so you don't want anybody else to be either? Get over yourself."

"You can't just take whatever you want from people," I say. "Especially me."

"Girls," my mother says.

"Oh, because you're so special," she says. "I forgot."

"Why do you have to be this way? You're such a—"

"What?" she says, inching closer. "Say it."

I bite my lip.

"Say it!" she barks, and shoves me with one hand. "What are you so afraid of?" She steps toward me, invading again, and blood pounds in my ears. "Say it, Maggie. You can't play the victim forever."

I slap her hard across the cheek and her eyes widen. We stare at each other for a moment, and I feel like I'm going to be sick. Then she grabs my hair and we fall to the ground, a ball of pounding fists and kicking feet.

"Girls!" my mother yells. "You stop that this minute."

We ignore her, rolling each other in the dirt, pulling hair and screaming curses. All I can think about is how I've wanted to do this for so long, how I've wanted to hurt my sister like she hurt me. But every second of it makes me feel more hollow, so much so I figure I'm doing it wrong. Then I feel the blast of cold water and hear Kylie shriek.

I slide away from her, shielding my face from the water. My mother stands by the steps, the garden hose dripping by her feet. "That's about enough of that," she says. "I didn't raise y'all to roll around like dogs."

"Happy now?" Kylie says. The dress is streaked with mud. "Now you've ruined it for both of us."

"You don't care about anybody but yourself," I say.

"How am I supposed to know this dress is so important to you? You don't tell me anything anymore. You act like you wish I was at the bottom of that river." She glares at me, the anger in her face turning to something else.

I stay silent, staring at her bare feet in the grass, her pale, perfect calves.

"I used to hate you for things like this," Kylie says. "But now I just feel sorry for you, because it's never going to change."

"That's enough," my mother says.

Kylie picks up her shoes and stalks back to the house, the door slamming behind her. My mother plods through the grass and stands over me. The floodlight blazes behind her like some spooky halo.

"Maggie," she says. "People with good hearts shouldn't let things eat away at them. The world's got enough heartless people in it. It needs people like you for balance."

We stay like that for a moment, two women slowly being devoured by something that we can't see, fighting against ourselves. I know what she's trying to tell me, and it makes my heart twist to think that she might not have time to tell me all the other things I need to know in order to survive without her.

After I pull myself out of the mud, I change clothes and drive straight to the factory, as if my body's been taken over by someone else. I let myself in through the back door and stride down the dark hallway, past rooms where perfectly-proportioned bodies stand like sentinels, lit by flickering security lights. When I open the door to the production room and flip on the light, my heart flutters like a bird. Someone's left a model with arms akimbo right by the door, no doubt as a practical joke. She's wearing a cowboy hat and a grass skirt. I leave her and walk to the back of the room, where I find the clay master of

Kylie. Why had they kept it? Usually they recycled the masters immediately, using the clay to make the next figure.

After staring for what feels like hours, I open a can of maroon paint that we use for lip color. I pluck a small brush from the table and begin to draw my own lines over her ribs, down her back. The lines become rivers, highways from her heart to her toes. They loop and curl until they become words that I've been too chicken to say aloud. To Kylie. To everyone.

I never wanted to be that girl who hated her sister. It's difficult to pinpoint when it started, when that ugly part of me took over, when I gave up on us ever being the way we were when we were kids. It was after we came out of the river, after she seemed to heal and I didn't. After she left me behind.

I hated myself for not standing up to her, not taking those keys. I hated her for making me lie.

"You have to tell them you were driving," she'd said. "I can't get a DUI. They won't let me into college. Please, Maggie. You have to." I hadn't been drinking. I wouldn't get into trouble like she would.

I hadn't argued hard enough then, either.

I'd let her charm me. Again.

On the mannequin, the words become tangled and illegible, but still I write with the brush on the smooth surface, inscribing all those words I've wanted to say to her for so long, those words I'm too proud to say now.

Soon there are only tiny flecks of tan clay peeking through. I slouch on a stool and stare at her. Mud still clings to my fingernails, my sneakers. Does Kylie ever feel remorse for that night? Does she ever feel like it was her fault? Does she ever think of it at all?

We never talked about the crash, and part of me thinks we never will. What would be the point? Kylie never took responsibility for anything, and I don't see that changing anytime soon. We came out of that river different people. Since that night, she's lived more recklessly than ever, not caring about the repercussions of anything she does. I'm the opposite, choked by what ifs.

What if we hadn't been fighting?

What if I had been driving?

What if she'd been the one to pull me out instead?

Probably, none of that mattered.

Probably.

Writing all of those words with the brush, though, it shakes something loose in me. I've been holding onto those words for so long, and now, seeing them covering her form, I see how much space they take up and what a burden they are.

"This has to be over," I whisper. "No more."

I cross the room to the steel tool cabinet and dig around inside until I find a sledgehammer. Gordon and the other guys will use it tomorrow to break the other clay models apart so they can be recycled. My arms waver as I heave it over my shoulder like a baseball bat.

I take a deep breath, and then I swing.

Bits of clay explode in front of me and scatter onto the floor. With each swing more of the model falls away, exposing the wire frame beneath. I swing again and again, until I hear someone shouting my name.

Fischer stands in the doorway, his eyes wide. "Maggie," he says. "What are you doing?"

He steps toward me, but stops when the hammer clangs against the frame.

"She shouldn't be here," I say. "We weren't supposed to end up like this."

I swing again, but my arms are tired and I miss completely, spinning myself halfway around and stumbling to the floor. I sit in a heap, in a fine layer of silt and chunks of clay, and laugh until I feel a throbbing in my ribs.

He will run, I think. He'll tell Luke I'm crazy and have me fired. But instead Fischer kneels beside me and brushes his hand across my cheek, wiping away tears that have begun to fall. My head is swimming, my ears still full with the sounds of smashing clay, splintering glass, gurgling water. I close my eyes to stop the spinning, but the darkness only heightens the sounds, filling me with the chill of the river. "I never wanted to hate her," I tell him. "How did I end up like this?"

And then I'm telling him about that night of the party, the cold bite of the river, the glass that cut me as I struggled to pull Kylie from the wrecked car.

When he takes the hammer, my hands feel numb, like they did that night.

He pulls me to him, wraps his big arms around me. My head rests against his chest, and the thumping of his heart fills my ears.

"How did she turn me into this person?" I say. "How did I let her?"

"I'm an idiot," he says. "I should have told her no. I'm so sorry, Maggie."

His lips move against my forehead, soft as velvet. I close my eyes, wishing he would hold them there.

After a while, the room seems to right itself. I sit up straight, and his hands slide from my shoulders. "I'm sorry," I say, though for what, I'm not quite sure. I know I should stand up, dust myself off and clean up the mess I've made, but part of me wants to stay there on the floor with Fischer until the sun comes up. Encircled by clay dust and debris, it's like we're the last survivors of some disastrous event that will leave us changed forever.

But deep down, I know I'm just another girl with a scarred body and a bruised heart. There's nothing special about that.

"Come on," he says. "Let's get out of here."

"They'll fire me for this," I say.

He looks around the room for a long moment, then walks over to the plaster cast that they'd used to make the Kylies. "Then they'll have to fire me, too," he says, and shoves the chunk of plaster onto its side. There's a crash like thunder, and it splits apart when it hits the concrete floor.

"Oops," he says. "It seems I've had quite a clumsy night."

I stare at the broken mould and shake my head. "You can't take the blame for this, Fischer."

He shrugs. "I'll make them a new one. A better one."

"Luke's going to be pissed."

"I can smooth it over," he says. "Don't worry."

"We should clean this up."

"Later," he says. "Come here."

He pulls me to my feet and holds onto my hand as he leads me down the hall, to a section of the building I thought was off-limits. He flips the bolt on a door that warns of an alarm and turns on lights that flicker and buzz. It's another studio, smaller than the others, filled with clay sculptures in various states of finish. "Luke lets me use this space," he says, shoving his hands into his pockets. "I work here some nights when I can't sleep."

"Why can't you sleep?"

"I don't know. It comes and goes."

"This is incredible," I tell him. "This stuff should be in a gallery." All around us are sculptures that look like beings out of old mythologies: part human, part animal, all haunted and raucous, starving for something they can't quite find.

"Maybe someday," he says.

I recognize number 7, her ballerina-like pose. But now she has birdlike wings, patches of scales like a crocodile, as if she's transforming into something else, in the darkness of this studio when no one's watching.

"You keep the masters," I say.

He shrugs. "Sometimes."

I bite my lip. "That's why the Kylie hadn't been recycled." I feel terrible. I destroyed what Fischer made, an object he would have transformed into a sculpture even more remarkable. It seems so stupid that I hadn't even thought of it that way. I'd only been thinking of the model as something of my sister's.

Fischer reaches into a mini-fridge and pulls out two craft beers that I recognize from the local brewery. They pack more of a wallop than the average beer. In one smooth motion, he hooks the two caps together and they both pop off and clink against the concrete floor. He hands me a bottle and says, "I think we could both stand to relax a little."

I take a long drink. I should sip, because this is strong, and I skipped lunch, but I'm annoyed and embarrassed. "I'm sorry," I tell him. "I didn't know."

"It's fine," he says. "It was just clay. For me, anyway."

I nod, and take a sip of the beer. "Tell me about your sculptures."

He leads me through the maze of figures, telling me bits of folklore that inspired him. In the back corner of the room, past all the figures, there are two wingback chairs, set up like a miniature lounge. Between the chairs is a baseball bat, pieces of PVC pipe, and a leg that I recognize as one from a broken mannequin. "What's all this?" I say.

He sighs. "It's for a commission that's been driving me crazy."

"A commission?"

He points to a line of photographs pinned to the wall behind the chairs. "You'll laugh," he says. "But it's roof tiles."

"Clay roof tiles?"

"Spanish style," he says. "Like the old missions in California and Texas. There's a guy here, a historian, who wants to build a replica of an old mission and have authentic hand-made roof tiles, like the Franciscans used to make them." He waves his hands in front of him, says, "I know, it sounds ridiculous. How hard can it be to make roof tiles?"

I sit back in one of the chairs, my head beginning to spin. "Okay, at the risk of sounding like an idiot, why is it so hard to make roof tiles?"

"Nothing is the right shape. You're supposed to mold the tiles around something cylindrical to get the right curve—they have to fit together just right, and curve enough to shed the water, but not so much that it gets trapped under them."

"If you haven't noticed, I'm way too tipsy to solve engineering problems."

He smiles and sits next to me on the arm of the chair. "According to old Franciscan stories, they used to make tiles by molding clay on the legs of the women they loved."

I scoff. "Impossible."

"Why would you say that?"

"Too romantic," I say.

"Monks can't be lovesick romantics?"

"And imagine how long those women would have to sit there, waiting for the clay to dry."

"It would give them time to share their most delicious secrets. Their deepest desires." His eyes widen and there's that impossible blue again.

I laugh. "Your fairy tale has serious flaws."

"They say the monks wanted to be sheltered by the legs of the women they loved," he says. "The archaeologists say that the curve's not right on the tiles, that the women's legs weren't big enough."

"But you think it's true."

"That they wanted some small trace of the women they adored and couldn't have? Absolutely. People have done stranger things for love."

"I didn't take you for a hopeless romantic," I say.

"What did you take me for?" When he fixes his eyes on mine, something in my brain snaps free. My heart hammers in my chest, my skin tingling everywhere, and for an instant I think this might be the same restless feeling that compels Kylie to do those reckless things she's always boasting about.

I move closer to Fischer, so there are just inches of air between us. His eyes widen just before I lean in and kiss him. His lips are softer than I expected. He's still for a moment, and then his hands are moving. I slip my fingers into his hair and he kisses me harder, his teeth pinching my lip. He slides his hand to the small of my back, pulling me against him, and it's magical.

It's like nothing I've ever felt, and I want this moment to last forever.

He tastes sweet like sun tea, and there's a hint of bitter from the beer, and I feel warm all over, like I'm sunbathing at the beach.

And then he abruptly pulls away.

"Maggie," he says, his voice almost a whisper.

I think he's just paused for a breath, but then he pulls his hand away, and my back is cold.

"What's the matter?" I say.

"I didn't mean to—" His eyebrows arch in that sad way, the same way he looked at me when he first caught me smashing the model. I'm a fragile thing again, and I can't stand it.

I feel like I'm going to be sick. I was stupid to think I could take risks like my sister. I'm not reckless like her, and especially not with people like Fischer, with things like kissing.

I get up from the chair and he says, "Hang on, Maggie."

"Forget it," I say, scrambling to get away from him and out of the studio. I push past him and stumble past the sculptures, dodging their outstretched arms, their beckoning fingers. I'm dizzy from the beer, or maybe from sheer embarrassment, and I feel one of the arms brush against me as I hurry to put more distance between us.

"Wait," he says, following me towards the door. "Please."

I feel tears coming, and I don't want him to see them. I don't want him to see me this way, like whatever was holding me together has given way to leave me falling to pieces.

My boot heels pound against the concrete as he calls my name again. It echoes and fills the room.

I bolt down the hallway, past the flickering security lights, and out the back entrance into the parking lot. The metal door bangs the wall as I shove my weight against it. I'm down the steps in a flash, fumbling for my keys and unlocking the car door. By the time I'm inside the car and starting the engine, Fischer is standing in the doorway, the fluorescent light pooling around his feet, his expression unreadable. He calls after me once more, but the tires are squealing, my foot stomping on the gas, and then I'm on the highway headed towards home. My vision blurs with tears, and I feel like an idiot. I shouldn't be driving, either, and I think once more of Kylie, driving us that night.

Halfway home, I step on the brake a little too hard, getting just under the speed limit. It's late, and the small town cops will be lurking, waiting for some driver who's made a bad decision. The streets are empty, except for the occasional cat slinking into the shadows. The moon is bright and nearly full, turning the lawns a pale blue hue. Most of the porch lights in our neighborhood have been turned off for the night.

When I pull into the driveway, I'm still shaken up. Our house is dark, except for one light in the kitchen, a lamp in the corner that Mom always leaves on. I sit in the car for a few moments, brushing away my tears. It's after midnight, but it's possible that Kylie or Mom might still be up. With a little luck, I can slip into the house and into my room unnoticed. I don't want to explain anything about the last few hours.

I close the car door quietly and trudge up the walkway to the front porch. My key is barely in the lock when I see headlights cut across the hedges. A car pulls into the driveway and stops behind mine. I twist the key in the lock and the car door opens.

Fischer climbs out and walks towards me, and time freezes.

For a split second, I consider slipping inside and locking him out, but then he'd just knock on the door and wake everyone up. This is the last thing I want Kylie to see. She'd never let me hear the end of it.

"You followed me home?" I say, keeping my voice low. The key hangs in the lock. The porch light flickers as moths flap against it.

"Maggie," he says, "You didn't let me finish."

I stare at him, just wanting this to be over, so I can crawl into bed and get up tomorrow, and maybe feel like all of this was just a bad dream.

"So you drove over here? It couldn't wait until morning?"

"No," he says, raking his hand through his hair. He climbs up onto the porch, staying on the step below me so we're eye to eye. "I didn't want you to feel like I was pushing you away. I'm not."

"It felt like you were."

"I figured. That's why I'm here." He shoves his hands in his pockets and looks away for a moment, gathering himself. When he looks back at me, his eyes are blazing. "You were so upset," he says, "I felt like I was taking advantage or something."

"I can make my own decisions," I say. "I'm not some fragile, broken thing."

"We're all fragile," he says. "Broken is different. You're definitely not broken." He glances down at the steps, like he's the one who's embarrassed. "It just felt like you were trying to prove something, and I didn't want it to be like that with us." He shrugs and says, "I like you, Maggie."

I stare into his eyes, trying to read them.

"Is this the part where you tell me you just want to be friends?" I say.

"Hell, no," he says. "I've thought about kissing you forever."

I laugh, steadying myself on the porch rail. "I can't believe you just said that."

He smiles. "Life's too long not to say what you mean."

He steps closer then, and takes my hand in his. "So how about we go to dinner one day soon. We can talk some more."

His thumb slides along my palm, and it's electric.

"Sure," I say. "I'd like that. You can tell me some more things you mean."

He leans into me, his face just inches from mine. My skin tingles, and I feel like I'm being pulled towards him. His hand slides up my arm, and my heart speeds up. I want to feel what I felt back in his studio. I want him to kiss me like before, but I'm afraid he'll pull away again.

He dips his chin, and then his lips are on the corner of my mouth. It's a lingering kiss that threatens to unravel me. He smells like leather and sawdust, and I want to tangle my hands in his hair, pull him closer.

He steps back and releases my hand, slowly.

"I'll see you tomorrow," he says, and his eyes don't look sad anymore.

I nod and he walks back across the lawn to his car, his pace slow and deliberate.

When he's inside his car, I slip into the house, closing the door so it doesn't creak. I leave my shoes by the door and pad through the kitchen and down the hall to the room that Kylie and I share. Mom's door is open just a crack, but her room is dark.

I half expected Kylie to still be up, but my room is dark, too. Inside, I sit down on the bed and ease out of my shirt and jeans. I lay them on the floor by the bedside table and pull the sheet over me.

"How was your date?" Kylie says, her voice low.

"What?" I say.

"I knew he liked you."

"I wasn't on a date."

"I saw you two outside," she says.

My heart bangs in my chest. "You can't say anything about this," I tell her. "You can't tell anyone at work."

Silence.

"I mean it, Kylie." I struggle to keep my voice low, since I don't want Mom to know about it either. I don't know what's happening between me and Fischer, but I'm certain I don't want the whole world to know about it and start offering me their opinions.

"Speedbumps," Kylie says.

"What?"

"Like when we were kids," she whispers. "You remember how it went?"

I can barely make out her silhouette in the darkness. She's lying on her back, staring at the ceiling.

"Sure," I say.

She's quiet for so long that I think she's dozed off. But then she says, "I'm sorry, Maggie. Really sorry."

"For what?" I say, because there's so much.

There's another pause, and then she says, "Your dress, for starters."

When I don't answer, she says, "But not just that. I'm sorry for all of it. There ought to be a better way to say it. But all this time, I haven't been able to think of the right way. And now it's been too long, and it's been too much, and maybe I just don't have any other way to say it. I was scared, Maggie, and I was hurting, and I didn't know how to fix it. I'm your big sister—I'm supposed to know how to fix it."

"You could have told the truth," I say.

She lets out a heavy sigh. "I should have. I was terrified, but that's no excuse." After a long moment she says, "I'll tell Mom. She needs to know."

We lay that way for a long time, but she doesn't say anything more. Outside, the katydids thrum in the trees, filling the night. It's started to rain, one of those sudden spring showers that rolls in from nowhere.

"I don't know what to say," I whisper.

"You don't have to," she says. "But I needed to tell you."

I know I should tell her something, like *It's okay,* or *I forgive you,* but those aren't quite true, not yet. And we've already spoken too many lies.

"We can do better." I say at last. "We can be better."

"I'd like that," she says.

The rain beats harder on the roof and I roll onto my side. Lying on her back, Kylie looks just like she did lying on the bank of the Catawba, and my heart squeezes like a fist.

"I don't wish you were at the bottom of the river, Kylie. If I had it to do over again, I would."

"I wish that night never happened," she says. "Some days I hate you for pulling me out of that river. Most days I just hate myself."

I can tell she's crying, so I don't say anything more.

One day we'll be able to talk about these things. We may be

fragile, but it'll take more than a river to break us. Someday, I'll know how to use the right words, and not let others weigh so heavy on me. We will learn to be patient with each other, and we'll tell our stories in the dark. We'll keep telling them after our mother is gone, and after we no longer live between these walls. Listening to the slap of raindrops on the roof, I think again of what Fischer said about the Franciscans. I imagine them sleeping under their clay roof tiles, sheltered by the people they loved most.

It doesn't seem so preposterous anymore.

A Thousand Holes

AMY HYATT FONSECA

Amy Hyatt Fonseca is an Appalachian-born writer currently navigating the suburbs with her husband, two children, and overly enthusiastic Golden Retriever. Her essays have appeared in *Motherhood Realized*, *The Bitter Southerner*, and *Power of Moms*.

Before taking the writer's plunge, Amy was a speech-language pathologist (SLP) in the public schools. With a B.A. in communication and an M.Ed in communication disorders, she also worked as a research SLP at Georgia State University where she co-authored multiple articles on communication interventions for children with disabilities.

In her spare time, Amy is co-founder of Women@TheFrontier, an Atlanta-based nonprofit that shares stories of diverse women in STEM and their relentless pursuits to solve our world's most significant challenges. This experience has allowed her to meet and interview some of her role models, including Mae Jemison, the first African American woman in space, and Mildred Dresselhaus, the queen of carbon science. Her articles and blog posts have appeared on Women@TheFrontier, Women 2.0, and Points of Light.

Amy is a member of the SCBWI and The Atlanta Writers Club. When she's not planning her next project, you can find her hanging out in yoga class or procrastinating on Twitter.

I've buried my life in holes. Deep, round pits that bleed Georgia red clay when I tear them open and drop trinkets into their mouths. Holes so bottomless I'm pretty sure my shovel touches Dante's first circle of Hell when I've hidden our stuff from Daddy in the garden. The shiny silver locket Mama gave me when I turned six. Crinkled dollar bills from Gran's Social Security checks. The pain meds the doctor prescribed for her back. My sanity. Our lives. All entombed in clay and guarded by a maze of decaying roots and wiggly earthworms.

It's noon. My best friend, Violet, and I have been searching for Gran's pain pills for the better part of three hours.

"You're sure you buried *Abuelita's* pills here?"

"Positive," I say. Then I tell her what happened last night. How I counted ten pills and planted the bottle somewhere between the twisty pole beans and the towering stalks of corn. At least, I think I buried them here. It was dark.

When I admit the second part, Violet pitches her shovel in the dirt and mutters a Spanish curse word under her breath. I don't blame her. Our junior year of high school starts in a week, and if my Instagram feed is any indication, we should be snapping selfies at the beach or minimum in the Wal-Mart parking lot. Instead, we're hanging out in Gran's garden and choking under a blanket of Miller family drama and Southern-fried humidity.

Sometimes I wonder why Violet hangs out with me.

But she does.

See, Violet's smart. Pre-med smart if she can get a scholarship next fall. And despite her petite frame and soft features, she's identical to the mama cat that hangs out near Gran's barn. Cute and furry until you piss her off, and then she's all hisses and claws. Trust me on this one. We've been best friends since we were eight years old. The same year Mama died from the big C-word, and Daddy found true love with meth.

Anyway, Violet never cared much about playground gossip. Or maybe it was because her second-language English caused her to miss the word-grenades the other kids tossed at me for fun.

Regardless, I still see Violet standing near the book corner in Ms. Sullivan's class. Dark hair braided and eyes infinitely dark. "Alma," she said. *"Ese es tu nombre?"* *Alma is my name.* I nodded. She laughed, and her face lit like a constellation of stars. "What's so funny?" I asked. *"Me gusta.* An American with a Spanish name." I nodded. I had no clue what she meant. "OK. What's your name? "Violeta." The syllables flowed like a river from her mouth. I grinned. "A Mexican with a flower name." "Not Mexican. Honduran," she corrected. My cheeks burned. I'd never been farther than Mason's Store on the other side of town. I guess Violet recognized the particular shade of pink on my cheeks because she led me to the computer and pulled up a map. "Here, I'll show you."

Eight years later, I wish I could see Violet's face light up again. But these days, when I look at her, her mouth falls in the corners. I get it. She's worried. It's impossible to ignore the shiny bruise that circles my left eye. The imprint of Daddy's high school football championship ring so perfect, Violet says she can almost make out the year 2000 near the bridge of my nose.

I told her the story before we started digging. *The buttery biscuits browning in the oven. Daddy sitting at the table and twirling that stupid ring on his finger while he complained Gran's chicken tasted funny. Me popping off, telling him to cook his own supper next time. The cracking of his hand across my face. The exposed light bulb buzzing overhead. Gran watching us. Stoic. Quiet. Blue fire igniting in the calm of her eyes.*

"And this morning, when I woke up, he was gone," I finished.

Violet raised a thick eyebrow. *"Dios,* Alma. Do you think he left for good?"

Wishful thinking, we both know. Basically, Daddy's the eczema on Gran's elbows—he goes away and always comes back worse in a couple of weeks. Still, Gran loves him. Every so often she reminds me good people live in these mountains. Daddy used to be good too. But now he's the reason Violet and I fashion a thousand holes in the garden. Our hands tattooed with splinters and cuts.

"How's your mama doing?" I ask to change the subject. I already know the answer by the inky caverns beneath Violet's eyes.

She shakes her head. "She needs a doctor, but she's scared to go. Afraid they'll report her or something."

Or something. Violet's daddy got deported over a year ago for speeding in town without a license. She cried for two straight weeks after they took him. That's the day I realized if I live close to Dante's first level of Hell, Violet camps out in the second or third.

At least nobody can take Gran.

Except for Daddy.

I heave my shovel into the dirt. It strikes a rotten root and vibrates to the end of my fingertips. Somewhere in the distance, Gran's cat meows. I freeze. Wait. It's not the cat. A whistle carries in the breeze. My stomach lurches. Oh god, I recognize that tune. *You are my sunshine, my only sunshine.*

Then I catch a glimpse of Daddy, creeping behind the corn.

I don't remember much about Daddy before Mama died. Except for the gray cloud of cigarette smoke that circled his head. The way his eyes crinkled when he sang, his voice low and velvety in my ears. How he pushed Mama's hair behind her ear while she shivered and shook in the bed near the end.

Three days later, we buried her in the church cemetery. That's the day the devil snatched Daddy's soul, and Gran taught me to dig.

"He's coming," Gran says. "I can feel it in my bones." She stands from her recliner in the living room and ambles toward the kitchen to fix supper even though she and I ate hours ago. The warped floor creaks beneath her orthopedic shoes. They're spotless except for a smattering of mud on the left one. I keep my mouth shut, but I'm onto Gran. She's sneaking out to the garden at night to dig, *exercising her demons* as she calls it.

Still, I'm not surprised Gran knows my father is on his way to visit. Her eighty-three-year-old body is more reliable than the weather app on my phone. A knee grumbles when a summer storm brews from the west. Fingers stick when rare southern snow makes its appearance. And now, bones ache at the whims of my mad, mad father.

More than mad, he's gone rabid.

But I don't need a twinge in my shoulder to realize Daddy's coming our way. Wednesday's *Gazette* is spread out on the coffee table. Uncle Eddie stares from the front page with the headline: *Local Man Found Beaten to Death.* He's smiling in the photo, which is weird for a dead guy. Also, he's not my real uncle. He's Daddy's dealer.

My heart beats wild. I try to breathe. Uncle Eddie is dead. D-E-A-D. Daddy wouldn't hurt him, would he? Next thing I know, I'm sprinting to my room to retrieve the silver locket and then down the hall to snatch Gran's pocketbook from her dresser. I plop on the divot in her mattress and pour the contents onto the quilt. I count ten pills and forty-five dollars, barely enough to scrape by the rest of the month.

I shoot from the bed and grab the empty Christmas cookie tin in Gran's closet. Pictures of faded butter cookies cover the top and swirl around to make my mouth water. Since it's empty, I chuck the items inside and secure the lid. But I nick my finger on a rusty edge. Blood oozes, and I wipe it across my shirt.

My blood.

Gran's blood.

Daddy's blood.

Tired of digging, I want to lie in bed and dream I'm somebody else awhile, anybody besides the weird girl with the disappearing dad. Maybe Chloe Martin from my AP English class. After Mama died, Ms. Martin invited me to their house after school. She baked Chloe and me gooey chocolate chip cookies, and then we swam in their backyard pool until our fingers wrinkled into raisins.

Drifting.

Weightless.

Alive.

The smell of fried chicken wafts through the walls. I gag. Before I can think, I take off past the kitchen and bolt through the screen door. Outside, the moon hangs overhead. Gran's shack becomes a black and white snapshot, filtered with faded skin. I grab a shovel, the broken one that leans against the side of the house, and follow the worn path to the garden.

I'm not alone though. A whippoorwill sings beyond the pine trees. I usually chant along, but not tonight. The muscles in my throat tighten. Gran's right. I feel it. Daddy will bang on the front door soon.

"He's over there," I say to Violet. "Do you see him?"

Violet flicks her head toward the rows of corn. She stares for a good thirty seconds. "You're overheated. Go inside. I'll keep digging."

I blink. There's no one there. Oh god, I'm losing it. But before I freak out, my phone buzzes in the pocket of my cut-off shorts. I reach back and retrieve it.

Violet chews her bottom lip. "Your dad?"

"Nah, it's Emily Dawson. Her parents are out of town this weekend. She wants us to drop by her party tonight."

"The same Emily Dawson who hooked up with Will Davis after homecoming? I thought you hated her."

Actually, I despised her until we bonded while scooping ice cream at the Dairy Queen this summer for minimum wage. I swallow hard. I don't know why I haven't told Violet about Emily yet. When I start to mention it, my shovel scrapes against metal.

"Finally," Violet says, her voice textured with sugar and annoyance.

I give her a watery smile. Shit, I'm certain I buried the tin closer to the beans and farther from the corn. I shift my weight to my right hip and study the garden's layout. That's when I spot him. A scruffy headed man two or three feet behind Violet. *Daddy.* I gasp, and he puts a finger to his lips like we're kids playing hide-and-seek. The gold ring flashes like a blade in the sunlight. I raise my shovel over my head. I'll kill him. I will kill my father if he harms Violet.

Violet doesn't see any of this and stumbles back a step. "You OK, Alma?"

"Don't touch her," I yell. The sound echoes off the mountains, so I'm an army of five instead of one terrified girl with quivering knees.

But Daddy ignores my warning. He shuffles closer, closer, closer. His lips move, but the sound never reaches my ears. "Alma," he mouths. "Sweet Alma."

I squeeze the shovel's handle, ready to slug him when the screen door shrieks on the porch. Gran hollers from behind me. "Somethin' wrong out there?" I turn. Gran's poked her silver head out, watching me closely. Her voice is honey and dust.

Somehow, my muscles unstick, and I start to dig again. I shove the blade beneath the cookie tin. It pops up creepy jack-in-the-box style. I lean over to snatch it. Earth and mold choke me.

Violet stands steady beside me. "*Abrelo,*" she says. *Open it.*

Behind her, Daddy grins. A puff of air blows past us, and I catch a whiff of the poisons fermenting his brain. Sour. Rotten. Sweet. Decayed.

"Open it," Violet repeats.

For once, I listen. I dig my fingers beneath the rim of the lid until it snaps. Inside are four items: Gran's money, her pills, my necklace, and Daddy's ring. First, I take the bottle and shake it. *There's only one.* I pass it and the money to Violet. But when I glance up to ask Daddy about the ring, he's gone.

On the porch, Gran's cat tangles around her feet. She shoos her away with a hand. "No more digging. Come in before you get too hot, and bring me my pill," She waits for a beat before she slams the door.

Heat rushes through my body. I turn to Violet. "Did you see him?"

"Who?"

She hasn't put it together yet, but I have. My head gets woozy. I point to the bottle. "It was the chicken. Gran put the other pills in Daddy's chicken."

Violet's body stiffens. She grabs my shoulders to keep me upright. "Listen, *Abuelita's* right. No more digging. No more holes."

"Where's Daddy?" I need to know what she did to him.

"*Abuelita* took care of it. She always takes care of things."

My hands shake. I must have dropped the tin because it's on the ground now. Violet picks up the ring with her thumb and one finger, like it's a dead wasp that might come back to life to sting her.

She places it on my palm. Suddenly, I'm the Lady Justice—the shovel in one hand and the ring in the other—except I'm not blindfolded anymore. I study the chunk of gold with its bluish center stone. The color is Mama's favorite, a deep azure. It matches Daddy's eyes.

Heaviness and lightness hitch in my chest. I can't stand the weight any longer. I drop the ring into the hole. Violet grabs her shovel and covers the ring with dirt.

Please Don't Call
Me Mary

LAUREN FULCHER

Lauren Fulcher is a UNC-Chapel Hill alumna born and raised in NC. She's completing her MFA in Fiction at UNC-Wilmington. She's an unabashed YA devotee, with a special love for queer fiction. When she's not writing, she roller skates, collects tattoos, and eats more spinach than Popeye. If she had to have one giant face posted on her bedroom wall forever, it would be Karen O's.

W*hat about the hot girl at the counter? With the silver eyeliner and that cute bull ring?* Pooj texted me from across the restaurant. We weren't supposed to text until our break, but Pooj had a way of knowing when our manager, Mr. Rob ("don't forget the Mr.") wasn't looking.

Whenever I text, it's like I send out a bat signal for customer complaints. The worst was two weeks ago, when I got yelled at by an angry granny with a radiating blue perm who shoved a plate with a nibbled biscuit at me. She wasn't convinced that our buttermilk biscuits were really made with buttermilk. Which was a disgrace, she told me, at a restaurant called Buttermilk.

"It tastes like whipping cream," she'd said. "I'm from here. I can tell."

Here—i.e. the South, the land of biscuits and bigotry. I might not have been a biscuit-whisperer like her, but I've been stuck in small-town North Carolina for eighteen years. That woman was talking to me, but she was looking right at Pooj.

"I'm also *from here*, and I can assure you ma'am, we use real buttermilk." I'd returned her biscuit, letting the plate drop on the table with a crash. "We're all *from here*," I'd said.

Another goddamn racist Southern granny. I wanted to smack her so bad. I didn't care if she had false teeth. I hoped they'd go flying.

Waitressing isn't half as bad for me as it is for Pooj. I'm white, blonde, and busty in an Appalachian mountain town. Even though I'm baby-faced and dimple-less, with flat hair and a crooked nose, we live close enough to Dollywood that tourists tell me I look like Dolly Parton. This seems to make them feel good, like they've made my day. Like I haven't heard that bullshit a thousand times. But I always grin.

Pooj is Indian and has thick, dark hair that she crops into the cutest pixies. The angles change with her mood—slanty and emo one month, round and clean like a Nancy Sinatra backup singer the next. She also has the biggest brown eyes I've ever seen. She frames them with matte eyeliner on the outside and blots bright shadow into her upper and lower waterlines—fuchsia, indigo, safety-cone orange. I think some customers are stunned into politeness by the sheer bulging cuteness of Pooj's eyes.

Other idiot tourists make fools of themselves and ask her if she's Native American. "I'm the other kind of Indian," she used to explain. After a while she got tired of explaining and started to have fun with it instead.

"I'm a *direct* descendant of Pocahontas," I heard her say last week, three tables down from where I was taking an order.

It'd taken all my willpower not to snort as I wrote down requests from a tired mother in a Disney World t-shirt holding a fussy baby in her lap: pancakes for her and three hamburger steaks for her identical, buzz-cut little boys.

I'd glanced over at Pooj. The couple she was serving were two silver-hairs, well into their sixties, with Barney-colored fanny packs and Adidas tracksuits. I could picture the look in an Urban Outfitters ad. But these two were authentic vintage. They were probably on a bus tour of the Smoky Mountains, or on their way to Gatlinburg, looking for Southern charm, apple butter, and embellished history at every truck stop and country store.

Pooj had given them exactly what they wanted, playing up her authenticity with saucer-round eyes. "She's my great, great, great, great, great, great, great…great…Grand-maw-ma!" The twang at the end was the cherry on top.

I'd had to turn away. I couldn't look at her or I would break. I'd pretended to scratch my forehead, shielded my face from the customers, and barely made it to the counter where Rachel was filling sodas before I started laughing. Rachel had shaken her head, but smiled.

Pooj had told this kind of story before, always with a different ancestor—usually a local chief, even though the closest rez to our town is two hours north in Cherokee. It worked like a charm: Customers would ask for her autograph on napkins and give her enormous tips. That had been the first time she'd claimed descent from Pocahontas, though.

The real Pocahontas, Matoaka, had lived six hours east near Jamestown, on the Virginia coast. It was there that she was captured and held for ransom by the English when she was sixteen, converted to Christianity, married to a white man, shipped to England to be ogled, then shipped back to America to die before she was twenty-one . . . but tourists wouldn't know that if they'd only watched the Disney movie.

I didn't think anyone would believe Pooj, but the mother from my table rushed over to her. She'd handed Pooj her baby like an offering.

"I don't like babies," Pooj said. She'd held it a rigid arm's length away.

The lady seemed not to hear. She'd backed up and almost knocked over a sugar shaker, her butt folding over the edge of the table behind her. She'd held up her phone.

"Smile," the lady commanded. The baby cried, but Pooj was game. She'd held the thing skyward like little Simba in the Lion King. I'd half-expected her to break out into an a cappella "Paint with all the Colors of the Wind."

Pooj smiled at me. She'd mouthed, *suckers*.

When Pooj returned the squirming flesh ball, she'd walked by my tables and flashed a twenty.

Pooj was reckless, fearless—my complete opposite. That's why I loved her so much. *She* wouldn't just stand by the kitchen and twirl her hair, staring at the cute girl with the bull ring as the girl ate a piece of key lime pie. Pooj would have had her number by now.

To me, the girl might as well have been from another planet. First of all, I wasn't out, so I couldn't ask her on a date where I'd be seen with her anywhere in town. Second of all, what would I say to her? I wouldn't have the first clue. How do you gauge if someone is gay and flirt without making a complete fool of yourself if you're wrong? There's small talk, sure. *That pie looks good. My favorite's pecan. Do you go to McKinny High or Northside?* But how could I elevate small talk into flirting without making it weird? Could I slip her my number on a napkin? Invite her to make out in the bathroom?

I didn't have a chance to decide. The heavy cowbell tied to the door clanked as someone fell against it. In stumbled my namesake, the bane of my existence—Mary Ellen Webster the First.

My legal name is Mary Ellen Webster the Second, aka Junior, aka June. Mary Ellen the Second—sounds regal, doesn't it? That's what my mom thought. *It's rare you hear a girl with a title like that,* she would say. She was proud of being single, never marrying, raising me on her own. What she never acknowledged was how, in some respects, it was easier that way—like when she had no one (other than me) to tell her what a shitty job she was doing. And I was just an ungrateful kid whose complaints didn't count.

Mary Ellen worked at the idyllic Bellmont Inn, where doctors, lawyers, and politicians paid the equivalent of our trailer's monthly rent for a one-night stay in a "rustic" cabin, decorated in fur and taxidermy—complete with modern luxuries like Jacuzzi tubs and marble countertops. My mom was the ghost who cleaned up their spills and washed the sin off their sheets.

I went to school every day, brought home mountains of homework from my AP classes, and worked four shifts a week at Buttermilk to help out when money got tight, which was always. Mary Ellen wasn't the only one who made sacrifices.

I was done with her, especially on days like this, when she brought her random dates into the restaurant while I was in the middle of a shift.

She stumbled in on the arm of a beefy red-headed dude. The guy seemed sober. Mary Ellen did not.

Pooj saw her at the same time as I did. "Go take care of her and I'll cover for you." She tugged on my apron string.

"Thanks," I said, dropping off a ticket and speed-walking over to Mary Ellen. We'd lost our last car when she'd driven home drunk from a Christmas party at the Inn and totaled it against a tree. It was just a shitty 1998 Honda minivan, but it got me where I needed to go. I wasn't going to let that happen again.

I grabbed her skinny arm so tight her skin streaked red and white between my fingers. "Did you drive here?" I asked.

"Hi Mom, I'm glad to see you too," she mocked. The redhead laughed. I wasn't amused.

"*Did you?*" I grabbed her arm tighter.

She wriggled out of my grip. "No! Of course not. Roger has a motorcycle, a fuckin' Harley, June. The power of that motor, you can feel it from your toes to your scalp."

She rubbed the guy's back with the tips of her plastic nails and laughed that flirtatious laugh of hers that curled into wispy gasps at the end. I used to love when she scratched my back with those nails. Now I hated it.

"Can you eat somewhere else?" I asked.

Roger looked deflated, like he wasn't sure whether to respect me and leave, or defend my mom and get angry.

I spoke straight to him. "Rush hour's coming up soon. You'll have a better time at Cracker Barrel or Shoney's. Just drive a little ways down the mountain, you'll find something."

Then I stared at my mom with eighteen years of resentment concentrated into one unrelenting glare. I wished my eyes could operate like a magnifying glass and burn a hole where I directed my anger—her unfocused eyes, over-lined lips, overhanging cleavage about to jump off the ledge. It was four o'clock, and we only served beer, but I knew that wouldn't stop Mary Ellen from getting sloppy drunk—well, drunk*er*. That wasn't happening on my watch.

They argued over whether to stay or leave. When Roger casually cupped her ass, I turned away.

"Do what you want," I said.

I walked back to my tables, finished taking an order, and waited for pick-up on two cheeseburgers. The next time I walked past the entrance, they were gone. So was the cute girl with the bull ring. She'd left before I had a chance to ask her name.

I've known since seventh grade that I was gay, but I've never told a soul. Pooj guessed a few months ago, right at the beginning of senior year, when I was tipsy and slipped up at a party. The party was at her house with a couple of good friends, when her parents were gone. It wasn't a sloppy free-for-all with the whole school, just five or ten honors students and some of the guys Pooj bought weed from.

We were playing drunken truth-or-dare in her parents' basement. Pooj was half-naked, down to her sports bra and shorts. She had a beautiful belly button. I told her so.

"Thanks, baby." She lifted my shirt. Her hand tickled, and I flinched.

"So do you," she said.

Pooj always took dares. Her second dare that night was to lick ketchup off Henry the model UN team captain's elbow. Pooj suggested his nipple instead. He didn't complain.

I never took dares. Bodies grossed me out, especially the bodies of boys like Henry, who smelled like a radioactive combination of hair gel, Doritos, and Axe body spray.

"Truth," I said, when it was my turn.

Pooj was ready. She had a Jenga set with questions written on every block. "If you had to have one giant face posted on your bedroom wall forever, whose would it be?"

I took another sip from my Buttermilk Sweet Tea, a drink Pooj had invented that night. She said it was like a Southern version of a Long Island Iced Tea and suggested we sell it at the restaurant, but there was nothing particularly Southern about it. It was just a combination of every type of alcohol that Pooj had been able to sneak from her parents' liquor cabinet. She didn't want to take too much from any one bottle, so she'd mixed a little bit of everything they had—rum, peppermint schnapps, gin, orange liqueur, and even the creamy stuff, like Baileys. It tasted like cough syrup poured over a bowl of milky cereal.

"Cara Delevingne," I said.

I would have said Emily Adams, the girl I'd crushed on for three years at school, but I was still sober enough to know that would be a very bad idea. Emily was one of the few openly gay girls at our school. (Actually, the only one, after Ashley Perez moved to Charlotte.) She'd also starred in my daydreams for the past three years.

"You would want to stare at Cara Delevingne every night for the rest of your life?" Pooj cocked her head to one side and looked at me. Looked *into* me. I blushed.

The next day at work, the texts began.

Pooj: *What do you think of the girl by the windows, the one with the green crop top?*

Me: *A celebrity crush does not mean I'm gay.*

Pooj: *Lying doesn't work when you blush that hard.*

Me: *I have a boyfriend.*

Like that proved anything.

Pooj: *You can still be queer and have a boyfriend. There's a spectrum you know.*

I relented.

Me: *Those dimples though.*

Pooj: *(six heart eye emojis)*

Me: *If you tell anyone, I'll show your mom where you hide your weed. I'm serious.*

Pooj: *(six heart eye emojis)*

I couldn't stop smiling the rest of the day. I loved so much that she knew.

❄

I thought about Green Crop Top Girl's dimples the next time I kissed my boyfriend, Eli. Then I thought about Emily Adams. My default brain state was thinking about Emily Adams.

At eight a.m. every day before first period, Eli and I kissed at his locker. It was our ritual, our announcement to the school that we were still a couple. Eli was a deep puckerer, so I didn't have to stand too close. His mom had bought us both promise rings three months after we started dating. It was that kind of relationship, which was fine by me. I enjoyed minimal required physical contact with Eli.

He straightened the neckband of my thrifted Lacoste sweater. "Where did you get this?" he asked with a note of suspicion.

Most of my nice clothes were hand-me-downs from Eli's mom and older sister, or from other wealthy families at his church. I was their pet project. Their success story. A knotty Barbie they'd found in the dirt, bathed in baptismal water and dressed in name-brand sweaters.

I'd found the sweater I was wearing at Goodwill, but Eli didn't need to know that. "A cool little vintage store in Asheville."

"Good job, Mary. I like it," he said, like he was my dad or something. If he hadn't promised to give me his old laptop that weekend for my birthday, I would have gone off on him.

"Please don't call me Mary. That's my mother's name."

"It's your Christian name. It's a very Christian name. What's wrong with it?"

"You know my mother." I could feel my chest and face getting hot.

"Mother Mary," he chuckled. "What about Mary Full of Grace? That one's cute."

"Please. Don't call me Mary," I said again.

He frowned. "What can I call you then? I want a special name for you, one that only I call you."

Sometimes I thought Eli loved the idea of a girlfriend—the

idea of *me*—more than the actual me. I'd earned the title of girlfriend like a participation award—I showed up to places with him as a couple, we went to prom together, to the movies. But I kept him at arm's length.

Pooj didn't understand our relationship—or maybe it was more like she didn't approve of it. The Sunday after she'd figured out I was gay, when I was at church with Eli and his family, she'd texted me: *June, you can't lead him on forever.*

I'd shielded my phone in a Bible so that Eli's nosy twelve-year-old cousin sitting beside me couldn't see.

Me: *I'm in church. I can't text.*

Pooj: *Liar.*

I wasn't lying to Eli. I hadn't promised him forever. I was going to a state college next year, not to any of the private Christian schools where he'd applied.

Me: *I'm not leading him on. High school romances never last. Everyone knows that.*

Pooj: *He told you he loves you June.*

Ellipses appeared, disappeared, reappeared.

Pooj: *You lied when you said it back.*

Pooj knew that would sting. I'd shut the Bible over my phone and hugged the book to my chest, suddenly aware of how many bodies were in this room. I needed a minute away from Eli and his family and the dizzying kaleidoscope of a hundred different perfumes and Lily Pulitzer prints. I'd pretended to walk to the bathroom, then slid out the side door and took a big breath.

If I acted like a good girlfriend, and he thought I was a good girlfriend, isn't that what I was? It was so much easier to pretend it was true. Maybe if I pretended long enough, I'd feel something eventually.

Me: *I do love him, in a way. Relationships are a lot more than just attraction.*

I knew I wasn't being completely honest with Eli, but it's not like I was cheating on him. He wasn't allowed to be jealous of my thoughts. My desires. Those belonged just to me.

Pooj: *It's not fair to be with someone just because you need them.*
I hadn't responded.

Instead, I'd sat on the sidewalk and slid out of my sandals, rubbing my toes against the concrete until they burned. She was right. If I didn't break up with him, I wouldn't just be a liar, I'd be an asshole too. A cowardly, selfish asshole.

I had physics for first period. Emily was in my class. That day I walked in wiping off Eli's good-morning-kiss spit and almost crashed into her. She was crouching at the front of the room. A frazzled substitute had given up on figuring out a rickety VCR player rental from the library, and Emily was helping her reconnect the cords. I wished I could sit in the back and just watch her without it being weird.

Emily was tall and lean with long, frizzy red hair. She had freckles all over her arms and face, even on her lips. She ran an anarchist book club after school on Wednesdays and was starting a zine for her senior project. She wore oversized graphic tees that she sliced into midi shirts and bleach-dyed. She had Reeboks before they were cool again. I knew so many details about her that might have meant nothing to anyone else, but they meant everything to me.

I made myself stop looking at her and sat down in my assigned seat—in the third row, beside Bobby, one of Eli's friends on the soccer team. Bobby and I were both good at physics. We made great lab partners, because we didn't have much in common to talk about other than our work.

But that day when I sat down, Bobby stood up and moved. He didn't say a word to me. He didn't even move to a chair beside one of his friends. He moved to an empty seat at the back of the room.

I texted Pooj.

Me: *Bobby is acting like I licked some poison ivy. He moved out of spitting range.*

Pooj: *Yeah...so remember that chunky-hunky guy your mom brought into Buttermilk last week? That was Bobby's dad.*

Me: *Fuck.*

Fuck, fuck, fuck.

I often think there's nothing worse Mary Ellen can do to ruin my life. She always surprises me.

Pooj: *Emily's in your class. She's way hotter than Bobby. Go sit by her (wiggly eye emoji) (dancing stick figure gif)*

I didn't respond. My stomach did this panic thing where it makes tidal waves and then my whole body rocks like I'm sitting in the ocean.

Emily slid into her seat, but there was no way I was brave enough to go sit next to her. Instead, I left the classroom just as the lights were dimming. I went to the bathroom, rubbed my face with water, and sat by the window.

Me: *Want to smoke?*

Pooj: *Hell yea.*

Me: *The pig in 10?*

Pooj: *Already there (upside down smiley emoji)*

I walked five minutes to a deserted parking lot in front of the closed-down Piggly Wiggly. It was our sanctuary, forgotten and all ours. The white concrete of the parking lot was tinted yellow with veins of rain-washed pollen.

Pooj's was the only car in the lot. She was in there making out with her boyfriend-of-the-week, a cute stoner named Rafael who played the saxophone and liked the same first-person shooter games as Pooj.

I knocked on the passenger window. Pooj kicked him out.

He glared at me before opening the door. "Go ahead, she's all yours."

He held the door open with mock chivalry, then slammed it when I got in.

Pooj fished around in her makeup bag. She pulled out a black eyeshadow case that hid her vape. "Ignore him. You okay, babe?"

"Yeah..." I said, sighing and leaning my head back. "Sorry to interrupt."

"Don't be." She dug in her bag for a double-sided compact that had just enough room to slide a bud in the back. "He's so needy it's boring. I'm running out of decent male options at this school, June. Maybe I'll try out girls for a while with you."

Try out girls. I wished it were that easy. Like trying on a dress. Then I could decide not to buy it and go back to my normal life, no harm, no foul.

I watched Pooj grind and pack with practiced precision. She took a drag and handed me the vape. I took a long drag, like it was water and I hadn't drunk all day.

"Damn." She snapped her fingers. I always took tiny puffs. I was usually scared of overdoing it, of someone noticing that I was high. Not today.

I handed the vape back to her. I opened the door and stuck my feet out, then my hands, palms up. It was sprinkling, even though the sky was too bright to look at without tearing up. My skin glistened with dewy drizzle.

"It's not just something I'm trying out," I told Pooj quietly, with my back turned to her. My voice cracked a little.

She put down the vape and hugged me from behind.

"Hey, I know."

She started combing my hair with her fingers.

"I'm sorry."

I turned to her. She patted her lap and I lowered my head.

She took out a real lipstick, one without hidden compartments. She rubbed it across my lower lip. I let my jaw slacken, and she held my chin.

"We need to get you laid," she said.

I laughed and she almost smeared lipstick across my face.

"How about a kiss first?" I said.

"With Emily?"

I put my hand on my stomach, expecting it to do its panic thing, but it didn't panic at all. It felt warm. I rubbed up and down my navel. Pooj closed my eyes like a corpse and started with the liner.

"How did you know I like her?" I asked.

"It was pretty simple actually. When you spent free period in the Spanish room, I received an average of six cat memes an hour. Now that you draw in the library, you haven't meme-bombed me during school hours in over a month. When I found out a certain cute, queer redhead named Emily works behind the library counter...I put two and two together."

I smiled, careful not to open my eyes.

"What do I do?" My stomach ached then. Not panicky. A desperate, hungry kind of ache.

"Go check out a book and leave her your number. Or better yet, return a book with your number written on a slip of paper inside. That would be the cutest meet-cute in history."

"I can't do that," I said.

Pooj sighed.

"Then just ask her out for coffee."

"What the fuck Pooj, I have a boyfriend!"

"Break up with him."

"It's not that easy."

"Yes it is."

Neither of us spoke for a minute. She finished my face, and I handed her the vape.

I sat up and looked in the mirror. She had rimmed my eyes in a metallic gold that matched my hair and distracted from my crooked nose. It made my brown eyes look brighter, like dark honey.

Maybe it was the weed, maybe it was the fact that I trusted Pooj with my life, but in that moment, I believed everything she said. It wouldn't be easy, but I could do it. I could ask Emily out. I could break up with Eli.

There was just one more thing I needed to get off my chest. A legitimate fear. I sat up and straightened my shirt.

"What if she doesn't like big boobs?" I looked down at my inheritance with shame.

"Fuck you. Your boobs are fun. Just go for it." Pooj nudged one with her elbow and kissed me on the cheek. I hugged her and got out of the car.

I always went to the library after first period ended and my free period started. I knew Emily would be there working the desk. I liked being in her presence, even if on most days I didn't speak to her at all. She didn't have a girlfriend, but she'd never given any sign that she was interested in me. I was sure as hell never bold enough to make a move.

I usually tried to do homework or read while I sat in the library, but often couldn't focus enough to do either. Most of the time I drew and listened to music. Sometimes, if no one was around, I drew Emily, or Pooj, or Grey's Anatomy ships. Those were mostly romantic scenes between Meredith Grey and Cristina Yang. Like the two of them kissing in a supply closet, or Cristina wrapping her arms around Meredith teaching her how to cut the heart out of a cadaver. When I was done, I tore the drawings out of my sketchbook, took them home, and hid them away in the deep, dark corners of my nightstand.

That day, when I walked into the library and saw Emily, for a beautiful, weed-hazy moment I forgot my anxieties. I wasn't thinking about anything but her.

I leaned into the counter where she was Sharpie-ing a sign for her zine: *Accepting Submissions in May. Comics, Poems, Photography, Confessions, any and all things Radical.* At the bottom of the flyer, in all caps: *EXCLUDING ALL MISOGYNIST, XENOPHOBIC,*

RACIST, HOMOPHOBIC BULL****. Her font was old-school punk letters that resembled lightning bolts.

"That looks good," I told her.

I let my fun boobs rest on the edge of the counter, crossing my arms underneath, propping them up.

"Thanks," she said. "You should submit some of your drawings. If you feel like it."

She noticed that I drew? My skin felt electric. What else had she noticed? I combed my hair behind my ears.

Her eyes narrowed. "Are you okay?"

"What?" Did I look super high? Oh God. I stood up and smoothed out my shirt.

"You ran out of class earlier and missed the film."

"Oh, yeah. I'm fine. I just felt a little queasy." Queasy equals vomit. Why did I say that? Now she was going to picture me vomiting.

"It was a pretty cool film. Kind of trippy." She looked up at me and smiled.

I studied her for any signs of sarcasm. She seemed sincere. Then I got distracted by the freckles around her eyes. If I kept staring, she would definitely know I was high.

"I'll try and watch it sometime." I turned to leave. I couldn't ask her out, not like this.

She held up her hand, motioning for me to wait. "We have it here. The VHS. The sub just returned it." She leaned down into the return box and pulled out the worn tape. "It's in-school use only. But if you want to watch it here, we have a VHS player. Those are hard to find now."

This was the longest conversation we'd ever had without me choking up and darting to the nearest escape route.

"It's my free period," I said.

"I can set you up in the A/V room?"

"Sure," I said, coolly.

I followed her in a trance.

This wasn't real. It couldn't be real. Emily was leading me into a dark room. Me, Emily, and the smooth dip in her back that peeked out when her T-shirt lifted. And her hair moving like it was alive and joyous simply for being attached to her. I watched her hair for a minute that turned into an eternity as we walked. Then we were there.

She pulled out a key, unlocked the door, and held it open for me. The door was right behind my usual seat in the library, but I had never noticed it before. The room was small and cluttered with junk. I squeezed in by some boxes and lost my balance, catching myself on the jutting pole of a wall map. She reached out to steady me, and her warm hand brushed my neck. I could smell her body spray. Vanilla.

I ached for the possibility of her. I imagined kissing her freckles. I imagined more. It was a feeling bigger than my body.

Emily walked over to the VHS player and started to rewind the tape. She turned on the TV, and its high-pitched squeak made the air feel tight.

I got a text from Eli: *June, where are you? Reggie's driving to Bojangles for lunch and he said you can come.*

Then I heard Eli and his church friend Reggie's voices—inside the library, outside the door of the little room. Their voices got louder; they were walking this way. They were going to pass by the A/V room and see us. They would see me in a small, cramped room with Emily, alone. They would fill in the blanks with hypotheses that they would never forget, no matter how untrue they were. No matter how true.

Being alone with her was my dream, but I was scared the boys would imagine what I imagined: Me grabbing her hair, her lips tasting like vanilla. Everything tasting like vanilla.

Their voices grew distinct, and I panicked, turning off the lights.

"What was that?" Emily said.

I was quiet. Cold sweat dripped down past my bra into my underwear elastic.

"June?" Eli called my name out sing-song, like I was a lost dog who'd come running at the sound of his voice. I closed my eyes, playing the toddler trick of self-delusion—if I can't see them, they can't see me.

"She's always in the library. I don't know where else she could be." Eli sounded puzzled.

"What about that girl she hangs around with?" Reggie said.

"Pooj. I'll text her."

My fight-or-flight impulse was malfunctioning. I didn't want to run, I wanted to stand so still that time passed around me and I could catch up in a year or two, when Eli, Reggie, Emily, and all the rest of our class were long gone.

The boys' voices retreated, then faded.

Emily walked towards me and looked out of the doorway. Over her shoulder, I could see Eli and Reggie opening the door to the hallway. It clicked shut behind them, and she turned to face me.

"That was weird," she said.

She was so close, I could feel her breath.

She tested the lights and they turned back on. I averted my eyes.

"Did you turn off the lights?" she asked.

I didn't look at her. I stared at her elbow. I felt my cheeks burning.

She was quiet. I was quiet. I heard her breath slow as she figured out what I'd done.

"You're literally that scared to be seen alone with me?" She shook her head, angry.

I shook my head even harder. No. No. No, no, no.

"Don't worry. I'll leave right now." She leaned over and picked up the TV remote, looking like she'd rather spit on me than kiss me. "Here, you can figure it out."

She threw the remote at my feet.

"There are so many fucking homophobes in this town."

She left me alone. The VHS tape finished rewinding and started to play. The static turned to a rainbow and then the triumphant bloom of the PBS logo. The profile of a blue face with a big nose fragmenting. A splotchy, vinyl-like recording of a piano.

I wanted to call after her. I wanted to tell her everything.

But I couldn't.

The camera panned through space, following a star through pixelated galaxies straight out of an arcade game. The footage cut to a giant wave crashing in slow motion. I turned the lights back off and imagined kissing her there in the dark. A parallel universe.

Carl Sagan's ghost spoke calmly from a grassy rock above the sea. *"The cosmos is all that is, or ever was, or ever will be."*

I wrapped my arms around myself and squeezed so tight, I forgot to breathe. I was falling, crashing so hard I felt dizzy.

"I'm sorry." My voice was so weak, I couldn't tell if I'd actually said it aloud. *I'm sorry, I'm sorry, I'm so sorry Emily. Please don't hate me. I don't hate you. I love you. I am you. I hate myself. I'm a coward.*

I started to cry, quiet tears, then dragging sobs. I didn't care who heard me.

I got a text from Pooj: *How's it going? (happy cat emoji) (rainbow emoji)*

I typed: *I fucked everything up. I blew my chance. Emily hates me.*

Writing the words made me cry even harder.

I didn't press send.

I put down my phone.

The tape kept rolling in the dark.

I didn't talk to anyone the rest of the day, avoiding Pooj and Eli. I locked myself in a bathroom stall and cried during seventh period, then took the bus home.

When I got home, I was relieved to find the trailer empty. Mary Ellen must have picked up an extra shift. I poured a bowl of cereal, sat in front of the TV, and flipped through ten channels of commercials before turning it off.

I was exhausted from crying. Yes, I'd fucked things up. Yes, I'd blown my chance. But maybe I could fix the part where Emily hated me. I could invite her to coffee or lunch, buy her an apology gift.

Or maybe it would take something bigger for her to forgive me. Something like the truth.

I took out my sketchbook and turned to a blank page.

I started drawing a giant spiral, chaotic, like a swarm of bees. I erased two blanks for eyes and made a body for the swarm. Confession of a Girl Overwhelmed by Regret.

I turned to a new page. I drew a galaxy dotted with meteorites and constellations. I outlined a constellation of a girl fractured into stars. Confession of a Girl Who Wishes She Was Bigger Than Her Fear.

I drew for hours. I kept drawing until I got it right. The whole truth and nothing but the truth.

Me, on a hospital bed, leaning in to kiss sexy Doctor Yang while she attached my heart monitor. Confession of a Girl Who Loves Girls.

I drew and erased Dr. Yang's hair about sixteen times, until it looked suspiciously like Emily's. With a Sharpie, I colored in lightning bolt font on the cover of my sketchbook: For Emily. I hugged the book, my hands sore and inky, feeling the good kind of tired, like I'd run for miles. Then I stuck the sketchbook in my nightstand drawer, realizing how hungry I was.

In the kitchen, I boiled water and leaned over the pot, letting the steam condense on my face. It felt good after so much crying. Mac and cheese was all we had for dinner, since Mary Ellen had forgotten to buy groceries the week before. That was another item on the list of things to discuss when she got home: Hey Mom, please don't forget to buy groceries, and please don't sleep with parents or teachers at my school. Also I'm gay, and I might come out to my crush soon. How was work?

Mary Ellen walked in right as I was using my teeth to rip open the stubborn powdered cheese packet. I startled at the sound of the door shutting behind her and spilled neon-yellow powder all over the counter. She sat down and let her bags sag off her arms while she turned on the TV.

"What are you cooking?" She spoke in the direction of the TV, with her back to me. She sounded so casual, like she wasn't lying to me about fucking the dad of a boy who'd come to all my birthday parties since elementary school.

"When were you going to tell me?" I poured some milk into the pot without measuring it and started stirring the mess with a big wooden spoon. It made an awful squishing sound.

"June, what are you talking about? I'm too tired to play games right now."

"I'm tired too," I said.

She walked into the kitchen.

"Here." She handed me a few little bottles of half-used professional care shampoo and conditioner, the leftovers from guest rooms. The spring scent was lavender and charcoal. They smelled so good, I wanted to eat them. I was still angry at her, though. Little shampoo bottles weren't going to change that.

"Want some Coke?" She pulled out two plastic cups from above the sink and started filling them with ice.

"Everyone knows about you and Bobby's dad," I said.

She stopped filling the cups. Silence replaced the clatter of ice.

I didn't expect her to apologize. It wasn't her style.

She sighed. "He said he wouldn't tell anyone about it until after your graduation."

She was standing in front of the open freezer. I could hear the motor working extra to pump out chilly air, smoky frost falling around her like fog. "And you thought no one would see you riding around town on the back of his goddamn Harley? How stupid are you?"

She shut the freezer door.

"Just because you're going to college doesn't mean you've got the whole world figured out," she said, tears in her voice.

The look on her face made me cramp with guilt. "Mom, I'm sorry."

She started pouring Coke like it was no big deal. She cursed when the fizzy foam ballooned and spilled over the edges of the cups.

"There's no need to be. You're gone in a couple of months anyway," she said.

I was leaving, but it wasn't like I'd never come back. I needed a bigger life, a career that was comfortable and paid decently. A job in a city where there were things to do. Where I could be out and it wouldn't be a big deal. Maybe I could even meet a girl and fall in love.

I had to leave. I had no choice. I was suffocating. She didn't understand.

Unless. Maybe she did.

I started racing through memories of all of Mom's past boyfriends. Were any of them Elis? Was that why she'd never married?

My hands started sweating at the idea. Maybe I was more like Mary Ellen than I thought.

I didn't know much about my mom's love life, not much more than the gossip I heard at school. I was always the opposite of interested. I'd never thought to ask if she was like me. Or, I guess, if I was like her.

My neck grew hot under my hair. I braced my hands behind my back against the stove.

"Mom, did you ever…have you ever been with a woman?" I spoke carefully.

I'd finally gotten her full attention. She looked hard at me.

"Have people been talking about me?" She put down the Coke.

"No."

She pointed her finger at me, like my face was a news camera and I could telepathically communicate her fury to all the gossipers around town. "They can call me a whore if they want, but not a goddamn dyke. That's just not true."

Her eyes were so full of hate, it scared me. She stood so close to me, I could see them shifting—jittery fear morphed into anger and back into fear. I held my breath. I was scared she was going to hit me. I felt anxiety burning in my throat, then swelling in my chest like heartburn.

I wanted to run to my room. I wanted to shut my door until I left for college, so I'd never have to see Mary Ellen again, or Eli, or Emily, or the rest of the world.

But I'd promised myself a long time ago I would never become my mother. And in that moment, I knew I looked just like her. Scared. Stupid scared.

"What if *I'm* a goddamn dyke?" I said. The words hurt coming out, like I'd swallowed dry grits. I kept my face hard, but tears started falling. They glossed in silent ribbons over my cheeks.

She stood there for an unbearable minute, processing what I'd said, not saying a thing in return. I knew she'd been raised conservative and still voted straight-ticket Republican. But I wasn't sure what values she just went along with, and which ones she actually believed.

"Does anyone know?" she finally asked.

"Just Pooj."

"What about Eli? I thought you two'd end up married."

I shook my head no.

"There's this girl..." I started.

She held up her hand for me to stop.

"I don't want to hear it," she said.

I wanted to explain to her that Emily was out, and there were some idiots at school who provoked her sometimes, but it wasn't so bad. It might even be a little easier if the two of us were out together. And Mary Ellen didn't believe in marriage, so she shouldn't feel disappointed. Even though I still wanted to get married, just not to Eli, or any other Elis.

She fluffed her bangs and smoothed her hair, a nervous habit I'd inherited.

"If you don't give them reason to talk, they won't," she said.

She scooped out a bowl of mac and cheese and walked into the living room.

And that was it.

I stood for a minute by the oven and let the adrenaline pulse out of me. The sweat dried on my arms, and I shivered.

It wasn't as bad as it could have been. She hadn't disowned me. But I was still disappointed.

Don't give them reason to talk. Was that a warning? A threat? If that was advice, it was the most hypocritical piece I've ever heard. As if it was no big deal that she flipped through the guys in town like a stack of Pokémon cards, but it would be the end of the world if I asked out one girl on a date.

I was disappointed, but I also felt relieved in a way I hadn't for a very long time. I'd finally done it. I'd told the truth, and the world hadn't shattered. I'd done it once, and I was certain I could do it again.

I went to my room to eat. I read through all of Pooj's messages from the last seven hours.

Pooj: *Need a ride?*

Pooj: *This calculus homework is worse than when my dad sings Bon Jovi.*

Pooj: *Are you on problem 31 yet?*

Pooj: *Did you fall asleep?*

Pooj: *You haven't been on Instagram for like twelve hours. Are you alive?*

Pooj: *I'm seriously going to drive over soon to make sure you're still alive.*

I smiled and laid my phone on my chest, spreading my arms crucifix-style on top of my comforter. In a perfect world, Pooj would be gay and we'd get married tomorrow, because she is undoubtedly my one true love.

Me: *BREAKING NEWS, I just came out to Mary Ellen. And I'm still alive.*

Pooj: *What!!! Are you serious? What did she say?*

Me: *Not much. Basically, I should be careful, so people don't talk. So tomorrow I'm going to give Emily all the gay AF pics I drew for her zine. Everyone's going to talk.*

Pooj: *(fireworks emoji)*

Pooj: *I'm proud of you babe. Can't wait to see the drawings. Are they sexy?*

Me: XXX

I closed my eyes and smiled.

Love Is a Wild Creature

ROBIN KIRK

Kirk's young adult novel *The Bond* is forthcoming in December 2018 from Goldenjay Books. Her short fiction has been published in *Tomorrow,* an anthology of speculative fiction from Kayelle Press; in *Beyond the Nightlight,* an anthology published by A Murder of Storytellers; and in *The Moon Magazine.* She won an honorable mention in the Chicago Reader's 2014 Pure Fiction contest. She is also an award-winning non-fiction writer. Her essay on Belfast is included in the *Best American Travel Writing* of 2012; she won the *Glamour* magazine non-fiction contest; and she was featured in *Oxford American's* "Best of the South" issue. Her writing has appeared in the *New York Times, Mother Jones, The Washington Post, The American Scholar,* and *Sojourners,* among other publications. She writes a regular column for the Durham *Herald-Sun*.

Kirk has also published nonfiction books, including *More Terrible Than Death: Massacres, Drugs and America's War in Colombia* (PublicAffairs) and *The Monkey's Paw: New Chronicles from Peru* (University of Massachusetts Press). She coedits the *The Peru Reader: History, Culture, Politics* (Duke University) and is an editor of Duke University Press's World Readers series.

Kirk is a Faculty Co-Chair of the Duke Human Rights Center and is a founding member of the Pauli Murray Project. She is a lecturer in Duke's Department of Cultural Anthropology. She is a graduate of the University of Chicago and holds an MFA in Children's and Young Adult literature from Vermont College of Fine Arts. She can be reached on facebook.com/robinakirk or on Twitter at @robinkirk.

Working at Eversol's Rest isn't so different from a dentist's or a landscaper's or maybe a realtor's especially, since that is what the Rest really is, real estate, a piece of the earth to call your own until the world's actual end. When the dead come up to hold Jesus's hand, will it be as rags and bone or when they were young and beautiful?

I don't know. I think about that some.

Every so often, a person comes looking for a long-lost family member. Usually, it's the only one in the family who did something worth remembering, like start a store or kill a person or be killed in some oddball way. My job is to answer the phone, send bills, and hand out maps. I keep the candy dish full, too, with butter mints. They melt in your mouth.

The maps are yellow and brittle from baking so long on the shelf. Mr. Eversol, the owner, doesn't believe in the A/C. Before I hand a map out, I circle with a pencil the grave a visitor asks after. Number 58 east, I might say, or 12 center, right by the memorial gazebo. Off they run, as if I have a stopwatch to click that measures devotion.

Like as not, what they find disappoints. Our town, Wyott, is not made for big history. People live quiet lives here.

At least, until Travis and Hen.

The older headstones—pre-1940, not your grandmother, but her mother's mother, a Mavis or an Evangeline—are rubbed smooth by the wind and rain or erased altogether if they are really old, carved from pine and meant to crumble. It's as if the dead don't want to be a burden. They left, sort of, and don't want to make trouble.

To keep them from curling, I press the maps flat beneath boxes of pencils and staples and the shrink-wrapped adding-machine tape. But nothing halts their march to dust. Maps are like people that way. They become something else that you have no control over no matter what you do.

What do the great-great-grandkids find? Creeping Charlie weed. A jay feather. Somebody's cigarette butt. The Rest has built-in flower vases, but most plots haven't seen a real bloom in decades. The great-greats take a photo and scuff their feet. Sometimes, children pee on an azalea. There are faucets for the grounds-keeper, but even I won't drink from them.

Lee-Ann calls it corpse water, and I can't disagree.

In the summer, it's beastly hot. The winter in Wyott is gray, snowless, and cold. Pretty soon, the great-greats leave Wyott for good. As a rule, they don't come back.

I see love at the Rest, but never near old graves. Love breaks out when a child or young wife dies. Or when some Wyott High School student wraps a car around a tree after getting hammered. People bend over the casket draped in pink or blue flowers, and weep with love-hurt.

It's a thing: love-hurt. When I was little, I watched my mom carry Daisy, our dog, to the garden. My dad had dug a hole. She laid Daisy there, right on top of all the roots. My dad filled up the hole with his eyes closed because he couldn't bear to see the red clay spatter her beautiful black nose. We were love-hurt for weeks.

When I want to talk to Travis, now that he and Hen are gone, I sit at the bench by the water oak that spreads big as a house. I smoke. I always pick up my butts since no one wants their loved one resting in an ash tray.

At least I talk until Lee-Ann sees me and thinks I need a cheer up. Lee-Ann wants to be an accountant someday so she practices on Mr. Eversol's books. Some families buy multiples. Others get just one and layer themselves like a cake. Cozy and creepy at the same time, Lee-Ann says.

The first day I was back at work, Lee-Ann brought my favorite Bojangles egg and cheese biscuit.

"I know you miss Trav," she said, settling next to me. "He was your first love. It's hard to let go."

I shrugged. None of that was a secret.

Lee-Ann's eyes were full of pity and questions as she set the biscuit next to me in its wrapper. What was it like with Travis, she really wants to know. Who fired that shot? Was it Hen like people are saying? He was never very good with firearms, she's said before.

"If you don't mind me asking, why did all three of you go to the river? Travis and Hen, I mean, with you."

"It was always the three of us."

Lee-Ann blurts, "Always?"

I stood. "Don't be gross. There are different kinds of love, Lee-Ann."

Lee-Ann thought I meant friend love and boyfriend love, and I suppose that's one way of putting it. I also know about the love that rides just above the surface and the love that digs deep inside you like some sort of wild creature and feeds your daily will to live. It's a love that leads you off somewhere you never wanted or thought you'd travel. You don't ask for it. You don't invite it. You don't even want it. If you could, you'd lock your heart behind all sorts of gates and walls and then crouch, making yourself too small for that kind of love to see. Love like disease, like a hammer blow.

Like a gunshot.

I was lucky Lee-Ann couldn't see my heart thrum.

Some kinds of love can end you. But you can't help but unlatch the door when that love comes knocking.

"Cheri, I didn't mean to say…"

Of course, you did.

"Your biscuit," she said as I headed back to the office.

"I'm not hungry."

I know I don't look changed. I'm still small, still brown-eyed. I sleep light and smoke. Travis always tried to get me to quit. I still ignore him, though he's six months gone.

But I'm not the same Cheri. When I came back to Wyott High School after that day, I could feel the change inside me like something polished under my ribs. Like those fossilized bones in Science lab, still like bones but different, stone through and through. People look at me and maybe it's not just a hello they are expecting. They want to see the change in me, like a wound I can point to.

They want to know what exactly happened that cold afternoon by the river. They sense I'm not telling them everything and they are one-hundred-per-cent correct.

Love-hurt doesn't always mark you on the outside, I feel like screaming. Love-hurt seeps into your skin and scars you on the inside, where you have no defense.

When last I saw Hen, I barely recognized the boy I'd first seen in the Wyott High cafeteria. New kid from Chicago, people said. Red-haired, tall, a blast of freckles across his nose. He was slim-hipped and lean-muscled, a natural-born running back. Hen was the fastest boy in the state that fall. People thought he might just win the team the championship.

All the girls went ooooooh and aaaaah. A *hot property*, Lee-Ann called him.

Travis and I were going steady at the time. Travis: thick as a post, the blackest hair you've ever seen screening his blue eyes. Arms like saplings that wrapped around me tight. He'd played football since Pop Warner, a defensive back. His dad said it as three words: De *Fensive* Back. Already, the scout from N.C. State had come to Trav's house to talk about his future with the Pack.

The first time Travis and I did it, his mouth tasted sweet as gum drops. I'd loved him forever or at least since kindergarten. He had ambitions, of course. Once he got his football scholarship, he would study maybe business or communications. Sometimes, I imagined going to State with him, the two of us in a cozy apartment like my sister got after she left Wyott with her boyfriend. I'd cook and maybe take classes at community college. Every game, I'd be Travis's loudest cheerer.

We'd set a date. I'd be in a beautiful dress and Trav would wear a tux black enough to match his hair. I saw us with three little boys, black-haired like their dad.

Travis was a good boy, a kind boy. We would hook up by the river, our special place with the grill and the old picnic table and the rope swing with the tractor tire that sometimes moves all by itself. I'd feel the tree roots on my back as his hand found the inside of my suit, where the wetness had nothing to do with our swim. I shivered, then felt warm as toast. When he entered me, propping himself with his elbows, he was my anchor to the earth.

When Hen first came to Wyott, he stuck out. He was no hunter, but Travis took him out when deer season opened to get him to know the other guys. Coach even gave Hen the locker next to Travis. Pretty soon, Hen and Travis were best friends. After practice, the three of us would sometimes hang out at our river spot. There, the Wyott River takes a lazy turn south, brown and thick. On weekends, we'd pick a movie to watch in Hen's rec room. So many girls liked Hen he could have had his pick. Even Lee-Ann asked me who he liked, though she and Mark have been a thing since like forever.

But Hen didn't want any of them. Hen carried his silence with him like a second skin. Sometimes, I'd catch him staring at me with a kind of hunger. He wanted something, though for the longest time I couldn't tell what.

I know the moment I understood. I was leaving school right before Thanksgiving, heading for Eversol's. The air was pleasantly sharp, trees blazing orange and red and yellow. Travis and Hen were talking by the tennis courts. They wore their game day ties and black slacks since we'd had a pep rally for the Demons game that weekend. There was a kind of shimmer around them. Hen looked down at Travis. The look Hen got back was like he was the only living creature on that stretch of dirt. Everyone else was smoke. It could have been night quiet. It was like someone had carved the space around them with the sharpest point of the sharpest knife they had.

Henderson and Travis, Travis and Henderson. I knew why Travis had been slow to return my phone calls. Why we hadn't been alone together in a while.

I just knew.

What happened next I try not to think about. Though sometimes I can think of nothing else.

They didn't know I'd glimpsed them. That I understood in that instant that everything had changed. I followed them, Hen in his Colt and Trav in his Charger, to the river. I went to be angry and point my finger at Hen and yell at Travis and beg him to love me again, the way it used to be, and put everything back the way I thought it should be.

So stupid. That future vanished the moment Hen stepped through the doors of Wyott High, maybe the moment he was born and the moment Travis was born, since they were moving toward each other from then on. The Physics teacher tells us we are always looking at the past, at how things were right before they change and that they are always changing, every second of every day. I never understood that before I crept up on Travis and Hen, arguing and crying and holding on to each other like they were the only two things pinning each other to the earth.

Travis jumped back when he saw me. "Why are you here?"

"This is our place!" My hand jabbed at Hen. "This is us, not him. What are you doing?"

Travis broke. "I'm so sorry. I just…"

"How could you do this to me?" I burned with such shame I could have flamed up then and there, gasoline poured onto a fire. I bobbled my head and made a cry face, to mock him. "You'll never live this down. The whole school, the whole town," I said savagely, "will be laughing at you."

Travis sank to the ground. Hen kneeled, grasping his shoulder. The two of them there looked wrapped in Hen's skin of silence. They had no defense against me, and I knew it.

Hen finally spoke. "We can't stay here. We've got no choice."

How could I *not* see the wildness at that moment, something neither of them could tackle or outrun? Something neither of them wished for or in the end could hide from? Once they found each other, there was no way to deny it.

I felt my anger seep away. My hurt. Hen was right. There was no future for them in Wyott.

Then I saw the gun tucked under Travis's belt.

I wanted to be the river, wide and deep, to circle them at high flood and keep them safe. I wanted to slip into Hen's skin of silence and pluck out every word I'd said. But that's not how anything works. They knew without me saying: walking down the halls when everyone knows and whispers and points behind their backs. The two football players. What a riot.

Those little boys I wanted to make with Travis disappeared. Had he seen them, too, seen them wink out like a busted TV, replaced by pointing fingers and people smirking?

Sometimes, I can't sleep. I hear the backyard pines rustling and the hum of the freeway. I get all cold when I hear those sirens. I know what a siren means: heartbreak. Like the world has ripped in two. My heart is peeled raw and sometimes I wonder how it stays firm in my chest while all the rest of me is split open.

Did Travis still love me even though he loved Hen? Did he ever love me? Could he love us both, one who kept his silence close and the other who knew exactly how and where to hurt him most?

I tell myself not to think too much. I tell myself I can never really know. Love is a wild creature. Love doesn't ask to come in or tell you when it's going to leave. Love doesn't obey. It goes where it goes. It can't help itself.

I got mad. Mad times a hundred, mad to the maddest power the Physics teacher could put up on his dry erase board. I got so mad I grabbed the gun.

I've touched guns a hundred times in my life. My dad takes me out target shooting, and Travis too, with that same pistol. That minute, I might as well have been Hen. My finger slipped, and I stumbled.

An explosion knocked me back on my ass.

Travis was beside me, breath gumball sweet. "What were you thinking, Cheri? What have you done?"

"I thought you were going to kill yourself," I cried. "Kill Hen."

"What?" Travis gripped me so hard I couldn't breathe. "We're leaving, Cheri. That's what's happening. Hen's sister is coming for his car. We're leaving Wyott. Are you OK?"

Hen sucked in breath like he'd run his fastest race. "I think you killed that picnic table dead, Cheri," he said, starting to grin.

Just then, Hen's sister pulled up: hair red as fall maple leaves.

"You need to go," I said.

"Cheri, we can't now," Trav said. "The gunshot. The sheriff will come."

"I'll make something up. You have to go."

Something in Travis still wanted to protect me. It was my turn to do the protecting.

"If we don't go now," Hen said calmly, "we may never make it out of Wyott."

Travis took my head between his hands and gently kissed me on the forehead.

"Where will you go?" I whispered.

"Far enough. I'll call you," he promised.

When Sheriff Hall pulled up, I was ready. Sheriff Hall knows me from Eversol's since he sometimes leads motorcycle escorts for funeral processions.

"Hey, Cheri girl," he said, sauntering up. "Heard a report about gunfire. Any trouble?"

I'd lit up by then, never more grateful for my cigarettes and lighter. "Some kids from Green Level. You know those boys."

It was a pretty good lie. Green Level is known for pranking the Demons before big games. What is it that people say? The best lies are built on bits of truth.

Sheriff Hall sucked a toothpick. Right then, he wasn't Alison's dad or the middle school soccer coach. He was a place in space I was trying to tiptoe around. "Heard Trav's Charger was here. You still going steady? I'd hate to have him in trouble before the big game."

I pulled tears out of me like some extra tissue from a handbag.

It's been my experience that old men can't bear to watch a girl cry. Plus, I shook. "We broke up yesterday," I told him.

Sheriff Hall looked hard at the picnic table. He didn't see the fresh groove my bullet dug on the side. "Well, alright then." He tossed his toothpick in the dirt. "See you at the game."

Of course, the game was a blowout. Without Trav and Hen, the Demons rolled over Wyott like an old rug. A part of me wondered if Wyott wouldn't have overlooked Trav and Hen being together if they'd only been able to deliver one last thrashing of the Demons.

At the Rest, no one but Lee-Ann ever asks me any more about why Trav and Hen disappeared. Mr. Eversol is especially careful. Though you wouldn't think it by the way he looks, all stooped and with grey hair sprouting from his nostrils, I think he knows a thing or two about love-hurt. Sometimes, I see him talking to the gravestones. The ones of the people he knew, I guess. It's as if he's checking in on them, to see if they are liking their spot or if there's anything he can do for them now to make their stay more comfortable.

It's a silly thing, I know, but I talk to Travis even when he's not on the phone. I'll sit on the bench under the water oak and chatter about everyone's doings. Coach has a new running back who looks to go all-state. I see Hen's sister every now and again at the bank. The Physics teacher retired and moved to Florida. I graduate next month.

I'll be the one to go to State. Fashion, I'm thinking. I want to learn to make something Trav would be proud of. I want to make something with Wyott in it and also somewhere else, a place I'll go or even just dream about going. I want to make something beautiful for this world out of slow rivers and red maple leaves and benches under oaks.

Sometimes, I taste Trav's sweet gumdrop breath. Every time he calls, I end by saying, "Tell Hen *hey*."

The List

JOHN KLEKAMP

 John Klekamp has been writing since high school, contributing feature stories to the school paper. With encouragement from his high school journalism teacher, John graduated from Northern Arizona University and found work as a television reporter and anchor in the Phoenix, Detroit, and New York City markets, earning four Emmy Awards and numerous nominations for his feature and entertainment stories. "The List" is John's first published short story.

John is married to a super-supportive guy named Mike Huckman. Together, they spoil a golden retriever named Dory. Yes, she's named after the fish. John is currently working on his first young adult novel.

T he list is secret. Your secret.

You wrote down the first name even before a purple flower bloomed under your skin where your shoulder slammed into a metal locker. "Watch where you're going, faggot!" he growled even though you *were* watching where you were going.

Your shoulder was still sore when you added the second name to your list. Some guy thought it was hilarious, shoving his tray across the lunch table and into yours so your lunch spilled onto your lap.

"Oops," he said, smirking. You hustled to the boys' restroom to try to get the ketchup off your khakis.

But trying to clean the spill only made things worse. "Hey, look!" the lunch bully hollered so everyone turned to see. "He pissed himself!"

You hated P.E., not because you hated exercise, but because you hated the locker room. All those hard-to-monitor alcoves. Chaos and noise. A good place for bad things to happen.

He grabbed you from behind, squeezing your neck and forcing your head down—toward another boy's crotch. "You know you want it," the second kid sneered as he pretended to loosen his towel. They both cackled while your face reddened and you squeezed your eyes shut.

When you got home, you went up to your room, closed the door and wrote down two more names. You folded the list along its well-worn creases and returned it to its home on your messy dresser—next to some crumpled singles and a spare phone charger. In the morning, you slipped it into your front pants pocket. You carry it with you everywhere now.

One day during second period, you are called to the office after a particularly brutal shove in the hallway that sent you and your things flying. On the principal's desk is an unfolded piece of paper. You recognize the creases even before the handwriting. You jam your hands into your pockets, feeling around, heart racing.

The principal arches a brow when she sees your hands emerge empty. "Do you want to tell me what this is about?"

Your throat clenches. The inside of your mouth goes Death Valley dry. When you speak, the words come out choked. They sound like a lie. "It's not what it looks like."

"I certainly hope not." She sighs through her nose. Her eyes land on the lone chair facing her desk.

You plant your butt in the seat, thinking, *This wasn't the plan.* It's not the big reveal you'd been working toward.

It's not the ending you think they deserve.

The principal nods at the piece of paper. "Do you recognize this?"

"Yes."

"You made it?"

"Yes."

"Would you mind telling me why? Because frankly, I'm shocked by some of the names I'm seeing on your ... your list."

You're aware your lips are moving. You can hear the sound of your voice from far away as you answer her questions, trying to explain. But your brain is not entirely present. Every episode, every reason for starting the list in the first place is unspooling inside the theater of your mind.

You relive the impact, feeling the jolt of your shoulder slamming into the lockers. "Watch where you're going, faggot!"

"HEY! What's your problem?" There's a girl. In the boy's face. Yelling. He's got a foot on her, but she doesn't back down. She is fierce. You don't know her. "You alright?" she asks you after. "The guy's a total asshat. He's not worth thinking about." She puts her hand on your arm. "You sure you're alright?"

"I found out later her name was Lola Frasier," you tell the principal. "That was the first name I wrote down."

A vertical crease forms between the principal's eyebrows.

Next, the lunchroom bully. "Oops." His face smirking from across the table. Ketchup seeping through your khakis. You emerge from the boys' restroom with wet pants. A thousand eyes turn your way, followed by waves of laughter.

"Here," a freshman boy says as he fishes a sweatshirt out of his backpack and hands it to you. You tie it around your waist. "Instant stain-remover."

"He said it was no big deal. But it was." The principal's mouth is slightly agape. "His name was Hector Diaz," you say. "I believe that's the second name on my list."

This next one's the worst. Someone grabs the back of your neck, pushing your head down toward another guy's towel-covered crotch. "You know you want it." You wish you could fast-forward. Your face burns while they laugh.

"What the hell are you doing?" a guy yells, and you feel the grip on your neck loosen. You straighten as the neck-grabber tries to play it off. "We were just screwing around. No harm done."

"Really?" another guy says. "You think that's funny?"

The guy in the towel gulps hard. "Look, we're sorry, okay? We don't want any trouble."

And you're certain they don't because the two football players look like they could cause the bullies plenty of trouble without being late for Pre-Calc.

The principal blinks, horrified. "And the two who helped you were..." She checks your list. "Thomas Allen and Marcus Phelps?"

You nod.

"So, *all* these names..."

"They're all people who helped me out, yes."

You think the principal's eyes look a little shiny as she reaches into her desk. "But why keep a list?" she asks as she discreetly dabs under her nose with a tissue.

"My plan was to write a story for the school paper about what I learned my freshman year and all the people who helped me survive it—whether they realized they had or not. It was going to be my way of saying thanks."

"And what about the people who harassed you? No list?"

You shrug. "Nope. Like Lola said, they're not worth thinking about."

You have no idea how old the principal is, but you realize she looks way younger when she smiles.

A Handful of Seeds

KARISSA LAUREL

Karissa Laurel lives in central North Carolina with her son, her husband, the occasional in-law, and a very hairy husky named Bonnie. Her favorite things are dark chocolate, coffee, super heroes and *Star Wars*. She can also quote *The Princess Bride* verbatim.

Karissa writes science fiction and fantasy for adults and young adults. She's the author of The Stormbourne Chronicles, a young adult epic fantasy series from Evolved Publishing. Her short story "The Forest of Carterhaugh," a modern interpretation of the legend of Tam-Lin, appears in *Magic at Midnight*, a young adult fairy-tale anthology from Snowy Wings Publishing. As an associate editor, she also reads submissions for the young adult podcast, *Cast of Wonders*.

Kora Demetri grew up in Cypress Knee, a small farming community in eastern North Carolina where the piedmont's red clay hills gave way to flat planes, dark soil, and sand. The kind of land that preferred peanuts, cotton, and tobacco—seas of broad leaves that sprouted green before aging into rich gold beneath the summer sun. That same sun had affected Kora similarly, browning her skin like bread in the oven and drawing blond streaks through her long, honey-colored hair.

In the corner of one of Cypress Knee's numerous tobacco fields, the local high school's 4-H club had leased a garden plot. Kora and her classmates staked out rows of organic cantaloupes, heirloom tomatoes, and cucumbers in the summer. Collard greens, squashes, and turnips in the winter. On the weekends, they sold their harvest at a produce stand on the side of Highway 421, and that was where Kora met Hayden Rhea the day he and his little brother moved to town.

A gritty dust cloud billowed from the undercarriage of an old Ford sedan as it slid to a stop on the gravel shoulder. The driver's door opened with a groan, and a faded woman—dull black hair, wrinkled brown skin, worn slacks and blouse—stepped out, stretching her back until it popped. She looked up and met Kora's inquisitive stare.

It was a late Sunday afternoon near the end of summer break, and business was slow. Kora had been considering closing shop and taking the last of the produce home, but here was a curious customer: An older black woman with a young white boy sitting in the back seat. In the front was a boy—dark-haired and skin so pale it seemed translucent—who appeared to be about Kora's age. He glanced up from his phone, swept a lock of hair out of his long, narrow eyes, and peered at Kora.

When their gazes met, a crackling, prickling energy raised the hairs on the back of Kora's neck, leaving a trail of goosebumps down her arms. She'd never seen him before, she was certain, and yet she felt she knew him. As if something deep in her subconscious had recognized him.

"Excuse me, honey?" The faded, tired woman wiped a bead of sweat from her brow. "How close are we to Cypress Knee? My phone's dead, my charger's broken, and his"—she pointed at the older boy in the front— "only works for making emergency calls and playing some god-awful music." Her face puckered into a sour expression. "We've been on the road since this morning, and I'm half afraid we've spent the last hour driving in circles."

Kora wrinkled her nose at the thought of being cooped up in a car that long. She pointed down the highway, southward. "Five miles that way, take a right on Old Brevard Road. About three miles after that, veer left on Houndsditch. It'll take you straight into town. Don't blink, or you'll miss it."

"The turn?"

"No, the town."

The woman snorted as she eyed Kora's baskets of tomatoes. They were so red and plump they seemed on the verge of bursting. In fact, all of Kora's produce looked unbelievably ripe—almost surreal. "Those are some beautiful tomatoes."

"Picked 'em off the vine this morning."

"You use a special fertilizer? I don't think I've ever seen ones that fat and red before."

"Nope. I just have a knack for gardening." *More* than a knack. Ever since Kora's early childhood, all manner of flora had responded to her touch and care—not merely growing but flourishing. It was a trait she'd inherited from her mother. Actually, all the Demetri women in Kora's lineage had possessed a remarkable talent for agriculture. She'd never considered herself strange or exceptional—it was just the way things were in her family.

"How much for one of those little baskets?"

"Ten bucks."

The woman ducked in her car, found her purse, and traded a limp ten-dollar bill for a basket of Kora's extraordinary tomatoes. "You go to school around here?"

"Pender High." Kora frowned, thinking of the upcoming

hours of sitting still in stuffy, air-conditioned classrooms. The garden was her only escape, and lately even that wasn't enough to quell the sense of disquiet growing inside her. "Classes start back next week."

"You'll be, what? A senior?"

"Yes ma'am."

"So, what's your name, honey? ...If you don't mind me asking."

"Kora. Kora Demetri."

"Well, Kora, I'm Angela, and that one there's Hayden." She pointed at the front-seat boy again. If Hayden was aware he'd become the subject of their conversation, then he was ignoring them. "He'll be starting at Pender as a senior, too. The little one in the back is his brother, Zeke. Maybe..." She paused, searching Kora's face, although Kora couldn't guess what she was looking for. "Maybe you'll say hello to him? He'll be new to town. Won't know anyone."

"You're moving to Cypress Knee?" No one had moved to town in years. Mostly people grew up and left. Or grew old and died.

Angela chuckled. "Not me. Just the boys. Dropping them off at their grandparents' house...soon as I can find it."

A bushel of questions sprouted on Kora's tongue, questions about the boys and Angela's relationship to them. The presence of this unusual trio was an unexpected dash of red-pepper heat in her bland routine—waking up, working in the garden or produce stand, eating supper with her mom, reading a book until she fell asleep, then doing the same things again the next day. Church on Sundays and occasional visits to the farm supply store composed the majority of her social life. She was too polite, though, to ask anything except: "Who are their grandparents?"

"Parker and Ellen Rhea. Know them?"

Kora knew the Rheas, but she hadn't known they had kids, much less grandkids. "They live on Main Street. Ms. Rhea's been the town librarian for eons, and he's an auctioneer, does tobacco mostly."

"Didn't think anyone did that anymore."

"It's a dying breed." Kora shrugged. "Least that's what my mom says. She's the director of the local co-op extension office for the Department of Ag, so I guess she knows what she's talking about." Kora's mom was the reason Kora had started gardening in the first place. What began as a simple hobby for keeping a restless girl occupied during the summers had since developed into an obsession. Yet, even without her mother, Kora had a feeling she would have found her way into these fields. The land called to her, and the only time she felt truly at peace was when she was covered in dirt, surrounded by her plants.

Angela backed away, carrying her tomatoes like eggs that might split their shells if she jostled them. "Well, think about what I said, Kora. I hope you won't be a stranger."

Kora hadn't forgotten Hayden Rhea, but she'd been so busy and distracted during the week before the start of school, she hadn't given him—or her strange reaction to him—much thought. But on the first day of classes, she couldn't stop thinking about him as the rumor mill spread gossip faster than flames through a dry cotton field.

Cute... Quiet... Snobby... Probably has an old girlfriend... Probably gay... Probably a total wuss... Looks like some hipster guitar player... Looks like he needs his ass kicked...

Kora watched the sticky, oily whispers trying to cling to Hayden, but he seemed impervious and as hard as stone.

They shared English and Chemistry classes, but they didn't speak to each other until she spotted his tall, lean figure walking the ditch-line as she pulled out of Pender High's parking lot. She drove a battered truck, a hand-me-down from her brother who'd enlisted in the Marines after graduation two years before. One way or another, everyone left Cypress Knee. Hayden's arrival was an enigma.

Kora slowed, and her truck's squeaking breaks announced her approach. He glanced up, brow furrowed. She stretched across the bench seat and rolled down the passenger window. "Hey... Hayden, right?"

He cocked his head at an inquisitive angle, obviously wary, but then his expression cleared. "Vegetable girl."

"Actually, it's Kora." She huffed. "Get in, I'll give you a ride."

Hayden squinted. "I'm not going far."

"Yeah, but it's fixing to rain." She pointed at the darkening sky, clouds rolling in big black billows. In support of her argument, a stiff wind stirred Hayden's hair. Black and shiny, he wore it longer than most of the local guys who tended to prefer buzz cuts. It lay in stark contrast against his pale skin. *The farm boys will pick on him for that,* Kora thought. *He wouldn't last an hour in the field without burning to a crisp.*

Regardless, she found him beautiful, like some kind of rare moth that only came out on the darkest nights.

He exhaled a reluctant sigh and climbed in. Kora pulled out onto Main Street as he fastened his seatbelt. "How do you know where I live?" he asked.

"Everyone in Cypress Knee knows where everyone lives. You're new, so you're like a celebrity. By the end of the week, everyone will know all your secrets."

"Not if I don't tell them."

"They'll be happy to make up the parts they don't know."

"I heard small towns are like that."

"Hmm. Guess you don't come from a small town?"

He shook his head. "Charlotte."

"*Oooh.*" Kora popped her eyes wide and blinked, melodramatic and full of irony. "Big city boy, then. What are you doing in a place like this?"

"You getting all the details so you can take them back to your friends? Be the first one at school with the hot gossip?" His lip curled, nose wrinkling. "Will it make you popular?"

She returned his sneer. "I'm the vegetable girl, remember? My only friends are tomatoes and cucumbers. Have to be quiet around the corn stalks. They have big ears."

He rolled his eyes, but his sneer faded. "You're definitely too much of a dork to be popular."

"Not many girls my age still like playing in the dirt. They gave up making mud pies. I started making bigger ones."

"You're gonna be a farmer, then?" He muttered his next statement under his breath. "You should *love* it here."

"I do love it. And I'm not ashamed, so tease me all you want."

He didn't tease her, though. Instead, they rode the remaining distance in silence, and Despite her initial reaction to him—that inexplicable feeling of familiarity—Kora wondered if a city boy from Charlotte and a farm girl from Cypress Knee would ever have anything in common. He was nice to look at and might not be bad to talk to, when he wasn't so full of hostility. She could understand how he might feel like a black bear that had gotten its leg caught in a trap, though.

Kora loved Cypress Knee more than most kids in town, but even she felt the urge to look for something more, sometimes. Hayden seemed like the kind of person who might help her find it —whatever *it* was. She felt like it was a little unfair to assume so much about someone she had just met. And yet, there was something about him…

As she eased to a stop in the Rheas' driveway, Kora imagined that Hayden and his brother trying to weave their lives into their grandparents' routines was like trying to make the pieces from two different jigsaw puzzles fit together. "Tell your grandma I said hi. I'll be by to pick up those books she ordered for me tomorrow, maybe."

The Rheas lived in a modest brick ranch with a shallow porch and deep carport. A thick grove of pomegranate bushes, heavy with budding red fruit, bordered their small yard. Kora had never accepted one of Ms. Rhea's notorious pomegranates, although Ms. Rhea had offered them many times. The thought of those cold red seeds made Kora shudder with a revulsion she couldn't explain.

"Farming books?" Hayden worked the handle, but his door refused to open.

Knowing it sometimes took the right touch, she reached across to help. "Nope. Science-fiction—" Her hand brushed his, and her vision went blank like an empty movie screen. On a field of bright white appeared a girl, blurry at first, but sharpening into focus as a horrendous soundtrack boomed in Kora's ears: a scream, tires squealing, the shriek of rending metal. Kora recognized the girl lying like crumpled litter by the side of the road. Morgan Stafford was also a senior at Pender High, and her face was a rictus of death: eyes wide and sightless, mouth gaping, blood dripping from gashes in her forehead and throat.

Kora yelped and pulled back. The vision disappeared.

"What is it?" Hayden asked. "Are you okay?"

"Fine." She gasped for breath. "I'm fine."

"You don't look it."

"Just a dizzy spell." And a hallucination? Nothing like that had never happened to her before.

"Are you sure? You're white as a sheet."

She rubbed her eyes, trying to wipe away the horror of her vision. What was wrong with her that she would imagine such a terrible thing? "Could be low blood sugar. I skipped lunch."

He snorted. "Dieting?"

"Do I *look* like I need to diet?" Fit and strong, Kora harbored no delusions about herself. Hours of hard work in a field had a way of doing that.

He paused and looked at her as if seeing her for the first time. A deep blush stained his pale cheeks, but his gaze was warm when he said, "No. Not at all."

She reached across again, avoiding all contact, and popped his door open. "See you around, Hayden."

He slid out, clutching his bookbag, his gaze pinned to his feet. The storm clouds coughed, and fat raindrops fell, pinging the windshield and dampening his dark hair. "Yeah. See you around."

The next day at school, no one was talking about Hayden Rhea. Instead the rumor mill was grinding out theories about Morgan Stafford's fatal car accident.

Deer in the road... drinking and driving... lighting a joint... Texting... Giving her boyfriend a hand job...

Kora had watched the news report that morning while eating breakfast, and she'd been too stunned to respond to her mother's comments. Her mom had tried using Morgan's death as a teaching moment to discuss distracted driving, but Kora had felt like a stone at the bottom of a well—cold, hard, engulfed in darkness. She'd seen Morgan's death in her vision the day before, and now, impossibly, it was real.

But how? she wondered. *How...?*

In Chemistry class, she took the other seat at Hayden's lab table. When the girl who'd sat beside him the day before approached, Kora gave her a sharp look, and the girl scampered away. Hayden blinked like a surprised owl, but he said nothing to discourage Kora as she pulled out a stool. "Guess you heard about Morgan, huh?"

"Uh..." He blinked again. "Yeah. She was popular, I take it?"

"Shoo-in for this year's home-coming queen." Kora tugged her notebook from her bookbag and set it on the counter, trying for nonchalance. For the first time, she noticed his scent, cold and crisp like winter nights just before a rare, southern snow storm. None of that artificial musk in most teenage boys' deodorants.

"Was she your friend?" He drummed long, slim fingers on the countertop. His nails were short and clean, unlike her own, which were always crusted in dirt no matter how hard she scrubbed.

"When you grow up in a town this small, everyone's known each other since birth. But Morgan and I weren't friends. Still, it's... upsetting."

He nodded and a dark lock of hair fell over one eye. "I guess it's easy to forget we aren't supposed to live forever."

She wondered if he knew what had happened when she'd touched him in the truck, but how could she ask him without sounding crazy? *Hayden, I see dead people when I touch you. Could you explain that, please?*

The vision of Morgan's death was a splinter festering beneath Kora's skin. She planned to stick close to Hayden as long as it took to figure out if it had all been one disturbing coincidence or not.

"What are you doing after school today?" she asked. "Want a ride home?"

Blood rushed into his pale cheeks. "Even after I was such a jerk yesterday?"

"You were a jerk?" She scoffed. "I didn't notice."

He looked up at her from beneath a pair of surprisingly thick lashes. Her heart flip-flopped. "I'm sorry," he said.

"Apology accepted. I'll meet you in the parking lot after final bell."

Kora didn't touch Hayden again, not right away. Instead of taking him home after school, she drove to the local burger joint, a standing-room-only grill that sold hand-spun milkshakes. She ordered chocolate, and he chose peach. They sat together on Kora's tailgate, sipping and trying not to melt under the afternoon sun. "They don't use fresh peaches," Kora said. "They come from a can."

"Were they put there by a man in a factory downtown?"

She gave him a questioning look. "What?"

He flicked a smile. "Never mind."

"I don't buy the fruit shakes. They all taste fake to me. Like chemicals."

"You're seriously organic, aren't you?"

This time, it was it her turn to blush. No, she wasn't ashamed, but she knew how obsessed she could sound. "I know it's weird. But plants make more sense to me than people do."

Her garden was like a temple to her, and she was its priestess. When her faith was strong, she could perform all manner of agricultural miracles, ones that would put Jack and his beanstalk to shame. But that aspect of herself was something she never shared with anyone other than her mother. Experience had shown her that people feared what they couldn't easily explain or understand.

Maybe Hayden would, though. He harbored a few mysteries of his own.

"If that's true, then why are you being so nice to me?" He caught her gaze and held it, his dark eyes glittering and hard. "You feel sorry for me or something?"

"I don't know you well enough to feel sorry for you. What about you should make me feel that way?"

He arched a brow. "You aren't curious about why I'm here? Moving my senior year to the middle of nowhere to live with my grandparents?"

"And with your little brother in tow." She swirled her straw, blending melted ice cream with frozen. "Zeke, right? That's what Angela called him. I've been thinking about her. My guess is she's one of those, um, social workers, right?"

He didn't answer, just shrugged.

"If that was something you wanted to talk about, you would. Otherwise, it's not my business."

"Angela told you to be nice to me, though, didn't she?"

"She did." Kora sucked her straw, making a loud, rude slurp. "But that's not why I'm hanging out with you."

"Then why?"

"If you don't like it, say so, and I'll take you home."

"I didn't say I didn't like it."

"Then what's the problem?"

Hayden shrugged again, drew out his straw, and licked it clean. He reminded her of a lost, abandoned mutt sitting behind a gate at the county animal shelter. She suspected that like one of those forgotten dogs, Hayden had trouble trusting people. She wasn't trying to rescue him, though. She simply wanted to make sense of something terrifying and inexplicable.

Maybe it wasn't fair to use him that way.

Maybe it was fair for him not to trust her.

Before she could talk herself out of it or feel guilty about her intentions, she reached out and touched his shoulder.

That night Kora searched the internet for news of the death of a young woman who had died by jumping from a tall bridge. From the glimpse she'd caught while touching Hayden, she could tell the bridge was old, made of stone and wrought iron. Nothing like the concrete monstrosities spanning the Intracoastal Waterway, or the battleship-blue frame suspended over the Cape Fear River in Wilmington.

The news was silent, though, and Kora didn't know if that meant the woman hadn't jumped yet—or that she had, and her death had gone undetected.

Or maybe Kora had spent too much time alone in the fields, baking her brain in the sun's radiation.

Kora drove Hayden home after school every day for nearly two weeks, and during that time, neither spoke more than a few words to the other. She had so many questions, but not enough courage to ask them, and she was afraid if she opened her mouth, all the wrong words would come out. Besides, Hayden stuffed in his earbuds and cranked up his music the moment he climbed into her truck. He might as well have been a box turtle retreating into its shell, anxious to escape the outside world.

Today, however, he pulled out his earbuds, opened his bookbag, and withdrew a pair of library books.

"I almost forgot..." He waggled the books at her. "My grandmother told me to give these to you."

Kora glanced at the covers. "Tell her I said thanks."

"When you said you read sci-fi, I figured you meant the new stuff. The popular stuff that gets turned into movies the second it hits the shelf."

"What's wrong with that?"

"Nothing. I just..." He shrugged.

"A girl can't like all kinds of sci-fi?"

"I didn't mean—" His cheeks turned bright red. "I keep saying all the wrong things around you."

Knowing exactly how he felt, she let him off with a smile. "It's your grandmother's fault. She gave me *A Wrinkle in Time* when was I little. I've been hooked ever since."

"She gave me that one, too. It's one of my all-time favorites." He waved towards his house as Kora turned into his driveway and parked. "If you, um, want to come in, I'll show you our bookshelves. You can borrow something, if you want."

Curious and unable to resist his offer, she nodded. "Okay, but just for a second. I've got a ton of work to do in the garden this afternoon."

She followed him inside, and he led her into a space that was more library than living room. On every wall, a colorful mishmash of books lined each shelf from floor to ceiling. He selected an Octavia Butler novel and held it out. "Ever read *Kindred*?"

As she reached for the book, her hand brushed his, but she was so lost in the warmth of his gaze that she barely noticed the vague image of death—a middle-aged man clutching his chest—that drifted through her mind. Nothing she saw felt quite so terrible when Hayden smiled at her that way—like he trusted her.

Turned out that a month spent seeking out a certain boy and looking for excuses to touch him could have unexpected side effects. Somewhere along the way, Kora had stopped being shocked by the visions she saw—she'd developed a higher tolerance, perhaps, like a habitual drug user. She'd also discovered that touching Hayden could be lovely, particularly when he touched her back.

Standing in Mr. Rhea's dark garage after school, obscured among his collection of curiosities—antique farm equipment, old gas station signs, stacks of burlap bags stamped with tobacco logos—Kora savored Hayden's closeness as he trailed his fingers along her arm, elbow to shoulder and down again, exploring her skin with cautious touches that tingled to her toes.

"What are you doing this weekend?" he asked, his words a husky whisper. "Do you have to work?"

"We put in pumpkins near the end of summer, but they aren't quite ready for harvest yet. "There's nothing to sell."

He leaned in closer and breathed her in. "So that means..."

She grinned. He clearly wanted time with her, alone, away from school and nosy little brothers and over-protective grandparents. The Rheas welcomed Kora whenever she visited, but she could feel them watching, ready to intervene if she caused trouble. They probably thought Hayden's heart had been broken enough already—by his dad and whoever else had abandoned him in his past. Kora understood about absentee fathers. Hers had left before she was born, and asking her mom for more information about him was as futile as planting a pebble in hopes of growing a tree.

Kora didn't have many details about Hayden's past, but he'd dropped hints like breadcrumbs along a trail. If she followed them far enough, they might lead her to the truth.

"I want you to come somewhere with me," he said.

"Okay." The answer was easy. She wanted time alone with him, too.

He chuckled. "No questions? Just 'okay'? You trust me that much?"

"Probably more than you trust me."

He stiffened. "Why do you say that?"

"You keep secrets from me."

"There're things about me..."

You're not the only one, she thought. "I know. I have my suspicions."

His lips twisted into a lopsided frown. "Like what?"

"When I touch you..." She played out the rest of the sentence in her head and realized how ridiculous it sounded. He'd call her crazy. He'd tell her to go.

He gripped her shoulders, his fingers gentle but firm. "When you touch me, what?"

She swallowed. "I get a sense there's more to you than you want people to know. It's just a gut feeling, I guess."

"A gut feeling?" He sounded skeptical.

Visions of dead people dance in my head. "I'm not afraid of you, Hayden." And having said it aloud, she knew it was the truth. Whoever he was, *what*ever he was, she trusted him. "Wherever you take me, I want to go."

He touched his forehead to hers. "You might not like it."

"You'll be there with me?"

He nodded.

"That's all that matters."

Kora and Hayden left early Saturday morning, knowing neither her mom nor his grandparents would agree for them to be away together overnight. The four-hour drive to Charlotte was stressful, and Kora's knees trembled with relief when they left the truck in a downtown parking lot and took to the sidewalk. "I'm not used to driving beyond back roads and small towns. Maybe we should've taken the train."

Hayden took her hand, and she glimpsed an image of a little girl lying in a hospital bed, her heart monitor drawing out a slim, flat line. "You did fine," he said.

"Maybe you could drive back?"

"No, I don't drive."

"Why not."

"Too deadly."

She didn't think he was joking.

Summer had broken, making way for autumn's cooler temperatures and drier air—the time of year when Southerners could enjoy being outside without melting into a pool of sweat. Soon Kora and Hayden left behind downtown Charlotte's tall, modern buildings for a neighborhood of townhouses, old-fashioned homes, fancy boutique shops, and cute little restaurants advertising local beer specials and farm-to-table menus. Eventually they reached the entrance of what might have been a lovely park full of old shade trees, if not for the tombstones sprouting from the acres of green grass. Kora paused to read the sign at the entrance: Elmwood Cemetery.

She shivered as Hayden tugged her hand, pulling her deeper inside. A sense of foreboding filled her, making her feet heavy, her steps reluctant. "What are we doing here?"

"I want to show you something." At school Hayden was cool and aloof. She knew it was a mechanism he used to protect himself from scrutiny. But in this place, he was softer. Careful. Almost wary.

They followed a winding brick pathway toward the cemetery's opposite end where crumbling angels, obelisks, and mausoleums gave way to newer, sleeker monuments. Hayden stopped before a polished grave marker. He knelt and stroked the stone as though it were a loved one's cheek.

Kora crouched beside him, read the epitaph, and gasped. "Opal Rhea. Was she your...?"

"Mother." Hayden studied Kora from the corner of his eye.

She traced her fingertips across the date of his mother's death. "Five months ago?"

"We stayed with a family friend until we finished the school year, so things could be normal for Zeke as long as possible."

She wanted to ask how it had happened—illness, accident, or something more tragic—but she didn't know the right words.

That Hayden was revealing even this much seemed like an enormous gift of faith, and she didn't want to violate his grief. Maybe he read her mind, though, because he met her gaze, letting her see the anger glittering in his eyes. "It was my father. He killed her."

Fire raced through Kora, drying her throat, burning her heart to ash. "Y-your *father*?"

Hayden's shoulders stiffened, hands balling into fists.

"Is he...?" Again, she didn't know how to ask what she wanted to know. *Is he in jail? Is he a threat to you and Zeke? Is he dangerous? Is he a* monster?

"They never married. Mom left him after Zeke was born. He was... abusive."

Kora rocketed to her feet, furious on Hayden's behalf. "Has he been arrested?"

"No one could prove it was him. He's old-money rich. Has power. Legacy. He's smart."

"Won't he come for you?"

Hayden touched his mother's marker again and stood, facing Kora. He raised his head, jaw clenched, shoulders back. "If it were just me, I wouldn't be afraid. I could protect myself. But I have to keep Zeke safe, and I'm not sure I can."

"What'll you do if he does come?"

Hayden shrugged. "We'll run. That's all we *can* do against someone like him."

Kora slid her arms around Hayden and pressed her cheek to his chest, listening to the steady beat of his heart. She ignored her vision of an old man, lying still and cold in his bed, lips blue, eyes blank and empty. Hayden hesitated, then folded his arms around Kora and held her close. She offered him her comfort. He didn't refuse it.

❋

They ate a late lunch at one of the pubs nearby, and Kora ordered a fruit salad. She picked out pomegranate seeds from the dressing, and when Hayden questioned her, she blushed. "I hate them. I don't know why, but they taste horrible to me. Sour. Cold. Harsh."

He snorted. "Don't let my grandmother hear you say that. She's kind of obsessed."

"People in small towns tends to have their quirks." Kora's shoulder twitched. "I always figured hers was her pomegranates."

Hayden remained curiously quiet after lunch and said little during their walk back to the truck. He stopped, hand on her doorlatch, pausing before opening it for her. "Thanks for coming with me."

"You don't have to thank me. It was a privilege."

"Dumping my family drama on you was a privilege?"

"No, having you confide in me. Showing me something that matters to you." Could a girl love a boy after only a month—especially if she felt as if she'd known him forever? "Thanks for trusting me."

Hayden cupped her face and tilted her head back. She blinked away visions of death and grasped his arms, holding tightly as her world tilted. "This is going to sound really cheesy, but..." He bit his lip, hesitating. "There's something about you, Kora. Has been since the day Angela brought me to Cypress Knee and I saw you at your vegetable stand."

He'd sensed it as well? Her throat went dry. "I felt it, too, Hayden. If I believed in reincarnation, I'd say we knew each other in another life."

His warmth mingled with hers. "I'd like to kiss you, if that's okay?"

Her breath fled, and she couldn't have spoken if she'd wanted to. Instead, she nodded.

The moment Hayden's lips touched hers, a bolt of white heat streaked through her head. She cried out and pulled away, her vision spinning with images of Parker Rhea grasping his chest as blood welled between his fingers. It ran from his mouth. From his nose.

The image cleared, and Hayden's anxious gaze replaced the terrifying vision. "Kora? Are you all right—"

"Hayden, your grandfather." She panted, struggling to overcome her panic. "We have to get home. Now."

He grabbed her before she could open her door. "You saw something, didn't you? When I kissed you."

She covered her face, unable to bear the desperation in his eyes. "Yes."

"It's happened before, hasn't it? Why didn't you tell me?"

"I didn't think you would believe me."

"I told you there were things about me..." He pried her hands away from her face and held them locked together over his heart, which was pounding like the hooves of a fleeing deer. "I don't have time to explain. Tell me what you saw, exactly."

Kora stared into his eyes, wishing she could transfer her vision by telepathy to keep from having to speak such horrible words. "I saw your grandfather standing outside, under the carport at your house. He was clutching at his chest." She mimicked the motion, pawing at her own chest, at her heart. "There was blood." Her voice faded. "So much blood."

His grip on her shoulders tightened. "Was it day or night?"

She blinked and replayed the image again. "It was dark. The carport light was on." The blood between Mr. Rhea's fingers had glistened beneath the artificial light. "Do you think we have time?"

"I don't know how it works. Nothing like this has happened before."

"There were a few hours between the time I touched you and saw Morgan's death until she had her car accident."

He gaped at her, eyes wide. "You *saw* that?"

"First time I touched you."

He released her and stepped back, a look of horror washing

over his face. He stared at his hands as though they were covered in blood. "*Every* time we touch?"

She nodded.

"How could you stand it?"

"I've gotten good at tuning it out."

Shaking his head, Hayden spun on his heel and hurried to the truck's passenger side. When Kora climbed in beside him and started the engine, he kept silent. He didn't have to say anything —she could feel his urgency. His fear. He wasn't the only one who felt that way.

The inadequacies she'd harbored on the drive to Charlotte disappeared as they raced away from the city. If anything, her truck now went *too* slowly, and she wished she could trade wheels for wings.

"We have four hours," Kora said. "Maybe three and a half if I drive way over the speed limit and the cops don't stop us. That should be plenty of time for you to explain."

Hayden looked at the road as if, by staring hard enough, he could see all the way back to Cypress Knee. "One day when I was about Zeke's age—eight or nine years old—I found our cat in the backyard. He was dead. We just called him Cat. Mom wouldn't let me name him, didn't want me getting attached. He was beautiful, fur like smoke..."

Kora said nothing, waiting for him to decide how he would continue.

"I remember being... *overcome* with wanting him to be alive again. I *needed* him to be alive again. I closed my eyes and wished with all my heart and soul that he could be alive again, and—" Hayden drew in a sharp, ragged breath. "And he *was*.

"Cat *hated* being hugged. He scratched me, trying to get away. I dropped him, and he ran through a hole in the fence in our backyard. I never saw him again, and I might have thought I dreamed it, but my mom saw the whole thing. She made me swear to never do anything like it again. When I told her I didn't know how I'd done it, she said, 'Just let the dead stay dead. And don't ever wish for them to come back.'"

Kora glanced at him from the corner of her eye. If she hadn't seen the things she'd seen when she touched him, she might never have believed him. But she *had* seen. And she did believe. "And that's it? That's all she ever told you?"

"Oh, I begged her. Nagged her." The corner of his lip curled into a sad smile. "She'd get mad. Refused to talk about it. Made me promise to leave it alone."

"Did you?"

He nodded. "I did, eventually, but I would've broken my promise if it would've brought her back. I *did* try bringing her back—never wished for anything harder. But when my father takes a life, there's no getting it back."

The rode in silence a while longer before Kora worked up the nerve to confess her own secrets. "Maybe you're not the only one whose life hasn't made sense." Not that she could compare her life to his. He'd grown up knowing death as an intimate companion while she'd been privileged to have a connection to living, growing things. It should've made them complete opposites—incompatible. Instead, she felt it somehow made them two halves of a whole.

He frowned. "What do you mean?"

"My, um, obsession with gardening isn't just a serious hobby." Kora reached into her glove compartment and withdrew a packet of pumpkin seeds that had been rattling around for a while. "Open this and dump one into my hand."

Hayden took the packet from her without question. He selected a seed and pressed it into her palm. Keeping her gaze pinned on the road, Kora closed her fist. Moments later, several green curly shoots and leaves unfurled from her hand, poking between her fingers. One shoot thickened into a ropey vine. A yellow bud sprouted, bloomed, then curled up and fell off, leaving behind a small hard fruit—a premature green pumpkin.

Kora opened her hand and dropped the pumpkin plant on the

bench seat between them. Hayden's eyebrows arched high as he gaped at the pile of green leaves and vines. "I think you and I connected somehow," she said. "Like life and death. Unless it's just my imagination?"

He closed his eyes and let his head fall back against the seat. "No, Kora. It's definitely not your imagination."

"Then what is it?"

"I have no idea." He peeked at her through one slitted eyelid. "But I hope to God my father doesn't ruin our chance to find out."

The sun had set by the time Kora and Hayden reached the Rheas' driveway. It was empty, devoid of blood, but she didn't feel relieved, and she suspected Hayden didn't either. He raced into the house, calling for Zeke and his grandfather, and Kora followed close behind.

Zeke came out of his room, wearing an inquisitive expression, and Hayden threw his arms around him. "Where's Grandma and Granddad?" he asked his little brother.

"Grandma's at choir practice. Granddad's in the garage." Zeke peered at Hayden, concern etching lines around his mouth and eyes. "What's going on?"

"Dad's coming. We have to get out of here."

"Dad?" Zeke squirmed in Hayden's arms, struggling to get free as Hayden hauled him towards the front door. "How do you know?"

"Kora saw it."

Zeke dragged his feet, fighting against Hayden, his eyes like searchlights. When he found Kora, his face went even paler. "You saw my dad?"

"No, only your grandfather."

Zeke looked up at Hayden, questioning.

"If we don't go," Hayden said, "Dad'll kill him."

"Why do we always have to run?" Zeke gave a final hard shove and broke free. "We should stay and fight him."

"We can't fight Dad. You know that."

"We could if we stick together." Zeke scowled and folded his arms across his chest, a little kid full of spit and stubbornness. Kora might have laughed if the circumstances were different.

"Kora *saw* Grandad dying. We can't risk it."

"Maybe we can change things. It doesn't have to be this way."

"Quit arguing with me. We have to go." Hayden grabbed for Zeke, but his little brother darted away and dashed out the front door.

Hayden raked his hands through his hair and grumbled through his teeth. "He's an idiot."

"He's a kid, and he's scared," Kora said. "But I have an idea."

Hayden paused, arching an eyebrow at her.

"You said you could take care of yourself if you didn't have to worry about Zeke, so why don't I take him with me. I'll drive him out of town, and I won't tell you where we're going. Maybe..." She couldn't believe she was going to suggest Hayden put himself in danger, but she understood his fear for Zeke. If she could ease that concern, perhaps Hayden could take care of the rest. "Maybe you could lure your father away? Would he hurt you if he found you?"

Hayden's nostrils flared. "The last time I saw him, he promised to kill me if he ever saw me again."

"Why? *Why* is he so horrible?"

"It's hard to explain if you've never met him. He's not like regular people. He's not even like you or me, and he's convinced Zeke and I are destined to kill him."

She reached out for him, but he backed away. His rejection was bruising. She let her hand drop. "Just worry about saving yourself and your grandfather. I'll take care of Zeke."

He paused, considering her plan. "Aren't you scared? Of me? Of my life?"

She had asked herself the same thing over and over since she'd met Hayden, and the answer had always been no. She'd been confused and worried at times, but she'd never feared him or what he made her feel. "Whoever you are, whatever your life is... I accept it."

"You'll change your mind if you ever face my father."

She snorted. "Then I'll try to avoid doing that, okay?"

"I've spent my life surrounded by death." A pained expression, half fear and half wanting, crossed his face. "You're full of life. You should run from me while you have the chance and never look back."

She raised her chin, giving him her most obstinate look. "That's not a decision you get to make for me, Hayden."

He studied her one more time, huffed, then nodded. They rushed outside together—being oh-so-careful not to touch—and followed Zeke's trail into his grandfather's garage. Among the dusty stacks of antiques, they found Mr. Rhea clutching a shivering, sobbing little boy. Mr. Rhea glanced at Kora, then at Hayden. He nodded as if he understood everything. "I wondered how long it would take him to come after you."

"Kora'll take Zeke with her," Hayden said. "It's me who Dad really wants."

Mr. Rhea squared his shoulders. He was tall and lean like his grandsons, and his white shock of hair might have once been black like theirs, but he didn't look capable of lasting long in a fight. "I won't let Chronis have you, Hayden."

"He won't give you that option. The best thing is to head him off and lead him away. I'll get away from him—I've done it before." He crouched, gently wrapped his fingers around Zeke's arms, and pulled his little brother close. Zeke didn't resist. His fight had gone out of him like air from a punctured tire. "Please go with Kora. I need you to keep her safe for me, okay?"

Kora stepped forward, offering her hand. Zeke took it and looked up at her with big, watering eyes. "Where are we going?" he asked.

She smiled. "It has to be a surprise."

Zeke came willingly, and Hayden and Mr. Rhea followed as she hurried towards the carport.

Maybe, if they hadn't stayed in Charlotte for lunch...

If she had driven a little bit faster...

If they hadn't had to stop for gas, they might have made it back in time.

But they didn't.

The moment Kora stepped beneath the carport lights, her gaze landed on a colossal man who threw shadows darker than the night falling around them. His shoulders were as broad as a mountain range, his fists like blocks of granite, his eyes hard obsidian. His face was storm clouds and fury. "Thought you'd get away so easily, son?"

Clutching Zeke's arm, Kora shoved the boy behind her. Hayden and Mr. Rhea formed a wall in front of her. She studied their opponent, but Hayden's father defied understanding. He was merely a man, wasn't he? He wore a dark suit, and his hair was the same ash-white as his beard, but instinct told her the man was a façade covering something too horrible to comprehend.

Hayden's father raised his fist. His voice quaked like bombshells dropping on a war-torn landscape. "I told you, Parker. I wouldn't let you come between me and my sons again. Did you think I wouldn't keep my word?"

"Leave them alone, Chronis. They're just boys."

He sneered. "No, they are much more than that. They are the harbingers of my death."

Who even talks like that? Kora wondered. Was this man having trouble coping with reality—delusions and hallucinations–or was he pure, diabolical evil? The cold dread dripping down her spine made her think it was the latter.

Kora never saw a weapon, not a gun or a knife. She suspected a man like Hayden's father didn't resort to such mundane conventions. But there was a flash like lightning. A crack like a giant bullwhip. Then Mr. Rhea cried out and stumbled, clutching his chest. Blood welled between his fingers. It ran from his mouth. From his nose. It glistened beneath the carport's artificial light.

Horror blasted through Kora like an arctic gale, frigid and howling. It chilled her heart and turned her blood to ice.

Hayden's eyes, wide and full of terror, met her own. He mouthed a command: *Run!*

But there was no outrunning this horrible being who'd turned his dark gaze on his son. Hayden froze as if locked in an invisible grip. Not even the air around him moved, as if time itself had stopped. Chronis licked his lips and gave his son a hungry, predatory smile—not like a wolf, but like some prehistoric beast who'd avoided extinction by sheer force of will.

If she were the type to believe in self-preservation, Kora would've taken that moment to run, but a stronger impulse compelled her to stay. She trusted in the power of life, and her faith was strong. She crouched, jabbing her fingers into the soil at the edge of the carport. The earth responded to her touch, and in an instant, a barricade of leaves, branches, kudzu vines, and pomegranate thickets enveloped Kora, Zeke, and Hayden, wrapping them in a fortress of greenery.

Hayden blinked, shaking off his stupor. "W-what's happening?"

"I don't really know," Kora said. "It just seemed like the thing to do."

"It won't stop him for long."

Already the walls were shaking, branches cracking, leaves tumbling in a green blizzard. Hayden's father roared, and the ground shook. Behind her, Zeke had curled into a trembling, mewling ball of terror. Kora held out her hand, beckoning Hayden to take it. He hesitated.

"*Help* me, Hayden," she demanded.

"Touching you won't help. It'll only hurt."

"You brought Cat back to life, didn't you?"

His expression darkened. "What does that have to do with anything?"

"You think your world is only about death, but it's about life, too. You're like the balance between the two." Her hand darted out, grabbing his before he could pull away. "Help me tip the scales."

He wavered as he considered her words. "What do I do?"

"What did you do to bring back Cat?"

"I was just a stupid kid. I didn't know what I was doing."

Their green fortress shuddered again, and a crack of light from the carport's overhead fixture breached their defenses. Chronis was breaking through. "Hayden, *please*," Kora begged.

"I..." Hayden bit his lip. "I wished for it with all my heart and soul."

She closed her eyes, squeezed his hand, and reached for the place inside herself that connected her to the land and all the things growing in it. "Then that's what you should do right now. Wish with all your heart and soul."

Their fortress gave way with a resounding crash and Chronis roared. The air around them stilled, turning to mud, then to concrete, holding them in place, freezing time. But a force more powerful than Chronis's rage bloomed between them, filling the frozen air with the scent of a spring forest, a mowed lawn, a plowed field, sunshine, earth, and light.

So. Much. Light.

That force exploded, surrounding them in warmth and bright white brilliance.

Chronis's roar turned into a desperate scream full of pain and defeat.

When the light faded, Kora cracked open one eyelid. The massive man, the horrible beast who was Hayden's father was locked in a rigid pose, teeth bared in a grimace of agony. A thick branch bursting with pomegranate fruits had impaled him through the chest, but instead of blood, only darkness seeped from his wound.

His features faded until he was merely a dim shadow in the vague shape of a man.

And then...

He was nothing—a star that had imploded upon itself, leaving behind a trail of dark stardust swept away by a stiff evening breeze.

Deep in the 4-H club's vegetable garden, Kora sat on her knees, pulling up weeds and piling fat orange pumpkins into her wagon. A cool autumn wind tugged at her hair, and she huddled deeper into her jacket as she sliced her knife through a tough stem. The short bit of daylight between the end of the school day and the arrival of sunset left her little time to accomplish everything she needed to do if her club was going to have enough produce to open their stand that weekend.

The wind in her ears and the garden's soft soil muffled the sound of footsteps. She didn't realize anyone was approaching until his shadow fell over her. Her heart lurched, and she swallowed a scream. She skittered away, pulse racing, and blinked at the unexpected sight of Hayden standing over her.

Still clutching her knife, Kora rose on unsteady knees and dusted her hand off on her jeans. "You shouldn't sneak up on me like that. I thought you were..." She swallowed.

Hayden arched an eyebrow. "Him?"

She bit her lip, refusing to answer. She'd told Hayden she wasn't afraid of his life, and she wouldn't go back on that now, even if her nightmares suggested otherwise.

"What are you picking?" He eyed her wagon. "Pumpkins? They're already ripe?"

"Did you really come all the way out here to discuss fall harvest?" She'd seen Hayden at Mr. Rhea's funeral the week before, but afterward she'd given him space—room to grieve his many losses without having to worry about her feelings, too.

"I came to thank you for saving Zeke."

A lump rose in her throat. "I wanted to save your grandfather, too. I'm sorry I didn't—"

He waved off her apology. "You have nothing to be sorry about. My father..." He looked away, abandoning his attempt to explain a man who defied explanation. Hayden reminded her of one of her pumpkins after it had been made into a jack-o'-lantern: insides hollowed out and his face a carved grimace. "Now you see what my life truly is. There are no more secrets."

He reached into his coat pocket and drew out a familiar red sphere the shape and size of a softball. He presented the fruit to her like a precious gem.

"I hate pomegranates," she said.

"I know. But my grandmother gave it to me. Said I should offer it to you."

Kora squinted at the fruit as if it were poison. "Why?"

"I told her about your visions. About what you saw when you touched me. What you saw when I kissed you. She grabbed this from her fruit basket, told me it would help."

Kora arched a skeptical eyebrow. "A pomegranate? Really?"

He shrugged. "There's more to Grandma than meets the eye. She said just a handful of seeds, and the visions would stop. But there are strings attached."

"What strings?"

"Promises."

She snorted. "What kinds of promises?"

"A promise to me." She heard the want in his voice. "Only eat the seeds if you want to be with me, Kora. Otherwise, toss it aside. Never think about me again."

Tentatively she reached out and grasped the fruit. It was firm and warm from Hayden's hand. "It sounds so ridiculous."

"So does foreseeing death, and bringing a cat back to life, and watching my father kill my grandfather without even touching him. So does what you and I did to stop him."

She tossed the pomegranate like a ball and caught it. Up, down. Up, down. He stepped closer, and she felt his warmth, smelled his cold, crisp scent. The force of his gaze pierced her heart and held her captive.

It was so simple. *Too* simple. If she wanted Hayden, she only had to swallow a few seeds. She would have done more, if he'd asked. She *would* do more.

Together, they'd be two halves that formed a whole.

She clutched the pomegranate and set the tip of her knife against its leathery flesh. "Just a handful?"

He gave her a tentative, hopeful smile, which she returned.

Juice flowed red like blood when she drew her knife through the fruit's tough skin. She prized out the seeds, little rubies glistening under the autumn sun. When she crunched them between her teeth, they tasted horrible. Sour, cold, and harsh.

But Hayden was none of those things when he folded her into his arms.

When he kissed her, sweet and warm, she felt so much possibility, but the only things she saw were stars.

ALEX AND LORA: An Earthkeeper Novella

KATIE ROSE GUEST PRYAL

Katie Rose Guest Pryal is a novelist, essayist, and erstwhile law professor in Chapel Hill, NC. She is the author of the Hollywood Lights Series, which includes *Entanglement, Love and Entropy, Chasing Chaos, How to Stay,* and *Fallout Girl.* She also writes nonfiction, including *Life of the Mind Interrupted: Mental Health and Disability in Higher Education.*

As a journalist and essayist, Katie has contributed to *Catapult, The Chronicle of Higher Education, The Toast, Quartz, Motherwell,* and more. She earned her master's degree in creative writing from the Writing Seminars at Johns Hopkins, and she is a member of the

Tall Poppy Writers (tallpoppies.org). You can connect with Katie on Instagram, Facebook, and Twitter, all at @krgpryal; on her blog at katieroseguestpryal.com; and through her monthly letter at pryalnews.com.

1

Box

North Carolina, Mid-1990s

My sister Freya dashes into our parents' house. From my seat at the kitchen table, I see her throw open the door to the garage and run down the short back hall to the kitchen, her long skinny legs sticking out of her jogging shorts. She only left a few minutes ago, headed out to go running on the trail in the woods. I'm surprised to see her back so soon, her pale face flushed red, her blond hair in a tight ponytail with a few leaves sticking in it.

Freya looks disheveled, actually. A jolt of fear zips through me. I stand, worried she was chased by a dog, or something worse.

It's an unusually warm Friday afternoon in November. We got home from school a few minutes ago, and I wanted to chill out before starting my homework. I'm sixteen, a junior. Freya's fourteen, a freshman. She really wants to make the varsity basketball team even though she's only in ninth grade, so she's working out extra hard. It's the break week for sports, between the end of volleyball season and the start of basketball. I told Freya she has nothing to worry about because she's freakishly athletic, but she didn't believe me. So she went running.

"Lora," she says, heaving for air. "Come with me, right now. I have to show you something."

She seems frantic, but not afraid, I realize. Thrilled. Like she's made a great discovery. I relax, but only a bit.

"I thought you were in trouble, you stinker."

"Trouble? Why?"

I gesture at her. "You look like you were chased by a bear."

She giggles. Sometimes she still seems like a little girl. "No. But I did find something. It's kind of wonderful."

My curiosity piqued, I follow her to the door where we pile our shoes haphazardly. "What did you find?"

"I can't describe it." She sounds dreamy. "I have to show you. Put on your running shoes."

Puzzled by her tone, I tie my sneakers, and we run out the door together. I'm dressed like she is, in running shorts and a t-shirt, my typical after-school wear.

We race up our street toward the trailhead. Our street, like the rest of our neighborhood, is full of compact houses built in the last few years. The houses are on small lots, with lots of shared green space. Wherever there was a pond or a creek, the developer allowed green space to thrive. Everywhere else, our neighborhood looks like a new urban paradise. That's probably why our parents moved here. It's perfect for raising kids. Totally safe.

We turn right at Mrs. Lee's house on the corner. Mrs. Lee sits in her back yard, her greyhound sleeping at her feet. She waves as we pass, watching us intently.

The back of my neck prickles. "Hey, Mrs. Lee!" I call out.

"See you soon!" she calls back.

The prickling doesn't abate. *See you soon?*

If anyone who doesn't know us were to see me and Freya, they would think we were twins, even though I'm two years older. We're both tall, with blond hair cropped to our shoulders and pulled back in low ponytails. She's still skinny from her growth spurt, all bony knees and ankles, and she whines about it sometimes, causing me to roll my eyes. But for the most part, we

Box 177

look nearly identical. From a distance, even our parents mistake us for one another.

But we are very different people. Take Freya's worry about the basketball team. Everyone but Freya knows she'll make the team. If the rules allowed it, she would have made the squad as an eighth grader. She was like that with the volleyball team, too. Nothing I say can convince her not to worry.

She's always been nervous like that. Puking before big tests and games. But the strangest thing is, once that buzzer sounds and the game starts, she's in the zone. No more puking, no more nerves. She's a total rock star—unstoppable. No matter what sport, or which class the test is for. You just have to get her to the starting line. Like those racehorses in the starting gates, bouncing around, all jittery. That's Freya.

I never tell anyone about the puking. She's my little sister. I've protected her since the first day she got on the school bus.

And it's not like I'm perfect. Hardly.

She worries about tests and games, and then she doesn't worry enough once the action has started. Like right now, apparently. Where on earth is she taking me?

We turn off the road and into the trail entrance. I love this trail. I've been jogging on it since as long as I've been jogging, and before that, I rode my dirt bike on it and explored the forest and creeks and ponds that the trail encloses. This forested watershed was the land of adventure for my entire childhood, with Freya tagging along once she was big enough. We know every inch of this path. We know the ponds, the old dam up ahead that separates the big lake from the creek below. We know the maples and oaks and willows that grow down here. We've climbed most of them, and fallen out of half of those. This is our place.

The light of the winter sun breaks through the branches of the trees, lighting the path at sharp angles. The jogging path is covered in a sparse layer of gray gravel, replenished every few years by the town. Without the gravel, the path would wash away entirely whenever we have a big storm.

For a few minutes we jog side-by-side. Then I feel it. The tugging. Like a string is tied to my ribs and leading me off the trail.

I stop, resting a hand on my stomach. I don't like this feeling, like I'm being led someplace against my will.

I've always had problems with authority.

"Do you feel that?" I ask Freya.

"You can feel it too?" Her eyes are large.

I nod. "You came this way before? You know where it leads?"

She nods.

"Is it safe?"

She bites her lower lip. Then she nods once more. "At least I think so. I didn't get too close. I wanted you to come with me."

Well, at least she was smart enough not to approach whatever it is by herself. It feels like a giant magnet is pulling at me. I wonder if that's what's here, some sort of magnet, or magnetic stone—perhaps a meteorite. Perhaps we're feeling a type of radiation, something that would be harmful to us if we stood near.

The tugging pulls harder, but it doesn't hurt. On the contrary, as I take a step in the direction of the tug, joy fills me, as though I'm doing the right thing.

Freya's watching me for a cue. Whatever I decide, she'll do the same.

I start forward again, allowing the tug to lead me. Once again, joy fills my body, from my toes to my ears, as though the earth itself were pleased with my choice.

How ridiculous.

Following the tugging, we turn right toward the creek that runs next to the trail. We've played in this creek innumerable times during our childhood, gathering the smoothed rocks from the creek bed for our rock collection, or catching tadpoles in a bucket and watching them grow into frogs. Sometimes we argued and pushed each other into the knee-deep water, coming home muddy and angry. Those times, Mom would make us bathe

Box 179

outside with the hose. By the time we were clean, we were friends again.

As we leave the trail, we slow to a walk. Dry leaves crackle beneath our sneakers. We push scraggly bushes out of the way until we reach the edge of the muddy creek bank. Like Freya, I now have leaves caught in my hair.

"There," Freya says. "Do you feel it?"

Her finger points at a the corner of a metal box sticking out of the mud on the creek bank. It looks old, like it was left there decades ago but a recent storm has unearthed it.

We haven't had any storms recently.

We step into the mud and crouch on either side of the box.

"You didn't touch it," I confirm.

"Like I said, I wanted to wait for you."

"Why?"

"Don't laugh," she says.

I raise my eyebrows. I never promise that I won't laugh.

"Whatever it is—it seemed to want us both here," she says.

I don't laugh. Her words aren't funny.

"Should we get Dad?" Freya asks.

"He's not at home. He left right before you came in." Dad is a doctor, and he works unusual hours at the university's student health center. And Mom is at work at the bank where she's a loan officer.

We meet each other's eyes. We're alone.

We both look back at the box.

Only a few inches of one corner are visible above the mud. The box is made of a dark metal. Some sort of carving marches along the surface, but I can't make out the pattern, not while it's buried and filthy. All I want to do is yank the box from the mud, wash it off, and see what those carvings are.

"I want to do that, too," Freya says.

I jerk my eyes to her face. I know I didn't say my words out loud.

Simultaneously, we reach for the box. We dig our fingers into the mud, deeper and deeper, until we feel the box's shape through the viscous soup. Then we stand, lifting the box. It's not very large, only two feet long, but it's strangely heavy for its size, too heavy for one of us to carry alone.

Together, we carry the box to the shallow stream and set it on the rocky bottom, allowing the two feet of clear water to wash over the surface. My sneakers are soaked, but I don't care. The water cleans the box, revealing the patterns on its surface, and I'm entranced. The material glimmers like the inside of an oyster.

We lift the box from the water and carry it up the creek side to the leafy ground. Squatting on either side of it, we examine it closely.

Along the border, a complex vine pattern is pressed into the metal. At first glance the pattern seems Norse, and then Irish, and then something else entirely, like Egyptian hieroglyphs. I blink twice to clear my vision—the pattern seems to change every time I glance at it.

"It does. And yet it doesn't," Freya says.

"Freya," I say, exasperated. "How are you hearing what I'm thinking?"

"What are you talking about?"

"You just carried on a conversation about things I was saying in my head. And it's the second time it's happened since we've been down here."

Freya tilts her head, like she does when she's figuring out a problem. "Obviously it's the box," she says.

"Oh, obviously," I say, unable to hide my snark.

"Look, there are words, here. Inside the pattern." Freya leans close to read them. *"The two whom are needed will find me. And I will give them what they need."* She looks at me. "The two whom are needed by whom? And to do what?"

"Honestly," I say. "That is why I hate the passive voice."

"Should we open it?" she says.

The invisible line that was tugging me toward the box now pulls my hands toward the shiny silver latch that holds it closed.

Box   181

All I would have to do is lift the hinged latch and the box would open.

Every part of me wants to open that box.

But I know that sometimes the urge to do something reckless, like open a strange box that I find buried beside a creek, a box that seems to give off some kind of radiation, that makes my vision blurry, that makes me confused about whether I'm actually speaking words out loud, is not an urge I should listen to. I know that I'm impulsive. I've been working on being less so.

Freya, on the other hand, is not impulsive. Freya considers everything before she makes a decision, sometimes to the point of being unable to make a decision at all.

"What do you think we should do?" I ask her.

"I really want to open the box," she says. "But I think it's the box that's telling me to do it."

"I agree," I say. "And that's bananas."

"No," she says. "I think that's magic."

She reaches for the silver latch and flicks it open.

2

Guardian

Inside the box are two objects. Two ordinary objects.

"Well, this is a bummer," Freya says.

The box contains two smooth rocks like the ones that line the creek bed behind us. Each one is slightly smaller than my palm, rounded as though by years spent in running water, and plain gray in color.

"Why keep two old rocks in here?" Freya says. "How anti-climactic."

And why is the box so heavy if it only contains two rocks? I'm not taking physics till next year, but I can tell that the box shouldn't weigh so much. It's about two feet long, six inches tall, and one foot wide. It's about the same size as the box full of roses my dad had delivered to my mom on her birthday last month. The metal itself isn't overly thick. And, strangely, the rocks weren't rattling around inside while we carried the box.

"You're right," Freya said. "It's like the rocks were surrounded by padding. But there isn't any padding. Just rocks."

"You have got to stop doing that." I'm getting a little freaked out by her listening in my head.

"It might be useful to be able to know what you're thinking now and then," she says. "Sometimes it's hard to keep up."

"How are you acting like all of this is so normal?"

"It's not normal at all, Lora. But would you rather I have a meltdown? Barf in the bushes?"

I crack a smile. "Of course not." Freya is in the zone. It's good to have her like this. I'm feeling freaked out.

She nods. "I am too, don't worry." She points at the box. "Here's a question: why put two boring rocks in a magic box?"

I snort when she says the word *magic*, but I have to agree with her about the rocks. They do seem anti-climactic.

But wait a minute. As I stare at the rocks, one of them begins to glow, just a little. Around the rock closest to me, a faint light reflects off of the shiny metal it rests upon. "Freya," I say. "Look."

She leans closer. "Oh wow. It's glowing." Then she picks up the rock that isn't glowing and cradles it in her palms.

"Not that one. This one." I pick up the glowing rock. In my palms, it glows brighter, turning my skin a delicate green.

"Incorrect, sister dear," Freya says. "I'm holding the glowing rock." She glances at my rock. "Or," she says, "we are seeing things differently."

Of course she's right—one rock called to her, and one called to me. In the logic of our strange day, that is the only explanation that makes sense. I look at my rock again, smooth in my hands, and faintly green. I stand, my legs tired from squatting so long. "What color is yours?"

"Green," she says, standing next to me, holding her rock close to mine. Hers looks plain gray to me.

"Same here," I say. "What did the box's inscription say again?" I can't remember it, which is weird because I remember words really well. It's like the sentences jumped out of my head on purpose.

Freya closes the lid so she can read it. When the lid closes, the latch snaps shut of its own accord, the sound echoing throughout the forest. For a moment, not a bird sings, not a squirrel chirps. We meet each other's eyes.

"What just happened?" she asks.

"Something. I'm sure we'll find out." I nod at the lid. "Read the words again."

"It says, *The two whom are needed will find me, and I will give them what they need.*"

I sigh. "I guess we need these rocks."

Freya nods. "Let's put them back in the box and take it home." She reaches to unlatch the box, but the latch won't budge. She tries to lift the lid, but she can't. "You try it."

I squat down, pulling at the latch. It won't move, my fingers slipping on the shiny metal. "I guess we'll just carry it home like this."

We try to pick it up, but we can't lift the box from the ground. It's like it suddenly weighs a thousand pounds. If I wanted confirmation that ordinary physics weren't at play here, I just got it. But why go through all of the trouble to bring us to the box just to have us abandon it in the forest?

"Are we supposed to just leave it here?" I say.

"I guess so."

The box has accomplished its mission. It seems that Freya and I are the two whom are needed. Someone needs us for something. But we don't know who, and we don't know what for.

I read plenty of fantasy books when I was younger—I still read them. But I always knew they were fantasy.

The box, though, it's real. These rocks are real. And now, the words from the inscription are creeping around my head like a haunting and won't let go. I glance at my little sister, whose only worry until twenty minutes ago was basketball tryouts. We're in the forest alone, and I realize I'm afraid.

Suddenly, as though we're standing on a sinkhole, the ground softens beneath our feet. Freya and I jump back, away from the box, and clutch each other's hand. The dirt dips and dips under the weight of the box, and the box sinks down under the earth until we can't see it anymore.

I glance at the rock in my palm, then at Freya. She's holding her rock, too, her mouth slightly open, as though the earth swallowing the box was the first thing today that has astounded her.

"Let's get out of here," I say.

She nods, her brown eyes as big as a baby deer's.

As we turn to run home, I feel the line attaching me to the box stretch. A little farther away, it snaps, and in its place remains a prickling feeling that I can't shake.

We exit the trailhead, stepping onto the sidewalk. We haven't spoken a word to each other since we left the box buried in the ground.

"Did that seem to go a little faster than usual?" Freya asks. "Like, it's a mile back to where that box was buried. I realize we're kind of speedy, but we're not cross-country speedy."

"What are you saying, Freya?" My voice is snappish, my nerves frayed.

"I think we ran that mile in four minutes." She's looking at her watch.

"Don't be ridiculous."

She presses her lips together, as aggravated with me as I am with her.

As we pass Mrs. Lee's house, Mrs. Lee calls out to us. "Girls! Stop! This instant!"

We stop. Everyone stops when Mrs. Lee calls. She's one bossy lady, but she's also our mother's best friend. They take a walk together every morning at six a.m. If we were ever disrespectful to Mrs. Lee, our mom would make sure we never saw daylight again.

"Lora," Freya hisses at me. "The rocks."

We're both still holding the rocks in our hands. We don't have any place to put them—they're too large for the pockets in our jogging shorts. We hide our hands behind our backs as we approach Mrs. Lee's back patio. The patio is paved in brick, and Mrs. Lee sits at the black metal table with her greyhound, Namu. She has food laid out—enough for three, as though she were expecting us.

"Sit down," she says.

Freya cuts her eyes to me. *Should we stay?*

I nod.

We sit.

"Eat," Mrs. Lee commands. "You need your energy, and you don't have much time."

I'm still holding my rock behind my back. Mrs. Lee sets a plate in front of me with a cheeseburger on it, along with a side of macaroni and cheese casserole. It's like she went in my head and found my favorite foods. All I can think about is how I need two hands to eat that cheeseburger, but I don't want to put down my rock.

Mrs. Lee snorts. "Put the stones on the table, girls. They won't poof like the box. At least not today. Eat!"

Freya drops her rock—stone, Mrs. Lee called it—next to her plate. Her plate has four giant tacos on it. Tacos are her favorite.

I lean back from my plate and eye Mrs. Lee.

We've known Mrs. Lee our whole lives. She's from Seoul, originally, and her husband died before she moved to our street. She's about five-foot-five, the same height as our mom, with black hair cut in a bob. She has two grown kids, older than us, who live up north, in New York or something. We've never met them, but she goes to visit them a lot. She has pictures of them around the house.

Or maybe none of that is true.

Or maybe this isn't really Mrs. Lee.

I stand up. "Who are you?"

Mrs. Lee sighs. "You know me, Lora."

"Tell us what's going on."

"You eat, and I'll talk."

"You could be trying to poison us."

Mrs. Lee laughs a giant belly laugh. I've just said the funniest thing she's ever heard, apparently. "I've been watching over you for sixteen years, keeping you safe. Especially you, Lora, with all of your harebrained plans. That unsound treehouse you decided to secretly build in the forest, that was bad enough. And then you brought your sister! Without my help you both would have fallen to your deaths ten times over." She makes a rude noise. "Why would I hurt you now? Eat. You have to leave." She taps her watch, an overly large, gold, oyster-faced affair. It seems like an object that might tell more than time. "Bah! You should have left already."

Freya picks up a taco and takes a big, crunchy bite. I take a bite of burger. It's freaking delicious. Then I look at Mrs. Lee. I think at her, as though she really can read my mind, *Talk.*

She nods like she heard me. "I'm a witch, obviously," Mrs. Lee says. "Of the immortal variety."

I cough at her words, nearly choking on my burger.

"Your family?" Freya asks, far more serene than I am. She is definitely in the zone.

"Fake. I have no family." I hear sadness in her words, and I want to know more. But the urgency in her tone keeps my questions on track.

"And what about us?" I say.

"You are the bloodline I'm in charge of watching over. When there's an emergency, when we need you, I invoke you."

"You invoke us?" My voice raises an octave. "What does that mean?"

"I've invoked you. You are witches, too, of the not-immortal variety. And we need your help. Urushka, the loon, keeps losing track of things over in her territory."

"Urushka?" I ask. "Losing things?"

Mrs. Lee points to my plate. "Eat. Clean your plate."

"The box?" Freya asks through bites of taco.

"That's what does the invoking. A tool of mine. Like the stones."

"We ran that mile in four minutes, didn't we?" Freya says, hope in her voice.

Mrs. Lee nods. "Less than that, actually."

Freya fist-pumps and hoots.

I roll my eyes. Freya is seriously missing the big picture here.

"You can tell no one what you are. I'll tell you why when you return. You must go, now. Finish your food. Unfortunately, I don't have time to teach you anything. The timeline sped up. It's not my fault, of course. I'm not a disorganized person like Urushka." She stands. "You, Freya. You are a Traveler. Lora, you are a Speaker. Among the Earthwitches, you are Earthkeepers, as I am your Guardian. Your Third will meet you there. I don't know who Urushka is sending. Someone who isn't an idiot, I hope."

"Our Third?" I ask.

"An idiot?" Freya says.

"It always takes three." Mrs. Lee says.

"Three of what?" I demand.

"Three Earthkeepers. We don't have time for long explanations. You'll have to learn as you go. Your Third will teach you the rest." She points at the table. "Pick up your stones."

We do.

"Now take each other's hands. I'll send you this first time, but after this, Freya will know what to do." Mrs. Lee nods at Freya. "You will be an exceptional Traveler."

When I grasp Freya's hand, the world flashes white.

3

Traveler

I t might have been a moment, or a year, that Freya and I spent in that flashing white. I know she's with me, even though I can't see her, because I can sense her presence nearby. But I can hear nothing, see nothing, feel nothing.

Not hot, not cold. Just nothing.

And then we are on all fours in a grassy field, atop a small rise. It's nighttime—the sun has already set in the distance, the afterglow barely lighting the sky. My arms feel weak, barely able to support my upper body.

Freya barfs in the grass.

"I thought you were supposed to be a Traveler," I say. But I get it. I'm feeling queasy, too.

Slowly, I push myself to my feet. Freya joins me, wiping her mouth on the back of her arm and coughing. A cold breeze whips over the hillside, and I realize we are way underdressed in our t-shirts, running shorts, and soaking wet socks and shoes.

"What just happened?" I ask. I think of wormholes, of Einstein-Rosen Bridges, and of wrinkles in time.

None of those things are real.

"We don't know that," Freya says. She holds her stone in her hand, looking at it like it's the Hope Diamond and not a river rock.

Any dream that she might stop listening in my head is now crushed. I wonder why I can't hear inside hers. "How did we get here?" I ask.

"We traveled. Like Mrs. Lee said we would." She glances around. After a moment, her expression turns fearful.

From atop our small hill, we can see the lights of a city in the far distance. But in addition to lights, there are fires, and plumes of smoke rising to the sky.

The city looks like a war zone.

There are no people around us. In fact, our surroundings are oddly quiet.

"Where are we? Do you know?" I ask her.

"We're in Bosnia." She rubs her bare arms to warm them. "That city to the north; it's a United Nations safe zone. But all around it is war."

I stare at her, amazed. "How do you know where we are? And what that city is?"

"Don't laugh."

I tilt my head to the side. She knows I never promise not to laugh. But more than that—what is there to laugh about, here in a war zone in the middle of the night?

She won't meet my eyes. "I can feel it. Like, through my feet." She holds back a smile. "Um, the dirt is talking to me."

We can't help it. We fall into each other, cracking up.

"We're Earthwitches, right?" I say. "So maybe that makes sense."

"Maybe our mysterious *Third* will shed some light on all of this."

"We need better clothes," I say. "It's freezing here." November in Bosnia is far colder than November in North Carolina, and our running gear is not keeping us warm. "Can the dirt tell you where we can get pants?"

Freya suppresses a smile. "This way."

Over the hill's crest is a small cottage. We're on the property of a farming family, but the family is long gone. The cottage's exterior is made of stone and a beige stucco-looking material. The door is heavy wood. "This place is old," I say. "You can feel it." We don't have old places like this back home, not where we live. This cottage could be four hundred years old, easy. I pull open the door, and it moves on silent hinges. I leave it open so we can see by what little light the moon gives us.

I step over the threshold, listening carefully, worried others might be hiding inside. I hear voices and freeze. Then I realize the voices are coming from the walls—the stones in the walls—they mumble like old women and men, and their mumbling is soothing.

"I think we're safe here," I say. "At least for a while."

"How do you know?" Freya asks.

"So, those rocks," I say, pointing at the walls. "They're talking to me."

At least Freya doesn't laugh at me.

I reach for the light switch, but before I even try it, I know it won't work. I try it anyway. Nothing.

On a small wooden table by the front door is an oil lamp and matches, as though someone left them out just for us. The prickle of unease I've felt all afternoon surges again. I light the lamp, turning the wick so it gives off a strong glow, then close the front door. I don't want anyone sneaking in behind us.

Freya opens a wardrobe near the front door and rifles through the coats, looking for two that will fit us.

"We need pants, too," I say. "I'll look in the bedroom." I pause. "And Freya, be careful."

She nods.

Based on my exploration of the cottage, I discover that a husband and wife lived here, and children too. There's a large bedroom where the parents slept, and a second, smaller bedroom with two small beds and tiny shoes on the floor. My heart aches when I think about how they had to abandon their home. I wonder whether the family is alive or dead. I think about the safe zone to the north, and I hope they made it there.

I enter the larger bedroom. The moonlight through the window casts just enough light for me to see by. In a wardrobe, I find a few pairs of men's work pants in a brown canvas fabric. The pants are all the same—same color, same cut, same size. "Not much variety here, but I think these will fit us," I call to Freya.

She joins me in the bedroom, taking a pair. "Communism is efficient, but not very colorful," she says.

We kick off our sneakers, then pull on the pants over our shorts. The pants end just above our ankles.

She examines the high-water situation. "It's the best we can hope for, honestly," she says. "It could have been way worse."

She's right, of course. We're nearly six feet tall. Most men are shorter than we are. And we're lucky we found these pants at all.

We pull our sneakers back on, their flashy colors stark against the dull brown pants, then head back out into the living room-slash-kitchen-slash-dining room of the cottage. With only three rooms, the cottage might have felt crowded with a family of four. But with so much open land about, maybe it wouldn't have. Maybe it would have been an idyllic place to grow up.

No one will ever know, now.

War zone, Freya had said.

"I found coats for us. I'll wear the woman's coat. I'm smaller."

My heart sinks, thinking of the family again. "Why are their coats here, Freya? If they'd survived, wouldn't they have worn their coats?"

Freya takes my hands in hers. "Maybe they fled in summer, back when it was warm, and they didn't need their coats. Maybe they fled long before the army reached this place, and they're safe."

I nod, taking the husband's coat from her hand. It fits me perfectly. Freya's is a little short in the sleeves, but otherwise fits her well.

"These, too," she says, tossing me a dark green knit hat. "Tuck your hair in. I have a feeling we'll need to blend in better than we do right now."

I kneel at a wicker basket by the door, fishing out two pairs of leather gloves. "Here. It'll be cold out there in the middle of the night." We tuck the gloves into our pants pockets, where our stones are hidden.

We stand in the main room of the cottage, the black wood stove cold like an old ghost, the stone floor silent beneath our feet. The furniture is dusty, as though no one has been in the house in months—like Freya said, the family must have fled a long time ago.

I barely recognize Freya in her dull pants and jacket and the combat green toboggan on her head. I realize I must look the same. If only we had shoes that blended in better.

"Maybe we can rub dirt on them to dull the colors."

"Christ on a cracker," I say. "Having you in my head is starting to get old."

"I would think that you of all people would find it helpful," she says primly. "You're so impatient, after all. Now you can skip entire sentences."

I make a rude gesture, and she laughs at me.

"What are we supposed to do now, Traveler?" I ask her.

She stands still, as though feeling for something. "I think we're supposed to wait here."

I stand still and silent, too. I try to listen to the mumbling stones, but they've gone quiet now. They've given me their message. We're safe here for the time being.

And then I start to feel it. The tug on my ribs. This time, instead of pulling me in a particular direction, it's holding me in place.

"You're right," I say, meeting her eyes. "We are."

Then the wooden door flies open, and a man storms through, slamming it behind him.

4

Third

Not a man. Not really. A boy stands there in the entryway by the glow of the oil lamp. He looks to be my age, maybe a year older. I'm having a hard time guessing his age, actually, because he doesn't look like any boy I've ever seen. He's dressed an awful lot like we are, in what looks like combat clothing. Brown hair sticks out from the bottom edge of his green hat, and his eyes are a bright blue-green in the lantern light. He's handsome, sure, but a lot of boys are handsome. He's my height, so not particularly tall. No, what's drawing me to him is something more. It's the tug. It pulled me to that box. It anchored me to the floor of this cottage. And now it's pulling me toward this strange boy who may or may not be a friend.

I realize he's staring at me, too, and he looks like he's unhappy. Even unhappy, though, he's startling. Startling like the box, like the green glow of the stones.

I realize that, for as long as I live, I will never forget his face. That thought seems important somehow.

The boy looks sharply at me, frowning. Then he speaks to me and Freya in a brusque voice. "Urushka said you'd be here by noon. I've been waiting hours."

I do time zone calculations in my head. We left North Carolina in early afternoon. That means we arrived here in late evening. It must be eight or nine o'clock by now.

"Who are you?" I say.

"Alexander. Your Third."

"Is Urushka your Guardian?" I say.

He nods. "We live in a small town outside of Moscow. A Traveler dropped me here this morning, and I've been scouting by myself all day." He nods at the table with the oil lamp on it. "I see you found the lamp I left you. And you were smart enough to dress yourselves properly. We don't have to waste any time on that, at least."

Again, he runs his eyes over me and Freya as though we are very disappointing to him. Suddenly, I don't care how lovely his cheekbones are. If this Alexander is an ass, we're going to be having problems.

"If you're from Russia, how do you speak such perfect English?" Freya asks, amazement in her voice.

Alexander turns to her. "I don't," he snaps. "I'm Russian. I'm speaking Russian, just like you're speaking English. Your sister and I are Speakers. Don't you know anything?"

I interrupt. Only one person on this planet is allowed to insult my little sister, and that person is me. "Chill out, jerkface. How can we possibly know anything? We found a box and some rocks an hour ago and suddenly we're here."

Freya adds, primly, "With a very rude Russian boy."

Alexander pauses to glare at Freya until he's able to process what I've said. "Lee sent two untrained novices for *this*?" He almost yells the final word. "She invoked you *today*?"

Yep, he is definitely losing it.

"You'd be losing it too if you knew what we were facing," he says.

"Wait. You can read my mind, too? What is happening?" I'm so exasperated.

"I'm not reading your mind. You're a Speaker, like me. Speakers can send their thoughts into other witches' minds. It's part of our gift. You just don't know how to control yours yet, so you're sending your thoughts at us haphazardly." *Because you're an untrained novice.*

I hear the last part in my mind loud and clear.

Like a punch to my stomach, I realize that he was able to hear my thoughts when he first came into the cabin. I realize why he gave me that strange, sharp look. He heard me thinking about his *face.* Oh, god.

Alexander smiles at me so smugly I want to kick him.

"Freya," I say. "Take us home. Now."

"You can't leave," he says, worried. "You have to complete the task."

"Can't?" I say, adding some smug to my tone. "We can't leave? If Freya were to pick up her stone and hold my hand, and say, *There's no place like home*—we'd still be stuck here?"

Alexander presses his lips together in frustration.

"I see," I say. "Then what you mean to say is that we *shouldn't* leave yet. You mean to say that you need our help." I step toward him and poke him in the chest so hard he stumbles back. "Right?"

He nods sharply, once.

I'm starting to feel slightly less embarrassed that this guy heard me crushing on him when he walked through the door.

"I have an idea, Alexander." Freya speaks, her voice sickly sweet. Alexander is not from the American south, so he doesn't know that her tone means trouble. "Why don't you tell us what we were sent here to do, and then we can do it. After we're done, Lora and I will travel home and you will never have to see us again—since you apparently hate us already. Sound good?"

Alexander nods, obviously frustrated. He mutters words that sound like *stupid, impossible,* and *disaster,* and then turns back to us. "Let's introduce ourselves properly. My name is Alexander, but you can call me Alex. I was invoked two years ago, when I was fifteen. My Guardian is Urushka, as you know. I'm a Speaker."

"I'm Freya," my sister says. "I was invoked, like, an hour ago.

I'm still not clear what it means to be an Earthkeeper. Maybe you can clarify that for us. I'm fourteen. I'm a Traveler. I hope if I ask you questions you won't yell at me because it hurts my feelings, and also because it will piss off Lora. She's very protective."

Alex glances from Freya to me, eyes appraising. I raise an eyebrow. Freya isn't lying. I used to beat up boys on the school bus when they pulled her hair. What can I do now that I can run a four-minute mile? My entire body tingles with newfound power. I want to use it.

I kind of want to use it on Alex's face.

But I don't. Mrs. Lee told us we're going to need him. Besides, if he's like us, he'll be just as boosted as Freya and I are.

I speak. "I'm Lora. I'm sixteen. You know the rest."

Alex nods. "All right. You'll have to do."

I bristle at his words, but I keep my mouth shut.

He points north, to where Freya and I saw the smoke rising outside of the city. "Here's our task. We have to stop a nuke from falling into the hands of a madman. According to Urushka, we have until midnight."

5

Vision

"This way," Alex says, throwing open the door to the cottage and taking off at a blistering run. Freya follows behind him, just as fast.

I can't bear to leave the family's front door open. They'll want to come home someday, and it's bad enough that we've taken their things. I blow out the lamp—I don't want to start a fire—and close the door. As I leave, the stones of the walls mumble to me once more. They're telling me to be careful.

I chase after Alex and my sister. They're now mere specks in the distance, their dark clothing blending into the night. They've just about made it to a wind-break of trees that edges the rolling farmland.

I run, the ground blurring beneath my feet. I don't look down. I look for the shiny flecks of Freya's sneakers, the only thing visible of her in the distance now. She's right—we should rub dirt on our shoes to disguise them. No one around here would be wearing the latest Nike Airs.

After they enter the trees, Alex and Freya slow their pace. I'm able to catch up to them. They're moving silently now, and once I'm with them, I see why. About a half-mile past the edge of the small forest is a military camp.

We huddle in a circle, squatting on the cold ground strewn with pine needles.

"There are a lot of camps like this," Alex says. "Outposts along the roads. Once the general establishes control of an area, he sets up supply routes, and routes for...other things."

He eyes me, holding back information on purpose. With what I'm guessing are my Speaker skills, I can feel the thoughts he's holding back. They're pushing at me, just barely.

I really want to know what those *other things* are. I wish he weren't so good at keeping his thoughts under control.

"Well I am, so you're just going to have to deal with it," he says to me.

Freya gasps, then covers her mouth.

I feel anger rising. "First, if we're going to work together, you shouldn't hold back information, even if you don't think it'll be useful. You don't know how that information might affect outcomes in the future."

Freya nods. She's heard me say stuff like this before. Small things now can make big differences later.

Alex starts to speak, and I whip up my hand to his face to shush him. "I'm not done. Second. Instead of holding over our heads how much better you are at witchy things, why don't you help us? Wouldn't that make things easier?"

Alex doesn't say anything for a moment. "Are you done?"

I snort. "Jerkface."

"Rookie," he replies. He stands, gesturing for me and Freya to follow him. He lays his hand on the trunk of a tree. "Come on. Do this."

We follow suit, each yanking off a glove and placing a palm on the rough bark. The tree feels oddly warm given the cold air outside.

"Shut your eyes," Alex says.

I narrow my eyes at him in warning.

"I'm not messing with you. Just do it."

I shut my eyes.

"Now, ask the tree to tell you what you need to know. You don't have to say it out loud. Just, in your head. You've probably done this already, but you didn't know you were doing it."

Of course we've done it before. Freya said the dirt told her where we were and where to go. The stones of the house spoke to me, reassuring me that we were safe. We just didn't know what was happening to us, or how to control it.

With my hand on the tree, I think, *What do I need to know?*

I'm assaulted by so many thoughts and images I fall to my knees, suppressing a scream.

When I come to, I'm on all fours, barfing on the pine needles.

"Well, this is a nice change," Freya says.

"There are two kinds of Earthwitches: Guardians and Earthkeepers," Alex says. "You know your Guardian. She's immortal, mostly. We're Earthkeepers, or just Keepers for short. We live normal lifespans. We're normal people until we're invoked."

My stomach starts to roil again as the visions in my head spin, making me dizzy.

"But what do we *keep*?" Freya asks.

"The Earth. The Earth created us and gave us our power. The power is handed down through our families over centuries, millennia maybe. When there is a crisis that puts our planet in danger, it's our job to stop it."

"Isn't that Greenpeace's job?" Freya says.

Alex sighs, turning to me. "Are you done down there?"

"I hate you," I say, spitting out goop into the dirt.

"We need to know what you saw."

"Didn't *you* see anything?" I grumble, sitting back on my heels.

"Freya and I saw the same thing—the nuke hidden in the back

of a truck. We also saw the face of the driver." He squats down so he's near my face and the pool of puke. He pulls a face at the smell. "But you saw more, right?"

I nod.

"So that's why she sent you," Alex says. "Witches like you are rare. Some of us are a little stronger, or faster, like your sister."

Freya fist-pumps again. I roll my eyes at her.

Alex looks between us, trying to understand the joke. "Some have better sight, like you. We're not all the same. Lee must have known that we'd need your sight."

At the moment, all I can feel is how much my sight has kicked my butt. I need help to stand, but the nearest thing to grab hold of is the awful tree that messed me up in the first place. I reach for it, then pull my hand away. I sit back on my heels, realizing there are tears streaming down my face. Embarrassed, I wipe them away with the sleeve of my coat.

On the sleeve of the farmer's coat. The thought of the refugee family makes me want to cry harder, especially given what I saw in my vision. But I refuse to cry in front of Smug Alex.

"It's just Alex." He gives me a smile. "Although Smug Alex has a nice ring to it."

"I can't be the only one to have called you that."

He leans closer to me. "It's okay if you cry."

I look at him out of the corner of my eye. "You don't understand what I saw."

"I know what I saw earlier today when I was scouting. What I didn't want to tell you about." Alex holds out his hand to me. "Let me help you up." His hands are bare—no gloves. For someone raised in Russia, this weather probably doesn't rate as cold. My one bare hand touches his, and he hauls me to my feet. For a moment, he doesn't release my hand. He stares at my face, our hands locked, and surprise, mingled with fear, crosses his face.

I really wish I could hear his thoughts.

Then he lets go of me, and his expression resumes its familiar stern look.

Fear? Why would Alex be afraid of me?

Freya locks her elbow with mine, sensing that I need support. She isn't wrong.

"Tell us what you saw in your vision," Alex says.

"I saw the entire camp," I say. "It's not just a supply camp. They have prisoners, people like the farmers who used to live in that cottage. The army is torturing and killing people as they make their way across the countryside. They're a scourge, a disease."

"But you must have known that," Alex says. "This genocide has been on the news for years."

"You're right," I say. "But it's different to experience it like that, as though I'm right there. To live it."

"What else did you see?"

"I saw other deaths, but they were harder to understand. It was like I was flying above the Earth, or, and this doesn't make sense, flying above time itself. And I saw people fighting each other in ways I don't understand. But I know in my bones that these were Earthwitches fighting. They were killing each other."

Alex nodded. "The Witch War. Your vision showed you that, too."

"There's a Witch War?" Freya asked.

"Yes. There's no time for the long history, but a long time ago, a group of Guardians splintered off. They believe that what we do is wrong, and they want to wipe out the Guardians so no more keepers can be invoked, ending the Earthwitches forever. Some even want to wipe out the Earthkeeper families."

"Mrs. Lee didn't mention this to us," Freya says.

"Mrs. Lee didn't mention a lot, as you may recall," I say to her.

"Did you see the bomb?" Alex asks me.

"I did. I know right where it is, and I know how to get there." I take a step toward the camp. "Follow me."

6

Camp

"This way," I say, ducking low under a branch and leading my sister and Alex toward the camp. I feel a tug under my ribs and, before I can consider what I'm doing, I reach out to a tree I'm passing, brushing it with my fingertips.

I see more of the vision I saw before, more clearly this time, though not as fast or as ferociously. Now, the trees guide me.

In the first vision, I saw the refugees the army captured, farmers and others, people dressed in clothes like the ones Freya and I wore, most of the women in headscarves—Muslim women. I saw mass graves filled with entire families. I saw children's fingers covered in dirt, dead children, and bullet holes in their bodies. I saw women thrown on the ground by soldiers and raped, systematically, as though rape were a weapon of the war.

I shake my head, remembering headlines from back home. For the army we are approaching, rape *is* a weapon of war.

The generals of this army are brutal and without mercy. Their leaders are war criminals. And in that camp, where they are currently violating every line of every international war treaty ever signed, they are hiding a decommissioned Soviet nuclear warhead.

They're planning on sending it into the United Nations Safe

Zone to the north, carried by one of their own soldiers on a suicide mission. They will turn this entire area—and the entire U.N. military installation—into a wasteland. I know what it will look like after the bomb is set off because my vision showed it to me.

Freya, Alex, and I won't die if we fail. Freya will travel us out of there. But if the bomb goes off, the United States will retaliate with more nuclear weapons. Everyone, civilian and military alike, will die. All of this beautiful countryside, all of these centuries-old farms, these old trees, everything will be scorched from the Earth. And what will be left will be poison—for decades. These bombs, these aren't like the ones the United States used in World War II. They're ten times stronger—no, a hundred times stronger. The bombers would aim for military targets, but the collateral damage would be unavoidable. There won't be a Bosnia any more. A Serbia. No more Croatia or Dalmatian Coast. Not for a hundred years. The Mediterranean Sea itself will be poisoned by the water that will flow down from the rivers. All of this knowledge assaulted me in a flash when I touched that tree. It was too much, and I ended up puking in front of Alex.

I flush at the thought.

We have to stop that bomb.

We keep creeping closer to the camp, and I lead us left, to the north, where a fleet of trucks stand in a makeshift motorpool.

"I know which truck has the bomb in back. We need to climb in back and hide. Only one guy is taking the bomb north. He's leaving any minute."

"It's an hour's drive," Freya says.

We're still at the forest edge, waiting. "Which truck," Alex says. "Please say it's a close one."

"Sorry." The truck is about ten vehicles away. We'll have to walk a ways through camp, and we're likely going to run into soldiers.

"No, we're *definitely* going to run into soldiers," Alex says.

I groan. I'm never going to keep him out of my head.

"If we have time," he says, "I'll teach you how to shield your thoughts. For now, though, let's use the telepathy as a tool, okay?" *It'll make things easier when we have to communicate silently. Like when we're in an enemy military camp.*

I can tell by Freya's face that she heard him too.

We nod.

Come on, he says.

We follow him. Instead of sneaking like we expect him to, he walks as though he's a soldier: head up, shoulders back, confident. We do the same. From a distance, I realize, we would look like any other soldiers.

Exactly, he says. *Keep acting like you're supposed to be here. And tell me which truck it is.*

When we arrive at the truck with the bomb in the back, I think hard at Alex: *This one.*

Oof, he says. *I heard that loud and clear.*

Ass, I say.

"You there!" A voice calls from behind us, maybe thirty feet away. Alex turns to face the soldier, stepping in front of Freya. I stand just behind his shoulder, keeping an eye on the approaching soldier—and the AK-47 over his shoulder, its wooden stock gleaming in the camp lights.

"Yes, sir?" Alex says.

"Do you have authorization to be in the motorpool?"

"We are assigned to the motorpool, sir." Alex seems to know far more about military stuff than you'd expect a teenager to know.

"What are your duties now?"

"We are inspecting this vehicle before its trip, sir."

The soldier looks at me. "Is that correct?"

I pitch my voice low, doing my best to pretend to be a boy. Perhaps I can pass for one of the teenagers they've pressed into this army. "Yes, sir. Tire pressure, oil, and such."

The soldier nods slowly.

Freya stands behind us, frozen like a rabbit. I realize with a kick that she has no idea what we're all saying. She's not a Speaker.

I send a thought to her. *It seems to be going well. Alex is telling him we're supposed to be here to get the truck ready for the trip.*

The soldier crosses his arms across his chest. "I have a problem, friends."

"Yes, sir?" Alex says.

"No one but me and my driver knows that that truck is leaving tonight."

Now! Alex screams in my head. He moves like a blur, before the soldier can shift his gun from his shoulder to his hand. Alex rips the gun from the soldier's arm and tosses it to Freya, then wraps an arm under the soldier's throat in a chokehold. I launch myself at the soldier and elbow him across the temple, knocking him unconscious.

Alex looks at me, eyebrows raised.

"It was faster," I say, shrugging. But for a moment, I marvel at how the strength I felt grow in me earlier has melded with an instinct to move like a fighter. Sure I play sports, and I'm not uncoordinated, but it's not like I'm a superhero with martial arts training. Fighting off school bus bullies hasn't prepared me for anything like this.

"You get used to it," Alex says, reading my mind again. "We're all given what we need."

His words echo the words on the box so closely, I wonder if the words are some kind of special Earthkeeper motto.

Freya holds the gun with two hands as far from her body as she can, arms outstretched. "This thing smells wrong. Like skunk, but worse. Like a paper mill. Ugh."

"Keep your voices down," Alex says. He lifts the soldier's unconscious body like it weighs nothing and tosses it in the back of another vehicle, locking the man inside. He takes the gun from Freya and tosses it in the back of a different vehicle.

Get inside the truck, he says. *We have to hide.*

We climb inside the truck with the bomb. It's basically an

oversized pick-up truck covered with a canvas topper. We sit against the wall farthest from the back hatch, hidden from view by a package strapped to the floor and covered in a black tarp, Freya, then me, then Alex. I realize we're all breathing heavily. My heart is still racing from the confrontation with the soldier.

I saw that soldier in my vision, I tell them. *I didn't realize it at first, not until he was about to shoot us.*

Is that why you tried to take his head off? Alex asks.

Maybe. He's an evil guy. He murders families. He orders young soldiers to do it. I heave an angry breath. *We should have killed him.*

We don't kill. Alex's voice has an odd tone, like he's telling me something really important, like the words he's speaking have the power to change the world.

And if we do? I ask.

The killing changes you. And the way your power responds to it, it changes your power, too.

This has to do with the Witch Wars, doesn't it.

Alex nods.

"That's why the gun stank," Freya whispers. "No killing."

Alex nods again.

I hear footsteps then, coming closer and closer to the truck. If the driver chooses to climb in back and inspect closely, he'll see us. We have to simply hope he doesn't.

The footsteps approach the rear of the truck. Hands appear on the tailgate. Someone leans in, muttering too quietly for me to hear. Then footsteps sound again. The driver's door opens and closes, and the engine turns over.

Beneath where I sit I feel the truck shift into gear.

We're off.

7

Road

Once we're on the road, Alex unties the strings that hold the tarp in place over the bomb. He works efficiently, even in the low light, never losing his footing. His hands are the only thing I can see well in the deep darkness of the truck, and periodically his face, when he glances up at me. When he looks at me, his expression is hard, and that trace of fear is back. Am I such a liability that I make him afraid? Is that it?

He folds the tarp and shoves it into a far corner, his motions angry.

"What are you doing?" Freya hisses. "That thing is dangerous! Plus, ew. The smell!"

She's right. Once the tarp is off, the odor of the bomb is horrendous. It's like the smell of the gun but a hundred times worse.

"Oh god. I can't believe I have to ride an hour in a truck with the equivalent of raw sewage," Freya says.

"Stop whining," Alex says. "The driver might hear you."

"He can't, actually," Freya says. "The truck is too loud."

"How do you know?" Alex asks.

"Traveler thing," she says, shrugging her shoulders. "I think I could fly a plane if I had to."

"Who's smug now?"

"Let it go, Alex." I sigh, nodding at the tarp. "Is there a reason you're playing with a nuke?" We can't actually see the bomb. Under the tarp is a black metal box, maybe four feet long and two feet tall and wide. The box is stamped with letters and numbers, but they're just code. I realize quickly that the letters are probably in Cyrillic—but I can read them just fine. The box is tied securely to the truck bed with red nylon ratchet straps.

"I'm not playing with it. I wanted to be extra-sure that we were in the right truck." He nods at the box, pointing at the letters and numbers. "We are."

Alex must know what the code means. I do not. Mrs. Lee said that she hoped our Third wouldn't be an idiot. I have to admit that Alex isn't.

Why thank you, Lora, he says.

Get out of my head.

The road we're traveling was paved well once, a two-lane highway leading to the city to the north. But after years of war, the road is bumpy and covered in potholes and chunks of asphalt. I can see the debris out of the back of the truck, and I can feel the bumps through the floor of the truck. The ride is uncomfortable. I think about how much I'd rather walk than ride in this stinky, bumpy truck.

"Me too," Alex says. "And Freya, with her speed, could probably get out and run alongside of the truck without getting out of breath. But you and me, we'd be tired by the time we arrived. So we'd better ride."

I roll my eyes. "Teach me to control my thoughts, please."

"I only hear the loudest ones, the ones that are driven by your strongest emotions."

"That's right," Freya says. "What you'd normally say with the most snark, you know?" She laughs, turning to Alex. "The Lora snark-o-meter has to be specially calibrated though. She's not like a normal human."

"We get it, Freya," I say. "You always said you liked it that I'm snarky." Between her words and the fear I keep seeing on Alex's face, I'm feeling a little attacked.

"I do!" She rests her head on my shoulder, her warm body next to mine reassuring me.

I turn to Alex. "I'm not going to stop having emotions. So how do I mask my thoughts?"

Alex smiles then, for a moment the fear gone. His teeth glimmer in the dark truck, and I'm struck stupid by how handsome he looks, even in an ugly green hat, even in our dire circumstances, bumping along in the back of a truck in the middle of a hostile war zone, our feet pressed up against a world-ending nuke.

He stops laughing, his face turning serious. "I heard that one, too." He grabs my gloved hand and squeezes it, and from his touch I'm filled with calm and reassurance. "The world isn't going to end. We're going to stop this bomb."

I nod, thinking that he now knows that I'm afraid. He also knows that, even in the middle of a crisis, I'm thinking about how cute he looks. He must believe I'm the shallowest girl on the planet. I want to kick myself. "Forget about teaching me to mask my thoughts," I say. "It's too late for that. Let's figure out a plan instead."

So we do. Alex tries to listen to the thoughts of the driver. Apparently after you've gotten really good at Speaker things, you can learn to read minds, too, a little. But Alex is having a hard time. Someone gave the driver drugs before sending him on his suicide mission, and the drugs are scrambling his thoughts, making him unfocused. All Alex can make out is a fuzzy picture of a building—mostly rubble now—with a flag that still flies in front.

He doesn't recognize the flag, so he describes it to us. "It's got a white background, with a red striped symbol and black lettering. I can't tell what it is." He shakes his head. "If we could know what his target is, we could figure out how to get the truck into the hands of the U.N. without getting ourselves caught."

"What do you mean by *caught*? Caught by the U.N.?" Freya asks. "Won't they be happy when we turn over the bomb? It's the United Nations. Aren't they the good guys?"

Alex laughs, shaking his head. "In a place like this, there are the really bad guys," he points at the driver, "and the people who try to stop them. Those people, sometimes, aren't so good, either."

"You're cynical about the U.N. because you're Russian," I say, annoyed.

"Perhaps. But I've also done tasks like this before. The so-called good guys aren't always pleased to see three teenagers with deadly weapons."

I mull his words, trying to imagine what the three of us might look like to outsiders.

Alex continues. "We need to know his target, and then we need a plan to sneak the bomb into the U.N. compound."

I don't know about sneaking the bomb into the U.N., or even if that's the right move—what if a corrupt U.N. official stole the bomb?

But I know how to figure out the bomber's target. I don't want to do it though, thinking about what happened in the woods before. "You stay with the truck," I say to Alex. "It seems I need to go for a jog after all."

"No," Alex says. "It's too dangerous. You were knocked out last time. And there could be soldiers in the woods." The fear is back. And this time, he looks stricken.

"I'm not going to screw it up."

"I don't think you will."

"Yes you do. I can see your thoughts all over your face."

He leans close to me. *You have no idea what I'm thinking.*

Electricity jolts down my spine.

"Besides, Freya will be with me. She can catch up to the truck and bring you back to me if something goes wrong."

But I'm lying to him. Alex has to stay with the truck because we can't risk losing track of the bomb.

"You won't send her to get me. I heard your thoughts just now."

I smile. "Aren't you glad you didn't teach me to mask what I'm thinking?"

Alex rips his hat from his head, revealing shaggy, dark brown hair. He yanks on it in frustration. "If you aren't able to catch up to the truck on foot, then you travel to the target. Meet me there."

"What if she can't figure out which building it is with her sight?" Freya asks.

Alex looks grim. He doesn't like my plan at all.

Because it's a terrible plan, he says.

We don't have any other choice, I shoot back. *I know you think I'm a novice, but it's the best we've got.*

He meets my eyes. *That's not why I don't like it. I—*

And then I can't hear any more. He's shut his thoughts down.

Freya is watching us, and I realize she couldn't hear our silent conversation. When you're really good at controlling your thoughts, apparently, you can control not only what thoughts get out, but who hears them. Alex only wanted me to hear his thoughts this time, not Freya. I wonder why.

I speak to Alex. "Freya and I are going to hop the tailgate now. With luck, we'll be back in five minutes."

Alex meets my eyes, and I can feel that he's shielding his thoughts with all of his strength. His thoughts press against my mind, like fingers pressing against a blanket. His eyes look grim with worry.

For a moment, I wonder what he's not saying. But I don't have time to worry about what he's keeping from me.

Freya and I creep to the back of the truck, and we jump.

8

War

I roll when I hit the side of the road, popping to my feet in a fashion far too coordinated than I expected me to be. Freya is already standing. Judging by her clothing, it appears that she didn't have to roll at all, but instead managed to land on her feet. Traveler, indeed.

I rush to the nearest tree and press my bare hand against it. An onslaught of images hits me like a brick.

The city, filled with bomb craters. Families, dead in their homes. A defensive force, woefully small, from many nations, trying to hold a line. A building—a hospital—a flag. White, red stripes. Not stripes. It's the Doctors Without Borders flag. The truck, parked out front.

The driver wears a light-blue United Nations peacekeeper helmet. He's glassy-eyed, stoned on a narcotic given to him by his commander— the man we fought. He opens the back of the truck, opens the box, flips a switch.

The world. It turns red.

I'm on my hands and knees, barfing on the forest floor. My stomach is already empty from the first vision's vomit session, so not much is coming up at this point.

"No wonder Mrs. Lee fed us so much before we left," Freya says.

"I know where the truck is going. We have to catch up with Alex."

"About that," Freya says. "You've been out about twenty minutes." She holds out her hand to me. "Can you tell me where we need to go? I can figure it out from there."

I tell her, she takes my hand, and we flash away.

We flash back to the world in an alley adjacent to the hospital. I step around the corner and look at the front of the damaged building, a building still in use despite the destruction from the war. She has put us precisely where we need to be.

I slip back around the corner and turn to Freya. "You are amazing."

She smiles like the Cheshire Cat. "I know."

"How long till the truck arrives?"

She closes her eyes, then opens them again. "Only a few minutes."

The buildings around us are old. Most were once beautiful. This is our first time in any part of Europe—our family can't afford fancy vacations—and I'm grateful to see anything so beautiful, even under these circumstances. The circumstances are immense. Three children—because the three of us are indeed children, no matter how much I argue with my mom about my curfew—were sent to stop an apocalypse. For a moment, I feel the pressure, and I feel like I might break under it.

"Freya," I say, needing to hear her voice. "What are you thinking about?"

"I'm really hungry, actually. I was wondering if we could travel to a Taco Bell and get back before the truck gets here."

"You were not." I snort.

"I'm thinking what you're thinking. If this is a dream we're going to wake up from. And if it isn't, how is this real?"

"If we survive," I say, "how are we going to go to high school on Monday and act like this never happened?"

"How can I try out for the basketball team now that I basically have superpowers? That isn't fair." She sounds really, really sad. "You'll have to quit, too. How will we explain *that* to Mom and Dad?"

"Being a witch is really complicated."

"Alex has been doing this for two years," Freya says, amazed. "Maybe things are easier in Russia. Let's ask him after we save the world."

Yeah, right. I won't be asking Alex about his life if I can help it. Every time I'm near him I embarrass myself. I think of his blue eyes, of the immense fear I saw in them just before I leapt from the back of the moving truck.

Freya grabs my wrist. "The truck is coming."

"We have to knock out the driver and take the truck to the U.N."

"How will we explain who we are at the U.N. compound?" Freya asks.

"Maybe Alex will have a plan for that."

We creep around the corner until we're in the shadows near the front steps of the hospital, right where my vision showed the truck stopping. Not a minute later the truck turns onto the street in front of the hospital and rumbles to a stop in front of the steps. The driver door opens, and the driver steps out, blocked from our view by the truck. I gesture for Freya to intercept him, while I run around the front of the truck to surprise him from behind. I don't know what Freya and are going to do, not exactly. I just know that between the two of us, we ought to be better prepared than one intoxicated teenager.

Then it hits me. The soldier is a teenager—a child. I can see his face from my vision. I can see his history. He was captured as a child, and the commander offered him a choice. Join up, or die.

We need to save him, too.

I creep up behind the soldier just as Freya pops around the

corner of the truck, startling him.

"Whoa!" he yells when he sees her.

I snatch the light blue United Nations helmet from his head and whack him across the skull with it. He falls to my feet, unconscious. He never even knew I was there. I toss the helmet into the rubble.

"Well," Alex says, sidling around the corner of the truck. "If you two don't need a Third, I can head home now."

I look up from the fallen body of the soldier, meeting Alex's eyes. He grins at me, and my heart skips when I see him. I want to punch the side of the truck, knowing that Alex can hear my every thought, even those about him. Especially those about him. I wish I can make them stop, but I can't.

"Of course we need you, Alex," Freya says. "Who else will tell us instructions that we can ignore?"

"We have to save the kid," I say, changing the subject. "He's innocent. They threatened him and drugged him."

"He's hardly innocent." Alex scoffs. "He's a soldier in a war criminal's army."

"You have to trust me," I say. "He was in my vision."

"The soldier was in your vision?" He sounds surprised.

"Yes. I saw him captured. He was twelve at the time, maybe. They killed his family. It was—horrible. His name is Stefan."

Alex hefts the unconscious Stefan onto his shoulder and carries him to the back of the truck. He lowers the tailgate, tosses Stefan in next to the bomb, and closes the tailgate again. "OK?"

I nod.

Suddenly, there are shouts behind us. A group of soldiers in light blue helmets—U.N. peacekeepers, heavily armed—have come dashing around the corner in pursuit of the truck. Stefan's ruse with the stolen helmet must have been discovered.

"Everyone into the truck," Alex says. "We have to get to the U.N. compound before anything else happens."

"Slow down there, tough guy," Freya says. "If we're in a hurry, then I'm driving."

9

Safe

Freya hops behind the wheel of the truck. Alex takes in the passenger seat, and I'm stuck in the middle. Freya knows right where to go, zipping across the pockmarked streets with ease, even in the dark.

When we reach the gates of the U.N. compound, a military installation surrounded by razor wire and lights, two armed soldiers in blue helmets approach the truck.

"Still glad you drove?" Alex whispers to her.

I tense, worried. "What do we do, smart-mouth?" I say to him. "It's too late to sneak it in."

"Hello!" Freya says to the soldiers. "Do any of you speak English?"

"Of course," the nearest soldier says. He's tall, and white, even elegant looking, like the way a soldier would look in a movie. He sounds British, but he could be from anywhere, I suppose.

"We have something for you," Freya says. She leans close, reading his name badge. "We stole a weapon from the bad guys, Mr. Jansen."

Alex is shaking his head now. "This is always the hardest part," he whispers to me. "Get ready."

Ready for what? I ask him

Anything.

"Out of the truck," Jansen orders.

"Sure thing!" Freya says, maintaining her cheerful tone.

We all clamber out of the truck, lining up in front of Jansen. He tells his partner, who seems younger and of lower rank, to check the back of the truck. I can smell the stink of Jansen's assault rifle from where I'm standing.

When his partner starts swearing, I know he's found the nuke, and the unconscious Stefan. I'm pretty sure he knows what the nuke is. When he returns, he speaks rapidly to Jansen in hushed tones, but I can understand every word. Freya, from her face, cannot. They're no longer speaking English. The partner explains about the unconscious soldier and the bomb. Jansen orders his partner to call for help in the guard booth.

We'll be having company, shortly, Alex tells me and Freya.

"He was going to detonate it in the middle of the city, by the hospital," Alex explains to Jansen using a calm tone. "We intercepted the truck and brought it to you."

"And the soldier, he was kidnapped as a child," I add. "He was drugged by his commander. He was forced to do this. He needs help."

"Who are you?" Jansen asks.

Answer this, please, I tell Alex.

"We're friends of the United Nations protection force here," he says.

There's a moan from the back of the truck. Scuffling.

"Go!" Jansen orders his partner.

After a couple of minutes, the soldier returns with Stefan, who is awake and groggy. His hands are in zip-tie cuffs behind his back.

Jansen tries to speak to Stefan in English. Stefan shakes his head. He switches to a different language. Then a third. This one Stefan understands.

"Do you know these people?" Jansen asks him, gesturing at me, Freya, and Alex.

Stefan looks at Alex first. He shakes his head. Then he looks at me and Freya. His eyes widen.

"Those two. The twins. I only saw one of them before."

"You're working with them?" Jansen presses.

"I think one of them hit me."

"You think?"

"Is this the United Nations?" Stefan asks, sounding disoriented and hopeful, and also very young.

"You know that it is, you imbecile," Jansen says scornfully.

Except Stefan doesn't know. The boy never left his family's farm until the day the army swept across his parents' land. He knows nothing about this war except what his commanders have told him, and what his fellow captors have whispered: the U.N. is a safe place.

But I'm starting to worry. Jansen looks worn down from years in this awful place. He looks suspicious, and he has every right to be. But his exhaustion and suspicion aren't working in our favor. His eyes sweep across the four of us, calculating. I realize he's deciding whether we are working together, bringing a nuclear Trojan Horse into his base.

Suddenly, he slams the butt of his rifle into Alex's gut. Alex drops to his knees, gasping.

"No!" I scream, dropping to the ground beside him.

Arms are pulling me away from Alex. I grab Freya's elbow and lock mine through it, but the guards seem content to let us stay together. They drag us through the gates.

Leave now, Alex says to me. Even his voice in my mind sounds injured. *You are touching her. Travel now!*

We're not leaving you here.

They'll come for me eventually.

I don't believe you. And besides, I say, *I don't trust some of these soldiers not to shoot you out back to save themselves the trouble of figuring out what to do with you.*

Not such a rookie after all. His voice is fading as we're dragged farther from him.

I speak to Freya, knowing she can't reply, but knowing that we have to save Alex—and Stefan too, I realize.

So I tell her what we need to do.

Four soldiers lead us to our destination, one to the left, one to the right, one behind, and one in front. They seem to think we are a serious threat. All around us, soldiers go about the business of being soldiers. Men and women look at maps, clean weapons, prepare food, and repair gear. Freya gawks at everything. I shove my elbow into her side. *Pay attention,* I say, glaring at her.

She narrows her eyes at me, seeming to tell me that she is paying attention.

After a five-minute walk and a ten-minute wait, we enter a large tent near the back of the compound. A man stands from behind a desk. He has a United States flag on his shoulder and a bird on his chest.

"They told me two American girls drove a stolen Russian nuke into my compound, but I didn't believe it."

"I drove it, sir," Freya says. "We stole it from the military camp forty miles south of here and brought it to you for safekeeping."

"I suppose you knocked out that soldier to steal his truck?"

"No sir," Freya says. "My sister did that."

The colonel—I know what a bird means—trains his eyes on me. "What are your names?"

Don't say anything, I tell her. *I'm not sure why. I have a feeling.*

We both keep silent.

"Here's my problem," he says. "I have no reason to believe anything you're telling me. You could be agents of any agency on earth. Apparently you," he nods at me, "speak fluent Dutch. As does your friend out there. And you were able to steal a truck and take out a soldier, probably more than one, disrupting an act of terrorism that would have shattered half of Europe?"

"The whole world," Freya says. "Sir."

The colonel raises his eyebrows when Freya corrects him. "And now you won't tell me your names."

"We don't want to get in trouble," Freya says. "Our parents don't know we're here."

Freya is the most disarming person I know. I let her keep talking, hoping for a miracle, even though I know what the colonel is going to say next.

"You're already in trouble!" he roars.

I swear I can feel the rumble of his voice through the soles of my feet.

"Oh." She pauses. "Even though we stopped the bombing?"

"Freya," I say calmly. "He still doesn't believe that we weren't a part of the bombing plan in the first place." I place my hand on her arm as though to calm her. "He doesn't believe that you and I aren't here as part of some elaborate ruse to bomb the base. He's just more polite about it than Jansen was. Same suspicion, less hitting."

"Really?" she says. "This is the thanks we get for saving the world?"

"Really," I say. "Alex was right. We should have snuck the truck onto the base."

"What a bunch of crap," she says, her tone angry now.

The colonel's eyes widen. I wonder how many years—decades —it's been since anyone has spoken to him like this.

"We saved your life," she says, pointing at him. "You're welcome. Keep the bomb safe."

"Why don't we discuss this over a warm meal." The colonel holds up his hands, trying to sound appeasing, but he comes across as patronizing instead.

"No, thank you. We're leaving now." We flash out of the tent.

We flash back behind a building about a block away from the compound. Freya is still pissed off. "That jerk! Sitting behind his desk like he's some sort of king. Ugh!"

"I told you to travel as soon as they let go of us. I didn't say to mouth off to a colonel first." Not far away, alarms on the compound begin blaring. Freya and I have caused a frenzy.

"I thought maybe we could explain, make him understand."

"In this instance, Alex was right. I don't think the colonel was a bad person, but he—like most people—isn't going to be able to understand us and what we do."

Freya nods, frowning. "Now we have to rescue Alex."

"If we can travel the perimeter, I can reach out to him. Once we find him, you can travel in, grab him, and travel out again."

"I'm not leaving you alone," she says. "We'll go in together."

I nod in agreement, holding out my hand.

We flash to one point on the perimeter, staying just long enough for me to call out to Alex with all of the emotion in my mind.

No reply.

I reach for Freya's hand again, and I notice that it's shaking. I look at her face, pale under the compound's lights. "Freya? Are you okay?"

"I think," she takes a deep breath. "I think that maybe traveling is something I have to do more sparingly than I've been doing it."

"Are you all right?"

"I'm not going to puke, if that's what you're asking."

"No, that's not what I'm asking. I'm asking if you're all right."

She smiles at me. "Let's run the perimeter instead. See if you can keep up."

She takes off, not as fast as she was earlier in the night when she dashed from the cottage, but still faster than I am. I'm relieved to see that she's okay. We run the perimeter of the compound. Every hundred yards or so, I call out to Alex. After a while, I start to fear that he's unconscious. And then, after a few more tries, I fear that he's already dead.

I call out again. *Alex!* I shout with every power I can command. *We're coming for you. Where are you?*

I would have been able to tell you my location a moment ago, but now that I have a concussion from your screaming, I'm not sure that I can.

I want to cry with relief when I hear his obnoxious voice in my head. *Show me and Freya where you are.*

Before I can say anything about sneaking into the compound instead of traveling, Freya grabs my hand, and we flash to his location.

He's in a makeshift prison. It's like an animal cage, with a metal floor and bars on four sides and the top. "What if it rains?" I say with horror, glancing at the sky through the metal bars.

"The prisoner gets wet," he says.

"They are the not-so-good-guys," I say.

He nods.

"Where's Stefan?" Freya asks. She looks pale. The traveling is taking its toll.

"I don't know," Alex says. "They took him that direction, and they haven't come back." He points toward the back exit of the compound.

My stomach drops. No. No.

"You can't save everyone, Lora," Alex says. "We completed our task. We have to go."

"We can't leave him." I think of the small, skinny boy in my vision who watched his parents die.

"We have to. We can't put the Earthwitches at risk by displaying what we are so publicly." He points to the alarm blaring overhead. "I take it you've already done so?"

Freya shrugs. "The colonel was a jerk. Besides, no one will believe him."

"But they'll believe something. They'll get suspicious. There are cameras everywhere."

"You two didn't see what I saw." My voice catches. "You didn't see how his mother died in front of him. What the soldiers did to her, and how they made him watch. He needs medical care, not a firing squad." I squeeze back tears. I can't ask Freya to risk herself to save him, though. She's worn down. I can tell. I know her as well as I know myself.

Faster than we can see her move, Freya grabs my hand and Alex's, and we flash out of the cage.

We flash back behind a group of men in the farthest rear area of the compound. Stefan is tied to a post. He's crying.

"I confess it," he says to the soldier standing nearest to him, this one with a French flag on his shoulder and the stature of a high-ranking officer. "I was sent to bomb the city."

They're going to do it, I think. They are going to execute him. He's a prisoner of war, but it doesn't matter. Nothing matters. The stink of guns nauseates me. I begin to panic.

Then the dirt beneath my feet soothes me. Reassures me.

Freya flashes to Stefan's side, takes hold of him, and flashes back to me and Alex—faster than we can formulate a plan. Then she touches us all, and we're gone.

We flash back in front of the hospital. Doctors Without Borders —the only truly safe place in this city.

Freya and Stefan both collapse onto the street.

Alex! I scream in my mind. *Save Freya!* He can protect her better than I can. I don't know the first thing about being a Keeper, an Earthwitch. But Alex, he'll know what to do. *Hide.* I tell him. *I'll find you.*

If you're not in contact in five minutes, I'm coming back for you. Alex lifts Freya into his arms like she's a small child, and takes off at a run.

I turn to Stefan. He's barely conscious. He's been beaten, and the drugs are still in his system. I glance up the stairwell in front of us. There are few lights on in the hospital, but the light in the foyer shines brightly. As I lean Stefan over my shoulder and help him up the stairs, bearing most of his weight, I focus on that one light.

That light is hope.

"You're helping me," he mumbles. "You're one of the twins."

"I am helping you, Stefan. You don't deserve to die."

"I was sent here to kill everyone."

"I know," I say to him. "I know everything. And when you get inside, I want you to tell the doctors everything. I want you to start with your mother. Do you understand me? You have to start with your mother."

As I push open the metal door, he nods.

10

Choice

I rush down the hospital steps in search of Freya and Alex. I left Stefan with a medical tech who promised me that Stefan would be safe. She told me that the hospital has lots of experience with child soldiers. She didn't ask any questions, or wonder where I came from. She thanked me for bringing him to her, and then she said good-bye.

Where are you? I scream to Alex. I have faith that he's kept Freya safe, even in these streets crawling with both bad guys who'd kill on sight, and the not-so-good guys who have orders to hunt us down.

His voice is faint. *Follow the alleyway. We're in the abandoned bakery in a storage room in back.*

I run, turning left at the alley where Freya first brought us to meet the truck, then left again into a shattered doorway under a sign that says *Bakery,* although I know that I'm reading the sign in a foreign language. The room is dark, and I step carefully over broken furniture, the remains of years of looting. I head to the back of the store where a dark doorway beckons.

Alex? I call to him.

Through the doorway.

I head through. In the dark space that used to be a kitchen, another door swings open, and Alex stands there with a flashlight.

Hurry, he says. *We don't want anyone to see the light.*

I step through the second doorway and he shuts the door behind us. We're in a storage closet; looters have cleared the shelves. Freya sits on the floor, awake, inhaling a granola bar.

"Freya!" I drop to my knees in front of her and smother her with a hug.

"I'm fine," she says through mouthfuls of food. "Sorry I freaked you out. Alex has granola bars in his pockets. I'm on my third, and I'm already feeling better."

I sit next to her, leaning against the wall, then turn to Alex, who sits on the wood floor facing us. "Why didn't you tell us that she can't travel as much as she wants?" I'm angry and also scared. Watching Freya fall to the ground outside the hospital was the scariest moment of my life, scarier than riding in a truck with a nuclear bomb.

"I figured she'd know," he says. He turns to Freya. "Didn't you feel it when you traveled the first time?"

"Feel what?" she says. "I puked, but that's nothing unusual."

"You should have told us," I snap at him. "You knew we were rookies. You were too busy taunting us to give us the information we needed."

"No, Lora," his voice is soothing. "That isn't it. Every traveler I've ever met has known his limitations the first time he's traveled. Traveling drains you." He looks at my sister. "Freya's special. She is overpowered in lots of ways it seems, not just foot speed. I never thought I'd have to tell her to preserve her energy." He squeezes my hand. "I promise I would never put her at risk."

Tears sting my eyes at his calming words, at his unspoken apology, and I turn my face away. "I'm glad you had the granola bars."

"Me too," he says.

"Me free," Freya says through her stuffed mouth.

"Stefan's safe?" Alex asks.

I nod.

"Good," he says. He pauses, then speaks. "Remember earlier, when you said that small things now can make big differences later?"

I thought back to our argument in the forest before we ever found the truck with the bomb. "Actually, I didn't *say* that. I thought it, and you read my mind without my permission."

Oh whatever, Alex says, looking at me with a smile and a glimmer in his eyes.

My heart skips at that glimmer.

I want to die of embarrassment.

"The point is, you were right," he says. "One of the things we learn as keepers is that when a chance to do the right thing crosses your path, you do it. Your vision showed you Stefan's life story for a reason. You were supposed to save him." Alex rubs his hand in his hair—he'd lost his hat somewhere at the compound and he never got it back. "I wonder why."

"And we may never know and the Earth knows and blah blah blah, right?" Freya says.

"Well," he says, "Urushka would put it more eloquently, but yes."

"What do we do now?" I ask.

"Now Freya travels us to my rendezvous point, where I'll wait for a Traveler from home to pick me up. And after she's eaten and rested again, you two will head home to Lee."

"The cottage?" Freya asks. She already knew Alex's rendezvous point. Of course it's the cottage. The cottage is a safe place.

Alex nods.

I look at Freya, examining her. "We don't have to go yet. We can take as long as you need."

"I'm fine," Freya says. She grabs us and we flash away.

We flash back just outside the cabin's front door, and I stumble into Alex. He uses two hands on my shoulders to help me catch my balance.

His hands seem to stay on my shoulders a moment longer than they need to, but I'm sure I imagined it. I step away from him.

I wish I didn't imagine it.

"New rule, Freya," I say. "You have to *ask* before you do that."

Alex nods in agreement. "It's the more polite thing to do."

Freya rolls her eyes.

Sometimes she really seems fourteen years old.

As Alex opens the door, I glance at Freya's profile. She looks tired again. We're definitely resting before heading home. Maybe Alex has another granola bar.

Inside the cabin, Alex lights the lamp. The rumbling stones greet me as we enter. In the lamplight, Alex's eyes dance. He looks a little sleepy—it's late at night for him—but he's still a handsome witch. His eyes meet mine. He's heard my thoughts, again.

Well, it's true, I say to him.

Come on, he says, tilting his head toward the farmers' bedroom. *I need to tell you something important. About being a witch.*

Just me?

Just you. His hands are stuffed in the pockets of his pants, and he looks afraid again. This time, though, the fear could almost be described as nervousness.

I turn to Freya. "You need to rest before we travel again. Sit." I point at the small sofa in the living room.

Alex hands her another granola bar. "Eat."

"Where are you two going?" she says, and I know she's being deliberately obtuse.

"We're going to have a private talk in one of the other rooms."

Freya yanks me toward her, looking at Alex. "You go ahead, Third. I need a minute to talk to my sister."

Now that we're almost safe, I can tell that Freya is getting conscientious again. I'm about to get lectured. She does this to me at least once a week. Last week's lecture was about how I drove with my gas tank on empty too often.

"What are you doing?" She points to the room where Alex is waiting, probably able to hear every word we say. "You're going into a bedroom with a boy we just met? There's a bed in there!"

"We're just going to talk."

"Lora, you are not stupid. Can you really not tell?"

I pull my brows together. I have no idea what she's talking about.

"You can't. Oh my god." She bites off a big mouthful of granola bar and pushes me toward the room where Alex is waiting. "I warned you."

I narrow my eyes at her, then I follow Alex to the bedroom. I shut the door behind me. I take a step toward him, and it surprises me how hard it is to do considering all of the scary things I've done today. The wood floor of the cottage is covered with a braided rug, and it muffles my footsteps. In the light of day, I think the rug would be colorful, cheerful even.

Alex stands near the window, his face outlined by the moonlight. "I've had to listen to your thoughts all day."

I nod. His words are true.

"You weren't able to hear mine."

I shake my head. Also true.

"At first I was really pissed off that Lee sent two novices."

"I didn't have to read your mind to know that."

"Two eye-catching novices. Doesn't she have any sense at all? You don't send you," he gestures at me, "into a war zone. You stick out like a macaw."

"No we don't. We put on clothes just like yours."

"I'm not talking about your clothes, Lora." He jerks on his hair like he did earlier, obviously frustrated. "I'm talking about *you*."

Oh. He's talking about me. "Is that a compliment?"

"Yes." He sounds almost annoyed.

"Well, I can't help the way I look."

"I know that." He takes a deep breath. "This isn't coming out right."

"Some Speaker you are."

He snorts. "And then you insisted on putting yourself in danger over and over. I was terrified."

"I'm sorry you thought my plans were bad. But I didn't see another way."

"I wasn't terrified because they were bad plans, Lora. Listen to me. I was terrified you would get hurt. I was worried for you. You. Do you hear me?"

I nod, but his words are still making their way into my head. He was afraid for me. He was worried about me. "So when you looked afraid?"

"I was terrified you'd get hurt, yes. And I wouldn't be able to save you."

"I didn't need you to save me." The words come out automatically. I've never needed a Prince Charming.

"You haven't been a witch for twenty-four hours. Of course you need someone to save you."

"I didn't end up in a cage like someone else in this room."

"Lora." He sighs, and I swear I can feel that sigh up and down my spine. "This isn't supposed to happen."

"What isn't?"

He steps close to me, putting his hands on my shoulders. Then he leans forward and kisses me.

And when he does, he lets down the curtain that has kept back his thoughts. All of the thoughts that I've sent his way, how handsome he is, the jolts of energy I've felt when he looked my way or touched me, I feel thoughts like those now, but from him. About me. And now that we're kissing, those jolts of energy grow and grow. I put my hands around his neck, feel the ends of his hair. He pulls the hat from my hair, cradling the back of my head.

I could go on kissing him forever.

But we don't have forever, solnyshko.

Solnyshko. Little sun.

Why not? With traveling, we can see each other easily.

Keepers can't be together like this.

I break away from him, heart pounding. "Why not?"

His eyes are sad. "When you return, ask Lee about the Earthkeeper's Choice."

"No, you tell me."

He shakes his head. "I can't. It's your Guardian's job."

I shake my head. "When Lee sent me here, did she know I'd feel like this about you?"

"Maybe."

"Definitely!" I'm angry now. I feel set up. I'm being ripped away from the first boy I've ever cared about. I jerk my eyes at him, worried he heard my thought.

He's smiling sadly. *I heard you. I agree. There's something between us. It's...unique.*

He pulls me to him, hugging me while I cry.

We arrive on Mrs. Lee's patio just after dinnertime. She has food laid out on her patio table for us when we arrive—the same food as before. She knew we'd be hungry.

I know my eyes are still red. I cried because of the stress of the day, because of the visions I saw, because of the horrors the visions forced me to feel, and because I had to leave Alex, apparently forever, if what he said is true. I want to know what this Earthkeeper's Choice is. I want to know so many things.

After we sit around the table, I start talking.

"We don't need the stones, do we."

"No," Mrs. Lee says. "They're mere talismans. The power lies in you. In fact, the stones were gone before you left the enemy camp."

Freya frowns. "I thought it was pretty."

"Why did you wait so long to invoke us?" I ask.

"I wanted to keep you safe from the Witch War."

"Tell us about the War. It seems we're a part of it now. I had a vision that showed it to me."

"Before you were invoked, you were invisible to those who used to be Guardians. Once I invoked you, you lit up like firecrackers. They can find you now. They can kill you."

"Can we fight back?" I ask.

"You can. If you learn how. But there is another choice."

"If the ex-Guardians are so dangerous, why invoke us at all?" I ask.

"I needed you for this task. It was very big, very important. You both had special skills—Freya's Traveler speed, your sight. With Alex, you three made a special team. You saved the entire planet. The Earth," she smiles, closing her eyes, "it thanks you. Can you feel it?"

I close my eyes as well, feeling the ground beneath my feet. It whispers gratitude and peace.

"I can feel it," I say.

"So can I," says Freya.

"Now tell us about this Choice. The reason I can't see Alex again."

Mrs. Lee smiles sadly. "Yes. Alex. Every task has its risks and rewards."

I grit my teeth. She's not the one with the broken heart.

Mrs. Lee nods. "Every Keeper is given a chance to become a Guardian."

Freya's eyes widen. "We can become like you?"

"Yes. You would get eternal life. The ability to change your appearance. The power to travel and speak. And more."

"That sounds pretty awesome," Freya says.

"There's a catch, sister," I say. "There's always a catch."

Mrs. Lee nods. "Very wise, Lora. As you can see, I have no family. I have few friends. No one except other Earthwitches knows who I am, not really. And no other Guardians live nearby. Guardians are few, and with this war we grow fewer still. We have large territories to cover. I am...lonely. I cannot marry. I cannot have children. I have one duty—to watch a bloodline, forever, until the day I decide to return to the Earth, or until another witch kills me in this war."

"Does anyone ever say yes to becoming a Guardian?" Freya asks.

She smiles. "Rarely. But yes, they do. Immortality has perks."

"What happens if we say yes?" I ask.

"To your family, it will be as though you were never born. Your existence will be wiped from reality. You will travel to the Guardian stronghold to train. Then you will take over a territory."

"Never *born*?" Freya screeches.

Mrs. Lee nods.

"Why did you say yes?" Freya demands. "Who would say yes?"

"Not every family is as loving as yours," Mrs. Lee says quietly.

Freya's mouth rounds into an O.

"What happens if a keeper says no?" I ask.

"Keepers who turn down Guardianhood must forget being a Keeper. You must forget the tasks you completed. You must forget your relationship with your Guardian. You must forget everything about being an Earthwitch. You return to your normal life, and you live on. Better still, that flare that lit you up, revealing you to our enemies? It goes out. You are hidden once again."

"You forget everything? Forever?" I swallow hard, thinking of Alex. He'd known in that bedroom that we didn't have a future together. One day soon we will either be Guardians, or we'll forget each other's existences. My heart clenches in my chest. I want to cry, but I won't in front of Mrs. Lee. I feel like she toyed with us, and I won't give her the satisfaction of my tears.

"There are exceptions," she says. "In certain, dire circumstances, the Earth will grant back a retired keeper's memories, even her powers. But we don't ever want to encounter those circumstances."

"You said you watch our bloodline," Freya says.

I gasp. "You were our mom's Guardian!"

"Yes." Mrs. Lee nods.

"She doesn't remember you," I say.

Mrs. Lee shakes her head. "I don't look like the Guardian, or the person, she once knew. So with or without her Keeper memories, she wouldn't recognize me." She smiles wistfully. "But spending time with her now, even as her neighbor, is pleasant. I have always liked your mother. Guardians can't have children, but we watch over Keeper families for centuries. I loved your mother when she was a girl, and I became her friend again now. She doesn't know who I was to her then, so when you were born, I started a friendship with her anew."

"When you knew her when she was young, you were, like, someone else?" Freya asks.

"Yes, I was someone else."

"Weird," Freya says.

"And once this day is over, if you choose to forget, you won't know I was your Guardian. I'll just be your neighbor and your mother's friend. And then you and I will meet again in the future, and I will watch your children. And like your mother, you won't know me because once again I will wear a different face."

"We have to make the choice now?" I say, my voice rising to a yelp. My heart races. I'm not ready to decide.

"We'll have children? You already know?" Freya asks, mouth agape.

"If you don't choose Guardianhood, you both will have children, and those children will be Earthkeepers. I will be their Guardian."

"How do you know?" I ask.

"It's my job to know." Mrs. Lee makes her pronouncement with certainty.

"Fine," I say. "You know that I'm going to have children. You must know whether I have a chance of finding someone like Alex again."

She shakes her head. "What you and Alex have is one of a kind."

I frown, but mostly what I do is hold back tears.

"This is your choice. You must decide." She looks at her strange watch. "Now."

It's the first day of school after the winter holiday break. Freya and I are standing at the bus stop, on the sidewalk at the corner in front of Mrs. Lee's house. We're bundled in our winter coats. Our basketball uniforms are in our backpacks. Freya made varsity, and the only person who was surprised was Freya. Tonight we have a big game, and she's looking a little green in the face.

"Please don't throw up on my shoes," I say. "I just got them."

"I shouldn't have had that second egg burrito." She sounds miserable.

"Actually, maybe you should throw up before the bus gets here, so you don't embarrass yourself at school again."

"Thanks for the support," she says.

"If you're going to barf, you should hurry. Someone's coming."

She rolls her eyes at me.

A person approaches the bus stop from the house across from Mrs. Lee's. The family moved in over the holiday break. Our mom told us that the mom in the family is a professor at the local university, and that the family moved all the way from Moscow so she could chair the Slavic Studies department here. Freya and I were appropriately impressed. Apparently they have a kid who's a junior in high school like me.

And now he's joining us at the bus stop for the new semester.

He steps up on the sidewalk, taking in Freya's peaked appearance, and then meeting my eyes. My heart stops for a second. This guy is grade-A hot.

He smiles shyly. "Hello. My English isn't super. I just moved in over there." He points at his house.

"Yeah, we know. Our mom knows your mom."

He smiles, and if he seemed cute before, the situation has just escalated. A lot. "My name is Alex," he says. "What's yours?"

I f you enjoyed ALEX AND LORA: An Earthkeeper Novella, look for the first full-length novel in the Earthkeeper Series by Katie Rose Guest Pryal coming soon. Sign up for her author newsletter (pryalnews.com) or follow her on Instagram (instagram.com/krgpryal) to stay in the know.

About the Editor: Emily Colin

Emily Colin is the *New York Times*-bestselling author of *The Memory Thief* and *The Dream Keeper's Daughter*. Her diverse life experience includes organizing a Coney Island tattoo and piercing show, hauling fish at the Florida Keys' Dolphin Research Center, roaming New York City as an itinerant teenage violinist, helping launch two small publishing companies, and serving as the associate director of DREAMS of Wilmington, a nonprofit dedicated to immersing youth in need in the arts.

A 2017 Pitch Wars mentor, she is the 2017 recipient of the North Carolina Sorosis Award for Excellence in Creative Writing and the 2018 recipient of the North Carolina Greater Foundation of Women's Clubs Lucy Bramlett Patterson Award for Excellence in Creative Writing. Originally from Brooklyn, she lives in Wilmington, NC, with her family. You can find her on Twitter at @emilyacolin or on her blog at www.emilycolin.com.

facebook.com/emily.colin.79

twitter.com/emilyacolin

instagram.com/emily_colin

About the Editor: Katie Rose Guest Pryal

Katie Rose Guest Pryal is a novelist, essayist, and erstwhile law professor in Chapel Hill, NC. She is the author of the Hollywood Lights Series, which includes *Entanglement, Love and Entropy, Chasing Chaos, How to Stay,* and *Fallout Girl.* She also writes nonfiction, including *Life of the Mind Interrupted: Mental Health and Disability in Higher Education.*

As a journalist and essayist, Katie has contributed to *Catapult, The Chronicle of Higher Education, The Toast, Quartz, Full Grown People, Motherwell,* and more. She earned her master's degree in creative writing from the Writing Seminars at Johns Hopkins, and she is a member of the Tall Poppy Writers (tallpoppies.org). You can connect with Katie on Instagram, Facebook, and Twitter, all at @krgpryal; on her blog at katieroseguestpryal.com; and through her monthly letter at pryalnews.com.

facebook.com/krgpryal

twitter.com/krgpryal

instagram.com/krgpryal

amazon.com/author/krgp

bookbub.com/authors/katie-rose-guest-pryal

goodreads.com/krgpryal

CPSIA information can be obtained
at www.ICGtesting.com
Printed in the USA
FSHW011124301018
53413FS